To Grandma Luella,

for showing me the grace of food

made with love and igniting my

passion for all things coconut.

• • •

To my husband—

may our magnet collection continue

to grow.

The Coincidence of Coconut Cake

AMY E. REICHERT

GALLERY BOOKS

New York · London · Toronto · Sydney · New Delhi

G

Gallery Books
An Imprint of Simon & Schuster, Inc.
1230 Avenue of the Americas
New York, NY 10020

This book is a work of fiction. Any references to historical events, real people, or real places are used fictitiously. Other names, characters, places, and events are products of the author's imagination, and any resemblance to actual events or places or persons, living or dead, is entirely coincidental.

First Gallery Books trade paperback edition July 2015

GALLERY BOOKS and colophon are registered trademarks of Simon & Schuster, Inc.

Interior design by Jaime Putorti

Manufactured in the United States of America

10 9 8 7 6 5 4 3

Library of Congress Cataloging-in-Publication Data
Reichert, Amy E., 1974-
The coincidence of coconut cake / by Amy E. Reichert.—First Gallery Books trade paperback edition.
pages cm
ISBN 978-1-5011-0071-0 (alk. paper)—ISBN 978-1-5011-0072-7 1. Women cooks—Fiction. 2. Food writers—Fiction. I. Title.
PS3618.E52385C75 2015
813'.6—dc23
2014039355

ISBN 978-1-5011-0071-0
ISBN 978-1-5011-0072-7(ebook)

I think careful cooking is love, don't you? The loveliest thing you can cook for someone who's close to you is about as nice a valentine as you can give.

—JULIA CHILD

PRAISE FOR

THE COINCIDENCE OF COCONUT CAKE

"Deliciously entertaining! Reichert's voice is warm and funny in this delightful ode to second chances and the healing power of a meal cooked with love."

—Meg Donohue, *USA Today* bestselling author of *Dog Crazy* and *All the Summer Girls*

"Reichert takes the cake with this charming tale of food, friendship, and fate."

—Beth Harbison, *New York Times* bestselling author of *If I Could Turn Back Time*

"*The Coincidence of Coconut Cake* is a delicious story of food, love, and a wink at what people will do to have their cake and eat it, too."

—Ann Garvin, author of *The Dog Year* and *On Maggie's Watch*

"*The Coincidence of Coconut Cake* is a read as satisfying as the last bite of dessert after a lovingly prepared meal. The novel is as much a celebration of the Midwest and regional food as it is a love story between chef Lou and food critic Al. I adored Lou and her quirky makeshift family of restaurant customers and co-workers. Their missteps and milestones kept me racing through the chapters."

—Susan Gloss, author of *Vintage*

"What a wonderful treat! Delicious descriptions of food and love and Milwaukee (I know! Who knew?). A sweet, endearing read."

—Megan Mulry, *USA Today* bestselling author of *A Royal Pain*

"Reichert whips up the perfect recipe for a deliciously fun read. Combine humor and romance with a dash of drama, then let it simmer. The sprinkle of Wisconsin pride is icing on an already irresistible cake. Warning: Do not read this book hungry!"

—Elizabeth Eulberg, author of *The Lonely Hearts Club* and *Better Off Friends*

"Reichert brings sweetness and substance to her scrumptious debut. Sign me up for second helpings!"

—Lisa Patton, bestselling author of *Whistlin' Dixie in a Nor'Easter*

The Coincidence of Coconut Cake

· CHAPTER ONE ·

Lou hoisted up her gown and winced as she tottered across the parking lot. The sparkly four-inch heels had looked so pretty in the box, but they felt like a mortar and pestle grinding each bone in her foot. She missed her green Crocs.

Lou plucked at the tight elastic, squeezing her under the sleek black dress her fiancé, Devlin, had given her. He walked five steps ahead of her, so she scurried to catch up.

"Overstuffed truffle and foie gras sausage," Lou said.

Devlin's face crinkled in confusion. "What?"

"It's a new dish, inspired by how I feel in these clothes. Maybe served over brown butter dumplings . . ." Lou tilted her head, visualizing the newly formed meal. Devlin frowned at her and sighed.

She wilted at the familiar reaction. "I'm sorry. It helps distract me."

His features softened as he looked at her. "You'll be fine. You look stunning."

Lou gave a feeble smile, stepping into the soft, yellow light of the Milwaukee Country Club's foyer, the cushy patterned carpet springing back with each step. Black-and-white pictures adorned the buttery walls, telling the club's upper-crust history. Many showed eager young men in white standing behind wealthy gentlemen in funny pants. Hunger for something more burned in the young men's eyes. Lou understood.

Lou turned toward Devlin, looping her arm through his.

"You didn't need to ship me off to the salon all day, or spend so much on this dress." She smoothed the fabric over her hips, the snug undergarments matching the tightness in her stomach. She wore a floor-length, black strapless column of jersey with matching elbow-length gloves—simple, elegant, and too expensive.

"It's my gift to you. You never pamper yourself." He shrugged his shoulders. "Get used to it. The future wife of a prominent attorney should enjoy a little spoiling."

"How am I supposed to top all this for your birthday?"

"For starters, you'll make your grandmother's amazing coconut cake. I'll tell you the rest later." He winked.

Devlin smiled down at her, and Lou's breath caught a little in her throat. He looked dashing in his tuxedo. Its classic lines fit his athletic frame, giving him an air of latent power and manliness; the faint smell of cloves lingered around him. His thick, dark hair offset his crystal-blue eyes—her very own Disney prince. He set her bejeweled arm on his and resumed their progress into the crowd. Lou clung to his Italian-wool-clad arm as if it were a life preserver as they wandered through the perfumed and primped throng of attorneys and spouses at the annual firm gala.

The private club swam with glittering women and powerful

men. Waiters in white tuxedo jackets swerved through the crowd, delivering twenty-year-old scotch and white wine to thirsty guests. Additional waiters carried trays with appetizers, the obligatory bacon-wrapped water chestnuts and peeled shrimp with cocktail sauce. Lou sighed at the dull offerings, imagining what she could do with this party's budget.

Devlin steered her toward a group of older men with elegant women by their sides.

"Bill, how are you?" Devlin said, extending his arm toward the largest man. "And you remember my beautiful fiancée, Elizabeth." All eyes turned to her. Lou gritted her teeth at his introduction.

Bill turned to Devlin and Lou. "We were just talking about the new restaurant critic for the paper, A. W. Wodyski. Have you read his reviews?"

Devlin shook his head. "I've heard of him but haven't had the time to read. The Churman case is taking more time than expected. Any good recommendations?"

"The opposite. He obliterates every restaurant he reviews. But he does it in the most entertaining way. Like Dennis Miller as a restaurant critic."

"Really?" Lou faked indifference, biting back the real commentary she wanted to share about such arrogance.

"He hasn't ever given a positive review. I've even heard a few of the restaurants he reviewed had to close."

"I don't buy that," said Devlin. "No one review could close a restaurant that was good."

"It could if they were struggling to begin with," Lou said softly, frowning. She opened her mouth to continue, but Devlin nudged her with his elbow. She nodded and stayed silent as the conversation flowed back to clients and billable hours. Lou flicked open her rhinestone-studded clutch and pushed a button on her phone. No new messages. She closed the bag.

A waiter appeared with drinks for the group. Lou looked at his name tag, then into his face and said, "Thank you, Tyler." He startled a little, then nodded in acknowledgment. Lou smiled. The rest of the small group continued talking about upcoming trials and the difficulties of finding good nannies. Lou watched the waiter flit into the crowd toward the bar, empty glasses appearing on his tray as he crossed the room, bobbing swift nods as he took new drink orders efficiently. He served without interrupting, moved quickly without rushing. Lou had turned to follow him when she felt a tap on her arm.

When Lou looked, Bill's wife stood too close, radiating musky perfume. "So how did the two of you meet?"

Before Lou could answer, Devlin turned toward them. "Elizabeth used to work at Giuseppe's years ago."

"They had a made-to-order-pasta station where people could sit and watch the chef," Lou added, smiling at the memory.

"I was there for a lunch meeting, but they canceled last minute, so I sat at the counter in front of this cute little cook." Devlin put an arm around her shoulders. "I came back every day that week." Devlin looked down at Lou and smiled.

"On Friday, he left a single red rose and his business card with the tip."

"She called the next day and soon she'll be my beautiful bride."

"Beautiful and she can cook," Bill said. "No wonder you closed the deal."

"I always close." Devlin wrapped her arm around his and said, "Excuse us; I see Susan and I need to ask her about a deposition she did for me." He guided Lou away, merging into the crowd and toward the French doors.

"I'm going to hit the restroom before dinner starts. I'll meet you at the table?" Lou turned and eased open the six-paneled bathroom door with her gloved hand, letting the silence melt some of her tension.

• • • • •

In the tiny room doubling as a bathroom stall, Lou struggled, realigning her undergarments to their original positions, trying to get her emotions under control. Devlin didn't understand what her restaurant meant to her. He seemed to think he was rescuing her from a life of hard labor, a life his mother endured as she worked two waitressing jobs to feed and clothe her academically gifted son. She touched her ring, a pristine rectangle like an ice cube that could melt into nothing. She tried to find comfort in Devlin's symbol of love for her. She shimmied her hips to slither the dress into place, picked up her purse, and left the sanctuary. As she scrubbed her hands, a slender young blonde emerged from another stall and joined her at the sink.

Lou smiled at her in the mirror and said, "Don't you hate having to use the ladies' room in these outfits? I feel like the Incredible Hulk in Catwoman's bodysuit."

The fresh-faced girl looked startled and tilted her head to one side. She must've been a summer intern, eager, ambitious, and idealistic. She wore a simple black cocktail dress accented with a pearl necklace and matching earrings, the uniform of the young and preppy. There were a dozen like her at the party, all with chin-length hair, minimal makeup, clutching small bags containing lip gloss and too many business cards. Probably not a superhero fan.

"Are you Mr. Pontellier's fiancée?" The young woman squinted her eyes, emphasizing her question.

"Yes, I'm Lou." She extended her unclad hand toward the pretty girl.

"Oh, I thought your name was Elizabeth."

"It is, but all my friends call me Lou. Devlin prefers Elizabeth." Lou half smiled and shrugged her shoulders.

"I'm Megan."

She shook Lou's hand, but instead of releasing after the appropriate number of pumps, Megan pulled Lou's hand closer, examining the skin. Lou looked at the shiny scars dotting her pale hands and forearms. It looked as if a makeup artist had been testing for the perfect shade of pinky-red.

"Occupational hazard." Lou pulled her hand back.

"What do you do?" Megan's face looked curious.

Lou rubbed the marks, feeling the smooth bumps.

"I'm a chef. My pastry chef says the more battle scars, the better the food."

"You must be the best chef in the city. It must be nice to come to events like this and get waited on for a change."

"You'd think." Lou's grin shook a little, the muscles tired from too much forced use. Her purse buzzed, and she almost sighed out loud with relief. "Excuse me."

• • • • •

Lou rushed out of the bathroom, pulling her phone from the purse. Devlin waited in the hallway holding a wineglass. She held up a finger while answering the phone and walked outside, Devlin following her.

"What's up?" she said.

"Need to be rescued?" said the confident voice of Sue, Lou's sous chef and best friend. Lou looked up at Devlin, cringing as she observed his tapping foot and raised eyebrow.

"Not yet. Something wrong?"

"No, just checking in. I know how much you love those events. I thought we could fake a catastrophe if you wanted to get out."

"I'll survive. At least the company is good."

"The lawyers and their spouses are good company? How much have you had to drink?"

"Not them. Devlin." Lou smiled at him as he pointed back to the building.

"Really?"

Lou sighed. "I gotta go. Text me later to let me know how the rush goes. Bye."

She slid her phone back into her purse and turned to Devlin.

"Sorry about that. Thanks for the wine," she said as she took the glass he offered.

"Can you not be a chef tonight?"

"I can try."

"You should hire someone to cook for you. Then you'd have more free time."

"I can't afford that. Besides, cooking is the best part."

"I'd think you would enjoy a night off."

"I do. But my idea of pampering doesn't involve high heels and elbow-length gloves. At least not with a gown." Lou gave him a gentle hip bump and a smile.

"The night is young." With a placating smile, Devlin held the door open for her and followed Lou back inside. "Soon you won't need to work anyway, and I can spoil you all the time."

Lou turned to look at Devlin, her eyes pleading with him to listen. "Business is improving. I love it. Why do you keep bringing this up?"

"Elizabeth, you work too hard and you'll need more time once we get a house and have kids. You'll still get to cook amazing food, but you won't need to worry about staffing and rent and bills. It's the ideal situation for you." Devlin gave her a kiss, took her hand, and walked right over her plans. Lou struggled to breathe under the weight of his version of their future.

. . . . .

After dinner, Lou escaped outside into the prematurely warm April night. She peeled off the gloves and stepped out of her shoes onto the cool grass of the practice green, moaning with relief as she texted Sue.

Steady night?

Lou looked up at the stars, waiting for the reply ping.

We hit a new record. 102 plates. Need another server.

Lou let out a whistle of appreciation.

From behind her, she heard voices beyond the edge of the green. Lou walked toward the sound to see a handful of white-coated waiters smoking cigarettes and rehydrating. One of them was Tyler, the waiter she had noticed earlier.

On it.

Keeping her eyes on the servers, Lou slid the phone into her bag, picked up her shoes, and walked toward the group, stepping gently as the soft grass switched to rough pavement.

"Ahem, excuse me. Tyler?" Lou said. Three startled faces looked up, eyes wide at the intrusion. "Sorry, I don't mean to interrupt your break, but do you have a moment?"

"Lou?" Devlin's voice cut through the darkness behind her.

"Crap," Lou said, digging her card out of her clutch. "I own a restaurant—Luella's. If you're looking for a steady job with good tips, give me a call." She pressed the stiff paper into Tyler's hand and turned to see Devlin standing behind her, staring at the waitstaff. She heard them scatter. Devlin's brow wrinkled as he spoke.

"I wondered where you disappeared to. Ready to go?"

Lou exhaled, realizing she had held in her breath, anxious about what Devlin might say. "Yes, please. My feet are killing me."

Devlin looked at her heels dangling from her fingers. "I see that. Why don't we walk around so you don't have to put them back on." He smiled at her, and she relaxed. He took her arm and led her to where his Jaguar waited for them. He guided her into the front seat, pulling a cream gift box from the back with the words "La Perla" adorning the top.

As Devlin slid into the driver's seat, Lou raised one eyebrow at him and said, "Is this part two of your own birthday present?"

Devlin winked, then started the car.

"You know, it's customary for other people to buy you gifts," Lou said.

"Consider it the gift wrap to what I really want."

Lou rolled her eyes and opened the box as Devlin drove out of the parking lot toward his condo. Inside, a tasteful nightgown of robin's egg–blue silk and creamy lace sat nestled in crisp tissue paper. As she lifted it from the box, the delicate material caught on the rough edges of her callused hands, the dainty lace ready to snag. Her spine tensed with worry about destroying the diaphanous fabric. She slithered it back into the box, swallowed, and said, "Shall I try it on when we get back to your place?"

Devlin pointed his chin toward the box. "Look on the inside of the lid."

Lou's eyebrow rose in question, but she flipped the lid over to see a key taped inside.

"A key? To what?"

"My place."

"I already have a key."

Devlin exhaled in frustration.

"I know you already have a key," Devlin said. "I'm trying to ask you to move in with me, and doing a piss-poor job of it. I don't want to wait until we're married, Elizabeth."

Lou swallowed and set the lid back in place.

"Maybe we can save the nightie until I move in—leave it at your place until then?" Lou asked.

Devlin smiled, certain of his success. Lou licked her lips, trying to unglue them from her suddenly dry teeth.

• • • • •

Lou squinted as she studied Harley, her pastry chef, between the shiny shelving separating his domain from the rest of the kitchen at Luella's. He didn't seem to notice her. She could see the amber bottle of vanilla on the shelf a few feet away in his station. She took a step closer, watching Harley's back, squinting at the glare of fluorescent lights off stainless steel. The whirr and snick of Harley's mixer kneading bread dough broke the silence. Another step. Another step. She reached her hand toward the vanilla. Whirr, snick. Whirr, snick. Just a few more inches. Almost there. Just an inch more.

Harley spun when Lou's shirt started to ring. He saw Lou's precarious position and shook his head, denying her. With a sigh, Lou fished the phone out of her bra and put a smile on her face.

"Happy birthday, handsome! You're up early." She turned her back to Harley, looking out the front of the gleaming kitchen.

"So are you," Devlin said. "I was planning to leave a message. I figured you were still sleeping."

"I have vendors coming early today," she lied.

"Fine. You're still planning on getting out early tonight?"

"Unless it gets busy, I should be over by ten. Is that okay?"

"Not until ten? I wanted more time to celebrate with you. Can't you leave that restaurant earlier?" She could practically hear his puppy-dog eyes over the phone. Lou tapped her finger on her lip and considered revealing the imminent visit she had planned, but any desire to appease him was outweighed by her excitement to witness his shock when she showed up in a few hours with the cake. Nothing beat cake for breakfast, especially early surprise birthday cake.

"Sure."

"Great. Can you get my dry cleaning, too?"

Lou sighed. "I don't know if I'll have time."

"Please? For my birthday?"

"Ugh. Sure."

"You're the best."

"I love you, too."

Lou stuffed the phone back into her shirt and returned to her mission. Now was her chance, as Harley layered fragile phyllo dough into a strudel, hunched in concentration. At over six feet tall, heavily tattooed, with teddy-bear brown eyes and a rumbly voice, he was more Jolly Green Giant than Hells Angel, but Harley protected the vanilla like a mama bear. Lou tiptoed toward the shelf, keeping one eye on him, the other on her target. She needed this cake to be spectacular, so she needed the best vanilla—Harley's. He knew a guy who knew a guy in Mexico who made small batches. It was the most potent vanilla she'd ever tasted. She'd seen him mark the sides so he could tell if anyone used it. As long as his back stayed to her . . .

"No," Harley said without turning.

"Hmph." Lou dropped her hand. Her shoulders sagged. She needed that bottle. "Please, Harley. I need your good vanilla for the cake."

"He doesn't deserve it." Harley turned to face her, shaking his head from side to side. "And I can't believe you're moving in with him."

Lou twisted her apron in her hands. "I haven't agreed yet. That's why I need the cake to be perfect."

"He won't appreciate the subtlety. He wants you to move in, so it's inevitable."

"I don't know. A ring is one thing. Moving in . . . it's too real." She reached toward the bottle again.

Harley watched her, waiting for her next move. His neat, blond beard covered his jaw like Kenny Rogers's circa 1985, and an ever-present black bandanna covered any hair he had. His full name was Harley Rhodes. Whether from predestination or paperwork, the name fit him.

"Dammit, Harley, as my pastry chef, I respect you. As a friend, I value you. But right now you're pissing me off. I pay for the stuff. I'll use it when I want." Lou grabbed the bottle and scurried back to her mixer. She could feel Harley smile at her retreating back.

She took a deep breath, blew it out, and began pulling ingredients off shelves, confident where each was, never pausing to think before grabbing. Lou set out a large bowl, then measured each cup of flour, leveling the top. A cloud puffed with each addition to the bowl.

"You should weigh it," Harley said, standing behind her. Lou jumped with a little yip.

"My grandma didn't weigh it."

"You're better than your grandma."

If only. Luella had been Lou's favorite grandma. Some grandmas took their grandchildren to parks, or bought them books and dolls, or shared their special stories. Her grandma shared her recipes. She taught Lou how to check when a roast turkey was done, chop veggies without cutting off a finger, and bake a coconut cake grown men swooned over. A fog of comforting smells had perpetually blanketed her kitchen—an expression of her love so strong you could taste it. Lou caught the culinary bug during those early days and loved that she was named after her grandma, even if Lou believed she'd never make food quite as delicious.

Lou rolled her eyes at Harley's overconfidence.

"I'll do it her way." Lou stared at Harley until he returned to his station. Back to the cake. She added the baking powder and salt and whisked them together. Next, Lou combined the coconut cream and milk in a separate small bowl, lifting it to her nose to enjoy the heady scent.

Lou used her stand mixer to cream the butter, blending until it was smooth. She poured in the sugar and kept mixing until the batter was pale and fluffy. Ingredients in baking were mixed in a specific way to create a specific result—a lot like relationships, Lou thought. If people didn't blend well together, you'd never get the outcome you wanted. Next, she added the coconut extract and Harley's vanilla. Before capping the vanilla, Lou dabbed a little behind her ears as if it were Chanel N°5.

She added the flour and coconut mixture, a little of each at a time, to the butter mixture. The key to a light, delicate cake was to not overmix; handling it too much made the cake dense and tough. If you tried too hard, you ruined it. She wanted Devlin to understand and love the restaurant as much as she did, but every attempt to involve him ended in anger and silence. Too much mixing, Lou thought.

She looked into the bowl. The perfect mix. At least she could get this right.

Lou divided the cake batter into the pans and carried them to the baking ovens. Harley heard her coming.

"Turn back around," he said.

"Harley, I need to bake them."

"It's bad enough you wear my vanilla like perfume; you can't use my baking ovens, too."

"Technically, they're my ovens."

Harley crossed his arms and stood in front of them. "I have bread proofing."

"Fine." Lou stomped back to the main cooking line and put the cakes into the small, yellow-doored oven behind the grill station. This was the oven she used when a dish needed roasting or braising, not quite as precise as the baking ovens, but it'd do. After all, her grandmother had never used a fancy oven. She walked the dirty bowls to the sink, using her finger to scoop up leftover batter, closing her eyes to fully experience the balanced flavors—not too sweet, plenty of coconut, but not so much you couldn't taste the vanilla. Perfect. Grandma would be proud.

"You want in on this?" Lou held out the bowl. Harley walked over, took a fingerful, and dabbed it on his tongue.

"And?" asked Lou.

"Should have used the scale." But Lou could see a faint smile in his whiskers. As his hand reached for another sample, she pulled it away.

"Then no more for you." She set it by the sink and walked away but saw Harley sneak the bowl back to his corner.

With the cakes baking, Lou made some breakfast for the two of them. She slapped a few slices of bacon on the heated griddle. Sizzling started immediately and the scent of rising coconut cake mingled with the smoky salt of bacon. "Heaven." She buttered day-old baguettes to toast, then cracked a few eggs for breakfast sandwiches. "Now some cheese. Brie? Emmental? Mmm, smoky onion cheddar."

The sounds of her cooking bounced around the empty restaurant like a Super Ball, reminding her of where she was and why. She still couldn't believe Luella's was hers, that she'd mustered the guts to open it. If Sue and Harley hadn't promised to work for her, she never would have done it. Going it alone was never an option. Each month she felt a thrill of shock when her balance sheet squeaked into the black. The profits were tiny, but they existed. After over a year of hard work, it looked like Luella's just might make it.

Standing at the sink to eat breakfast, Lou drained two cups of coffee laced with enough sugar and cream to make it dessert. She set her dishes in the sink for the dishwasher just as the timer dinged. Heat blasted out when she opened the oven; the sweet smell of coconut saturated her nose. The cakes glowed with golden perfection, tender to the touch—perfect. She had made four rounds, so that if she screwed up two taking them out of the pans, she'd have backups. Besides, her staff would devour the backup cake during prep. While the cakes cooled, Lou made the frosting: more softened unsalted butter, more fresh coconut milk—just enough to make it spreadable—powdered sugar, and more of the precious vanilla. So creamy and decadent, Lou used her finger to scoop out a Ping-Pong-ball-sized glob.

After frosting the cake and sprinkling on toasted coconut for a little crunch, Lou glanced at the clock. The little hand hovered by the seven.

"Damn!" Lou slid the freshly frosted confection onto the cardboard box, then folded it around the cake. She tied the box closed with butcher's twine, grabbed her keys, waved to Harley, and rushed to the door as Sue entered the kitchen. Lou noticed Harley stop and stare at the newest arrival.

"Morning, Lou. Hey, Harley. Coffee on?" Sue said in his direction, avoiding eye contact. Eyeing the box in Lou's hands and sniffing the vanilla-and-coconut-scented kitchen, she finished braiding her long, red hair. She always wore two braids while cooking. If things got really hot, she'd tie them on top of her head in an overexcited Pippi Longstocking look. Lou smiled at Sue's no-nonsense greeting.

"Yup," said Lou. "Gotta go, I've got to run some errands before I surprise Devlin with his cake. He's expecting it tonight, but I thought a prework birthday party would be a nice treat. I'll be back later. The backup cake is by the coffee—dig in." Then Lou leaned in to whisper, "Let me know what Harley says."

"Sure thing." Sue walked out to the coffee station, then, with a mouth full of cake, added, "He doesn't deserve you, Lou." But Lou rushed out the front door toward the corner, purse in one hand and cake in the other, eager to surprise her fiancé.

• CHAPTER TWO •

Al Waters stood at the corner of St. Paul and Milwaukee Streets, a crisp, white note card in one hand, irritation on his face, and the wind at his back. The snow-white, thick paper had two imperfections: blue-gray engraved initials, DP, in the bottom right, and a suggestion, "Mr. Wodyski, Consider visiting Luella's at 320 St. Paul Street."

In response to such a succinct directive, Al had made all the arrangements so A. W. Wodyski could dine incognito at Luella's tonight. Right now, he just needed to find the bloody place: "Three-oh-six, 312, 320. Here it is." On the back of the card, he scrawled,

Hours
S, T–H 5–10
F+S 5–12

Al studied the entrance. He liked to scout restaurants before dining to see what they looked like without the hustle and bustle of other patrons as a distraction. Through the window, he could see a woman with ginger braids near the kitchen doors. The chef, most likely. *Luella's—dull name—probably a grandmother*, thought Al. He looked at the menu posted in a small, bronze-framed box to the right of the restaurant's entrance. His mouth grimaced at the laundry list of ordinary French dishes. The review practically wrote itself.

Al shivered and headed back toward Milwaukee Street, scowling at the chill wind whistling between the city buildings, a contrast to the bright, blue sky above him. He remembered seeing a Starbucks a few blocks away and could use a hot cup of tea, even from there. As he walked into the crowded coffee shop, the caffeinated air slapped him in the face. Coffee had no subtlety. It was bitter at best, mud from a rubbish heap at worst. He could manage a latte or mocha, but that didn't count as coffee. Al shuffled to the counter to order his Earl Grey with a splash of milk. Starbucks had an absurd tea selection—Darjeeling and Earl Grey were the only reasonable options. The rest involved berries and herbs, which no self-respecting Englishman would order.

He waited for his tea at the pickup counter, tapping his foot at a rapid pace. Finally, he grabbed the hot drink and worked his way through the caffeine-deprived crowd toward the door, still polite and smiling at him as he pushed through. What were they so cheery about at seven in the morning?

Al left the coffee shop and crossed the street to the Milwaukee Public Market, the one small but bright spot in Milwaukee's culinary scene. He had heard about an outdoor farmers' market here in the summer, but after four months in the freezing, godforsaken city, he thought summer was a cruel joke locals played on new arrivals. It was supposed to be the first warm day of spring, which was why he'd left his winter coat at his flat. Foolish of him.

The Milwaukee Public Market consisted of one building the size of a small city block. Of the two stories, the first contained several booths for vendors ranging from coffee to beef to spices. All good quality and a decent variety for such a small market, though it was nothing compared to the meandering and never-ending food stalls of London, Paris, or even Vancouver's Granville Island. The second story had a small seating area for people to watch the action below and sample their parcels. A few of the stands catered to the downtown lunch crowd—business folks looking for a reason to escape their cubicles for a minute of sunshine and fresh air. On the rare occasion when Al wasn't eating out for work, he came to the Public Market to pick out the freshest ingredients for dinner. This morning, he just wanted to get out of the wind.

The queue at the newsstand where he liked to buy his newspaper was long, but Al had time. Because he worked afternoons and into the evening, he didn't have to be in the office until noon. While waiting, Al rocked back and forth, from his toes to his heels, sipping the hot tea. He closed his eyes and took a deep breath, savoring the familiar warmth and comfort. It almost tasted like home: fragrant, clean, just a touch of milk. Al took another deep breath to warm himself a little when coconut, vanilla, and bacon scents mingled with his Earl Grey. Al looked around, curious about the enticing smells, and nearly collided with a fair-faced, brown-haired woman standing right behind him, causing a few drops of tea to splash onto the pristine white box she held.

"So sorry," Al blurted out as he turned toward her, catching the cup before disaster. The woman's face warmed into a stunning smile—straight teeth, except one that was charmingly askew. Her nose crinkled a little when her grin reached its widest, making her faint freckles dance.

"No serious damage done," the woman said.

Al couldn't help but smile back—she had that kind of face. A ponytail, tied low on her head and not quite pulled through the last time, kept the hair away from her face. She didn't wear any makeup and, more importantly, didn't need it. She wore jeans—not too tight, not too loose—and a warm-looking brown quilted vest over a long-sleeve brown T-shirt. She eclipsed everything around them. He couldn't stop staring though he knew he should, but he wanted her image seared into his memory.

Al shivered again, despite himself.

"Cold?" the woman asked.

"Bloody freezing. The weatherman said it would be seventy-five today; it can't be more than fifty."

The woman nodded with a little smile. "It's the lake." Al frowned. "You know, cooler near the lake," she explained.

"What?"

"Cooler near the lake. I'm sure the weather report said that, too."

"Maybe. But we aren't on the lake."

"We're close enough. The lake's not more than ten blocks that way." The woman gestured over his shoulder. "Cooler near the lake can mean a few miles inland. Lake Michigan is so big, it does all sorts of crazy things to our weather. Wait until we get lake-effect snow." The woman's smile got even larger, with a hint of gentle teasing. "I suggest layers."

. . . . .

Lou tried hard to not laugh at the poor guy. He looked frozen in his neatly pressed tan pants and light blue dress shirt. His shirt pulled against his fit shoulders and arms as he crossed them, trying to stay warm. He wasn't very tall, so she could see his shocking blue eyes, the kind of eyes that would change based on how he felt. Right now, they looked like a blue winter sky: brilliant but cold. His frosty face said he spent too much time indoors, and his straight features reminded her of the private-school boys in movies like *Dead Poets Society* and *The Chocolate War*. His hair was a dark brown, short on the sides but longer and shaggier on top—the kind of hair you could bury your hands in during a really spectacular kiss. His scruffy face broadcasted he hadn't shaved for a few days and would probably scratch while kissing. Perhaps she should offer to warm him up. Lou shook her head to focus as he asked her a question.

"So what's in the box? Coconut?"

"A coconut cake." She adjusted the dry cleaning and coffee to get a better grip on the box. She had almost dropped it when the man turned around so quickly.

"Where did you get it?" The man leaned forward to get a good sniff.

"I made it." His eyes widened.

"Really? Someone is very lucky." With that, he paid the cashier for his paper and disappeared down the street, turning back once before disappearing around a corner.

With a sigh, Lou bought the gum Devlin preferred and a local paper because she wanted to see what this A. W. Wodyski was like. Her phone buzzed with a text from Sue.

Harley ate a piece the size of a suburban raccoon. I'd say he liked it.

Lou looked forward to teasing him later. With a grin, she tucked the newspaper under her arm and slid the gum into her vest pocket, adjusted the dry cleaning so it couldn't slide out of the plastic bags, took a little sip of Devlin's soy latte, and picked up the cake box from where she had set it on the newsstand counter.

Glancing at the clocks behind the counter, she realized she had thirty minutes before Devlin left for work. Clutching all the items, she hurried the few blocks to Devlin's apartment, arriving while the coffee was still hot, so hot she was thankful for her heat-callused hands. A little scalding coffee felt good on a chilly morning.

She hadn't given Devlin an answer to the La Perla question (as she liked to think of it), so the lingerie sat unused in his closet. Moving in seemed more real than the engagement. Since they hadn't even discussed wedding dates, Lou hadn't felt much different other than owning a sparkly piece of jewelry. Nothing else had changed. She liked the idea of sharing a life with someone, always having a date on Valentine's Day and someone to open presents with on Christmas, but moving in meant real changes. Leaving her apartment, melting her life into Devlin's—combining their books, their music, their clothes.

While she wasn't often home, she loved knowing her apartment waited for her, with her pictures, her cookbooks, her bed. She liked Devlin's apartment well enough, but it had too many nice things. He always reminded her to be careful so she wouldn't knock over a statue and asked her not to drink wine on his couch. All too often, she felt like an actor in a play, performing only actions outlined in the script. She needed her apartment as a place to spill food, be loud, break things, be herself.

But she also looked forward to sharing their days over a bottle of good wine, planning out Devlin's next career step, and laughing over the ridiculous antics of opposing counsel. Yes, the comfort outweighed her concerns. They would work out their disagreement over her restaurant—maybe she could convince him to bring clients in to dinner, perhaps a private dinner after hours. People loved to get special treatment at restaurants. Lou smiled, her decision lifting the worry off her shoulders.

She quietly slid her key into Devlin's lock and bit the twine so the cake box wouldn't topple out of her hands. With the door slightly ajar, Lou moved the box back to her hand to free her mouth and bumped the door wide open with her hip.

"Surprise!" Lou scanned the apartment for Devlin but only saw Megan, the blonde intern from the gala, standing in Devlin's living room and wearing Lou's blue La Perla nightgown.

Lou's jaw was still open and body frozen when Devlin ran out of his bedroom wearing only boxers and carrying an armload of clothes. He looked at Lou, then at Megan, then back at Lou.

"It's not what you think," he said, dropping the clothes and holding his hands out in front of him as if to stop a car crash. A pair of black lace underwear topped the pile. Her mind struggled to reconcile the scene before her with what she'd expected to find moments ago.

Then it hit Lou like an ice cream headache, cold and blinding. Lou dropped everything. Coffee splattered over the opened apartment door, dry-cleaning plastic slithered off her arm, the cake box broke apart as it hit the wood floor, splattering the frosted cake, soaking up the coffee, and staining the freshly laundered clothes with butter fat. Steaming coffee melted her beautiful coconut cake into slush.

Her heart lay in there somewhere, too, leaving an empty, lonely chasm in her chest. Lou closed her mouth to keep from being sick and took a step away from the open door and into the hallway, eyes still on Devlin. At last, she turned and rushed down the stairs and out of the building, bumping into a passerby as she reached the sidewalk.

"Sorry," she mumbled, and disappeared down the street.

. . . . .

Al staggered back as a brown-haired blur bumped into him. It was the coconut cake girl again. Al watched Miss Coconut Cake rush down the street, the frosting smeared on the toe of her shoe leaving smudges on the pavement. The pain on her face left smudges on him. He had the urge to follow her, make her smile at him like she had in line at the newsstand. A gust of cold spring wind whooshed down the narrow street, shoving him in her direction. He followed the frosting trail down the sidewalk. When he reached the corner, it disappeared into a busy throng of people rushing to work, with no sign of the cakeless Miss Coconut Cake.

Al shrugged and turned down the street, faintly let down at having lost sight of her. *Probably for the best,* he thought—he didn't plan to be in Milwaukee very long.

• CHAPTER THREE •

"Hey, Harley, has Lou called?" Sue asked. "I thought she'd be back by now to open." Now past noon, Harley had started baking bread and making the night's desserts while Sue worked on prep.

"Nope."

"I'm calling her cell—she's never been this late. I don't care what she's giving that ass for his birthday."

"Okay."

"I'm telling her you ate half the cake."

"Fine, I'm worried. Happy?"

Harley and Sue looked up as they heard the back door shut. Lou wafted in. Her hair looked windblown even though it wasn't windy, her coat hung open, and her face was as chalky as the chef jacket she reached for. She missed it four times before lifting it off the hook.

"What did he do?" Sue rushed from behind the prep counter. Lou dragged her face up to look at Sue, but her eyes were fixed on the kitchen behind her.

"I dropped the cake," Lou said.

"Ooooh, that sucks. Was he pissed? Harley will help you make another. Right, Harley?"

Harley grumbled a yes.

"There won't be any more cake."

"What did that jackhole say to you?" Sue asked.

Lou gave her head a little shake but couldn't quite get the lost look out of her eyes. "It's over. I don't want to talk about it. Where are we on prep?"

Harley walked from the pastry station and—without a word—engulfed Lou in his bare, tattooed arms. Once inside those sugar-coated pythons, Lou soaked Harley's T-shirt.

"I'll put her in the Lair. We're on our own tonight," Harley said, walking Lou toward the office door at the rear of the kitchen. Inside, recipes, pictures, and scribbled menu ideas hung from every surface; a mountain of paper covered the desk; and stacks of cookbooks, files, and supplies filled most of the spare floor space. A small cot sat in one corner and an open door led to a bathroom complete with shower. When the restaurant first opened, Lou had spent hours alone in there, only to emerge with a gleam in her eye and a new idea for the restaurant. Sue called Lou an evil genius, hatching plots in her Volcano Lair. Now everyone just called it the Lair. As they entered the room, the phone began to ring. Sue shoved a stack of paper onto the floor to reveal the caller ID. She looked into Harley's face and picked up the phone.

"If you ever bother her again, I will slice your bits off and serve it for the daily special." She slammed the phone down.

"Too nice," Harley said.

Lou took a deep, shuddering breath and unwrapped herself

from Harley's arms. She looked around at the clutter and shook her head.

"Thanks, but I can't stay in here. I need to work. If I sit still, I'll think too much." Lou yanked off her chunk of an engagement ring and tossed it on her desk, then walked past Harley and Sue, entirely missing the concerned look they exchanged.

• • • • •

Eleven a.m. and Al arrived at work, hustling through the newspaper's cubicle farm, passing faces he recognized with names he didn't try to remember. When he reached his desk, his cube neighbor already sat at his desk, adjacent to Al's.

"What's up with this cooler-near-the-lake bollocks?" Al asked.

"Bit nippy this morning?" said John. John wrote the style pages for the paper, but Al thought his appearance left something to be desired. His stoner-meets-mountain-man brown hair and beard made it difficult to discern facial structure and looked as if they hadn't seen water in a good month. John mentioned once he hoped to attract a girl who found facial hair sexy; a girl like that might be into some kinky stuff. He said there were websites.

Today, John wore a heavily wrinkled button-down shirt with a front pocket where he kept two pens (green and purple), wrinkly khakis, and red Converse All Stars. Al saw a little chest hair poking out the top of his shirt.

"Bloody frigid. What's with the hair?" Al gestured at John's neckline.

"I stopped manscaping."

"They're called T-shirts, mate."

"No, the ladies love the chest hair. There are websites devoted to it."

"Have you ever actually Googled any of those topics you mention, or are you all talk?"

"Not on work computers."

During the four months Al had worked at the newspaper, he'd been unable to reconcile his colleague's desk with his appearance. John's bookshelf had all the current fashion magazines neatly filed alphabetically. He separated his bulletin board into quadrants, each with a theme containing swatches, pictures, and street photos. A sleek copper lamp with a pale green silk lampshade stood on his desk and a chocolate-brown cashmere throw was draped from his chair. Neat stacks of boxes under his desk contained shoes and clothing samples from local stores.

Al swiveled around and pushed the power button on his computer. As it whirred to life, he set out the stiff note card with the address and hours for Luella's. His desk was gray and dull. The only clues to the owner's personality were several books on food and criticism residing on the shelf. He tried to keep a low profile given his secret identity, and a spare cube discouraged coworkers from extraneous conversations—though nothing seemed to deter the nearest one.

"Wanna grab a drink after work?" asked John.

"I've a restaurant to review, sorry."

"Which one?"

"Luella's."

"Can I come?"

"No."

"Why not?"

" 'Cause you've a big mouth."

"Some girls like that."

Al rolled his eyes and turned to his computer. John smiled behind his back. The screen finally displayed all the correct icons and had ceased its noise, so Al opened a blank document and started typing tonight's review, reveling in his scathing wordplay. He would fill in the details later, after he'd dined at the restaurant a few times to experience a variety of dishes and servers.

"Good morning, Al." The smooth, melodic voice of Hannah, Al's editor, spoke from above. Late thirties, blonde, and wicked smart. Semiframeless glasses perched on her nose, and her hair was tucked into a bun with a few pencils poking out at random angles. She'd taken a chance on hiring him as an unproven food writer, making her one of the few people Al respected. He'd been covering the royals, many of whom he'd attended school with at Eton, for the *London Journal*. While he hated the beat, the subject matter gave him room to hone his sharp-tongued writing style. After a few years reporting on vapid rich kids and their parents, he wanted out. With the goal of getting as far away from the royals as possible and, of course, following his passion, he applied for every open food writer position in the States. Hannah was the first to scoop him up. She knew talent when she found it.

"We've been getting some feedback on your reviews."

"And?"

"I quote"—Hannah cleared her throat, holding an e-mail printout in front of her face—" 'I've never had so much fun reading a food column. I love Wodyski's witty comments. Now I don't need to waste my time trying bad restaurants.' "

"At least I'm helping someone."

"I've got several more. A few think you're a little mean, but you can't please everyone. I've got more who love you. Keep it up, Waters—you've got fans."

After Hannah disappeared into the maze of cubicles, John asked, "So why Wodyski?"

Still facing away, Al rolled his eyes to the ceiling and took a deep breath.

"I couldn't use my real name, could I?"

"I get that—but why that name?"

Al whirled to look at him.

"Because it sounds Polish."

"And?"

"It makes me sound more local, like I can be trusted."

"You think us Milwaukeeans are that gullible?"

"It's working so far." Al gestured in the direction Hannah had gone, then returned to his work.

• • • • •

Al paused outside Luella's, remembering Miss Coconut Cake. He couldn't stop thinking about her infectious smile, freckled nose, and sad frosting trail. He shivered as a brisk wind blew from behind, nudging him toward the door. He entered two hours after Luella's opened and was greeted by a quietly crowded bar and dining room with a distracted hostess. *Unprofessional,* he thought.

Crisp white linens topped small tables, looking like chess pieces on the black-and-white-checkered floor. Black-and-white photos of famous French landmarks broke up the plain white walls. The cliché thickened with each detail—baguettes stacked behind the bar, fake grapes spilling out of baskets, and taper candles melted over empty bottles of wine. He could have found a French restaurant like this one in any city in the world.

"Reservation?" Al looked up as the hostess finally acknowledged him.

"Yes, one for Waters."

He dined alone tonight, as he did most nights. He hadn't established a dependable and discrete group of people he could take out for meals, though John asked about once a week—probably looking for a meal on the paper.

"Follow me," the hostess said, casting a glance over her shoulder.

The hostess sat him at a table with a view of the kitchen doors. He set out his iPad and typed, "Rude hostess," then looked around the room. He couldn't see into the kitchen, just glimpses when a waiter walked through. It looked clean and bright, but a clean kitchen should be the bare minimum standard. The hostess rushed off to a group of waiters near the coffee machine. While the restaurant had empty tables, it wasn't dead, so it seemed odd for the waitstaff to congregate. He looked around and saw other customers noticing the group. A few tables had empty plates ready to clear, others needed refills on drinks, but the staff kept gossiping. He typed, "Distracted waitstaff."

After more time than was strictly acceptable, a waiter appeared, took his order, and disappeared. He'd ordered the first item under each menu category: seared foie gras with a Bordeaux reduction, toasted-goat-cheese salad, sole meunière, and lemon soufflé. Al lifted his shirtsleeve to start the timer on his watch.

• • • • •

Focus on the orders, focus on the orders, thought Lou in a chant. She took a steadying breath, squinted at the tickets, called out the orders (two soles, three drunk chickens, and a special), and struggled to find her groove. The routine of the nightly rush started to kick in. If she kept moving forward, she wouldn't have time to look back. She bent down to open the cooler near the grill station, which she was working tonight. Sue hadn't let her near the sauté station, saying that too much could go wrong. She pulled out the chickens and a hanger steak for the special and tossed them on the grill, sprinkling them with salt and pepper. Lou noticed some plates waiting to go out, baking under the heat lamps—a pet peeve even on a good day.

"Why is table three's food still sitting here?" Lou said, much louder than normal.

"It's waiting on the grilled scallops." Sue raised an eyebrow at Lou.

"It can start going out while the scallops finish." *Why can't the waiters do anything without being told? They know better than to leave food sitting there.* Lou buzzed Tyler, whose first day on the job was tonight.

Tyler's head appeared in the window, and Lou pointed at the order with her silver tongs. "Get this food out."

"But—"

"Get. It. Out. Come back for the rest." Tyler grabbed the dishes and ran, looking over at Sue for reassurance.

"Little rough, don't ya think?" said Sue.

"Not when I have customers waiting for food."

Lou tossed up the finished scallop plate just as Tyler returned for the rest of the order. She stared at him until he took the food and delivered it, then she returned to the grill to pull the meat off. Instead of perfectly cooked chicken and steaks ready for plating, smoking remains poked at Lou's already wounded pride.

"Damn it!" She grabbed the food with her bare hand and tossed it into the garbage, wincing at what she knew would be another burn mark in the morning.

After Lou's outburst, everyone in the kitchen worked silently—college-library-during-finals silent. Sue and Harley flashed each other concerned looks. The dishwasher actually flinched when she tossed a pan in the sink. Her emotions roiled; anger, betrayal, and sadness all made her unstable, like two fronts crashing together on a stormy summer evening. She lit the air with profanities for every imperfection. Her glares sizzled and had the waitstaff avoiding the kitchen and gossiping by the coffee machine.

With each outburst, Lou hated herself a little more. What was wrong with her? This was her family and she was treating them abysmally. She wasn't mad at them; she was mad at herself for trusting Devlin, relying on him to be part of her life, part of her family. Assuming he cared about her best interests. But he had never loved the restaurant. Looking back, she realized he had only tolerated it. He had even tried to talk her out of it right when she'd finally saved enough money to open Luella's.

Lou remembered the night she told Devlin she had found her location. It was a year and a half ago, and they were dining out on one of the few nights she didn't work.

"I found it." Lou had chewed her cheek, head down a little so she had to look at him under her eyelashes, wrinkles forming on her forehead.

"My iPod? Great, I hoped you would." Devlin watched the businessmen at the next table, trying to hear their discussion. His head hadn't turned when she'd started speaking.

"No, my restaurant." Lou's voice barely carried over the restaurant din. Devlin turned now, his expression suggesting she'd just revealed she could fly using fairy wings she kept hidden using duct tape and gauze.

"I thought you'd given up on that. Besides, you don't have the money." His attention returned to the men.

"Dev, you know I—" Lou started to say.

Devlin held up a finger for silence, then a smile spread across his face. He turned to Lou. "Looks like I'll be making some calls tomorrow. A merger is in the works. Now, what were you saying?"

Lou took a deep breath. "I want to try owning my own restaurant. Sue and Harley think I'd be great at it. I saved enough. I found the perfect place."

"Why do you want to keep working in restaurants? I told you, I'll take care of you. With your support, I'll be one of the top attorneys in Wisconsin. That's where our efforts should be focused."

"Devlin, I need to try this. I'm sorry if you don't understand." He looked back at her, studying her face, her posture, as if she were a new car he might like to buy or a witness he wanted to break.

"Okay, Elizabeth, but I don't want it to distract from our plans."

End of conversation. For once, Devlin must have sensed her determination. But he'd ignored all her planning and had only eaten at Luella's three times since she'd opened.

"Lou, you okay if I take a quick break?" Lou looked over at Sue to see blood dripping off her wrist.

"What the . . . ?"

"It's just a minor cut, but I need to stop the bleeding," Sue said.

"Go." Lou waved her tongs at her, hearing Harley ask whether she needed help. Lou's attention turned to another ticket for sole meunière. Lou started the fish at the sauté station, then returned to the grill.

"Chef?" a quiet voice asked from the window.

"Yes, Tyler."

"Can you put a rush on the sole for table twelve? He's been here a while."

Lou saw red. She glared at Tyler.

"Fine."

Four more orders arrived. Lou flipped the damn fish, started two more orders of sole, then rushed to the grill to turn all the items before she burned more food.

"Where the hell is Sue?" Lou shouted. She slammed a pan down on a burner and lit it to start the sauce for the fish. She tossed in the ingredients, but as she reached for the salt, her sleeve caught the cooking brandy, spilling it across the lit burners and sending flames whooshing to the industrial vents above the cooking area. Lou jumped back, but not before singed hair crinkled around her face and her sleeve caught fire.

Food first. She pulled the flaming fish and sauce off the stove and covered it with a lid to extinguish the flames. By the time she used a damp rag to douse her sleeve, the ignited brandy had burnt low, then flickered out. Before she could finish assessing the damage, Tyler's face appeared in the window.

"Chef?"

She slid the rescued fish out of the pan onto a plate and dumped the butter sauce over the top.

Lou slammed the plate under the heat lamp and shouted, "Order."

"And that's enough," said Sue from behind her, her wrist neatly wrapped in duct tape. She grabbed Lou's hand and looked her straight in the eyes. "I say this as your best friend. You're a raging bitch right now. While I'd like a little more sass from you, that's not your thing. Go wash dishes until you can get your attitude under control. And what did you do to the food?"

Lou's eyes widened as she stared at the sauté station. She saw one overdone and one half-cooked fillet, both charred.

"I grabbed the wrong one. Get that order back." Lou peered out the pickup window, hoping to see Tyler holding it on the other side.

But it had already been served. Sue firmly pushed Lou toward the dishwashing area.

"I can handle it. The worst of the rush is over." Sue turned back to the line of tickets and started a new sole to remedy the complaint.

• • •

And stop. Al pushed a button on his wristwatch. Thirty-three minutes since his salad. He looked at the plate. The fish looked wan, drowning in its sauce. The capers were scattered haphazardly. A pathetic wedge of lemon clung to the edge of the white plate as if for its life. He nudged the empty salad plate away from the silverware so he could pick up a fork. On his iPad under "Decent salad," he typed, "Limp fish, poor presentation, slow service, no bread." Al cut into the middle of the fish to take a bite. The inside looked underdone. Perhaps the edge would be safer. He took a bite and gagged. Somehow the fish was over- and underdone, with a heavy alcohol flavor. He wasn't staying for soufflé.

"Check, please."

• • • • •

Lou took over washing pots and pans for the night, embracing the heavy, repetitive labor. She scrubbed every pan immaculately, pretending each was Devlin's lying face. Anger and hurt flooded her, blinding her to everything else. She scrubbed and scrubbed, expunging the indignation, the fury, the misery. Harley or Sue, she didn't look up to verify who, put more pans next to the sink and she scrubbed. Then someone else put them away. She didn't think, she just scrubbed, stopping occasionally to swab the damp off her face.

Devlin never supported her unless it aligned with his goals. His generous gifts, future plans, and lofty aspirations were always his, not hers. He made her feel safe, and sometimes sheltered, as if he stood between her and real life, as if she were a princess he wanted locked away in a tower, a beautiful but boring tower. But he had needed her, too, in his own way—needed someone to protect, to take care of, keep safe. Someone to help exorcise the demons left over from watching his mother deteriorate as she worked herself to the bone at restaurants. But this morning had shifted her understanding of their entire relationship. She held back tears as she tried to scrub him out of her life.

By the end of the night, she dripped from head to toe, every muscle ached, and her pots hadn't looked this clean since they'd come out of their boxes. When no more pots and pans appeared, she staggered to the Lair and closed the door behind her.

CHAPTER FOUR

Al never, ever got sick. He had eaten dodgy foods from Shanghai to Mexico City, from food trucks and back-alley counters. One reckless evening he even drank tap water in a small Indian village an hour outside Mumbai. During a college trip to North Africa, every one of his friends spent some time locked in their hotel room bathroom while he explored the vibrant souks and sampled more of the fragrant foods, uninterrupted. He was quite proud that he could eat anything, anywhere without negative effects—so the unsettled stomach ruining his morning made him particularly cantankerous toward Luella's.

His review was due to Hannah by three o'clock for the Friday edition. He'd mostly finished it last night while awake with stomach cramps. The discomfort sharpened his wit to a samurai sword; this was his most scathing review yet. A little smile twitched at the corners of his mouth. After this review, he hoped no one else would have to endure indigestion at the hands of Luella's inept chef. Serving undercooked fish should be criminal, outside of a sushi bar. And Luella's was most definitely not sushi.

"Why're you here so early?" asked John as he set his camouflage messenger bag on his chair, a perfect accompaniment to his shabby appearance. Then Al noticed the tiny print on the shiny silver buckles.

"Is that camouflage Prada? Where did you find that in Milwaukee?"

John looked pleased and guilty at Al's observation.

"Chicago. Though I find a lot of stuff online."

Al sniffed. "That's where I go when I want good food. And a promotion." He added the last part under his breath.

"We should take the Hiawatha down sometime. I can show you the great shops. You can show me the great eats."

Al stared. "You want to go to Chicago with me?"

"You can't be an ass all of the time. It might be fun." John shrugged. "So, why are you here so early?"

"Submitting my review from last night."

"Wasn't that your first visit? Don't you normally go a few times?"

"After last night, there's no need." He took a meaningful sip of tea and turned back to his monitor. His eyes settled on an e-mail he'd been avoiding. With a sigh, he opened it. It had arrived last week from his mother, but he hadn't had the stomach to open it then. Now on a high from writing his review, he was ready. Attached was a scanned article from the *Windsor Observer*, his hometown newspaper. Ian, his perfect older brother, had donated several million pounds to build a new library at Eton.

During their schoolboy days, Ian had always fit in effortlessly with the much wealthier families, comfortable with the sleek private jets, castle-like country homes, and watches worth more than most cars. He had embraced the privileged world of high collars with coat and tails while Al squirmed, drowning in the school uniforms, more dork than dashing. Everyone had expected him to come from the same Golden Boy mold as his brother, but he could never quite fit, never quite found himself. Instead, he was the awkward teacher's son who squirmed in the back of class, avoiding notice. Ian acted as if he belonged, so he belonged. Al had just counted the days until he could be free of his brother's long shadow.

So Ian would now be immortalized at Eton—fantastic for him. He was even putting Dad's name on the building, earning him another hash mark on the "best son" scorecard. He must have had a great year in investment banking. Al looked at the time—8:44. He moved his fingers, counting—2:44 in London. He dialed Ian's office number and heard the familiar ringback tones.

"Mr. Waters's office, Margie speaking."

"Hello, Margie. This is Al Waters. Is he available for a moment or two?"

"One moment, please."

The Muzak version of "Yellow Submarine" played as Al waited on hold. He sipped tea, watching John's back as he worked. From behind, he resembled a caveman fumbling with a computer, an image at odds with his elegant cube.

"Al! You saw the article, didn't you?" Ian's voice broke into Al's thoughts. He sat up and turned back to his desk.

"Mum sent it. Congrats, mate. Now Eton can never forget you."

"Thanks. Dad's a bit overwhelmed at the mo. They would have named a building after him sooner or later—I just made it happen while he could still savor it."

"You're such a good son," Al muttered.

"Don't be a twit. So, when should I come visit you in Milwaukee? I haven't seen you in ages. You can show me the sights." Al could hear papers shuffling in the background, Ian managing to work and be kind to his little brother at the same time.

Al thought about his first impression of Milwaukee—the gray lake, the boarded-up shopwindows down Wisconsin Avenue, the Milwaukee River, frothy like a bitter, dark beer. He imagined walking Ian past the graffiti-covered alley walls and up the dark, narrow stairs to his apartment. His view was of the busy street in front of his building, not the grand views Ian had in his many homes.

"There's nothing to see—trust me. And I won't be here much longer. Wait until I'm someplace better." Al took another gulp of now-cold tea. He never had anything that he felt was worth sharing with his brother, so their conversations dwindled into awkwardness. "I better be off. Just wanted to say congrats."

"Thanks, mate. See you soon, I hope."

Al set down the phone and rubbed under his too-tight collar.

• • • • •

Everything hurt, inside and out. Muscles on her back twitched from sleeping on the office cot, her hands were rubbed raw from the hot water and harsh soap used to wash the dishes, and her face hurt from fighting back tears. She remembered staggering into the Lair and tumbling onto the cot the night before, her aching body a testament to her hard work. Lou knew Sue had capably finished the night as the sole chef. Sue could run any kitchen, but she shouldn't have to run Luella's.

With a deep breath, Lou sat up, smoothed her hair, and opened her eyes. Her cluttered office surrounded her, giving her comfort. The shards melted a little; her heart reinforced itself. She told herself Devlin was no longer important. It didn't matter if she was alone. Her restaurant and, more importantly, her employees needed her. A pan clanged from the kitchen. Lou glanced at the round clock hanging on the wall—the little hand hovered near the ten. Sue must have come in assuming Lou would be useless again. Not today. Not ever again. A coffee-scented breeze wafted into the Lair, and Lou followed its trail out of her office and into the already-bustling kitchen.

It wasn't just Sue. Harley's bandanna-covered head bopped to a Katy Perry song as he vigorously chopped onions. All the busboys and dishwashers washed floors and walls. Lou grabbed Tyler's arm as he walked by with a stack of freshly laundered napkins. He jumped a little when he felt her hand.

"Sorry about last night," Lou said, and looked him straight in the eye. Tyler moved his shoulders.

"We all have bad days."

"But I'm the boss. I should have known better."

Tyler smiled. "We're cool."

Lou smiled back. "Is there a health inspection I don't know about?" She pointed at the bustling kitchen.

"No." Tyler shook his head. "We just wanted to do something to make you feel better. Harley wouldn't let us go after your fiancé. This seemed the next-best option." He continued out to the dining room, where the entire waitstaff were cleaning everything, from the light fixtures to the coffeepots. New tears misted her eyes.

"You gonna help or just stand there leaking all over the clean floor?" Sue noticed her late arrival and knew just how to get her moving. Sentimentality had no place in the kitchen. Her staff's actions showed her they'd forgiven her meltdown; they didn't need to say anything. Back to work as usual—exactly what she needed after the turmoil of yesterday. She lost herself in the kitchen; the smell of fresh bread and simmering veal stock, the hum of the kitchen vents over the stove and grill, the chatter of her staff as they worked—they were a healing salve on her still-throbbing wounds. She wasn't better yet, but she would be.

"Did Chris drop off the Bordeaux he promised?" Lou asked Sue, knowing her sous had stood in her place with all the early-morning vendors to pick out the best produce, meats, cheeses, or whatever hard-to-find morsels they might have unearthed. Sue's jaw clenched and her eyes tightened in response to Lou's question.

"No," she said. "He claimed he didn't have any in our price range."

"But I already paid him for it," Lou groaned.

"I know—that's why I told him he'll give us something better to make up for the inconvenience. Billy's putting the cases of wine in the cellar right now." Sue's smile implied her convincing involved unveiled threats, her favorite kind to make.

"You shouldn't have done that. He'll think we're cheap. I'll have to pay him the difference."

"I don't give a damn what he thinks, and we shouldn't pay him any extra. He's trying to screw you like he always does. It's time to find a new wine vendor who won't try to take advantage of your Midwestern good manners."

"You're probably right." Lou chewed her lip. "Anything good on the trucks?"

"Some beautiful lake salmon, fresh asparagus, and new potatoes."

"New enough their skin is peeling?"

"Yes."

"I know what we're going to do today!" Lou felt the excitement surge. This was why she loved cooking: getting amazing fresh ingredients and making something extraordinary. Luella's traditional French menu didn't leave much room for creativity, so the daily special had become Lou's canvas, where she was limited only by her imagination and whims.

"We'll keep it a simple spring dinner. Roast the potatoes in butter, salt, and pepper. Maybe some thyme or tarragon, too. We'll top the salmon fillets with hollandaise and roast the asparagus."

"Works for me," Sue said. "You know, you don't need to make it French. It might be fun to do it with a Latin flair. Or get all crazy and do Japanese."

"I wish, but we aren't there yet. We don't have that many regulars, especially ones who'd like a change. And the new guests come because they want classic French cuisine. I just don't want to mess with things now that we're getting busier."

"You can't play it safe forever."

"Someday, Sue, someday." Lou squeezed Sue's arm, then grabbed her favorite knife. She lost herself breaking down the salmon into generous fillets. In the background, Lou could hear her crew start their latest debate.

"You have to get out of the city," said Sue. "You need to avoid people."

"No, no, no," Harley disagreed. "Commandeer a huge boat and stay off the coast. You can get the resources of a big city—the water, empty stores, and fuel—but the zombies can't get at you. You have mobility, supplies, and shelter. And you can move around to different ports."

"You won't be able to get any supplies in a big city. The zombies will be where the most people are. You'll need to go somewhere more isolated, with water, food, and weapons. Like north to Canada. Not a lot of zombies in Canada."

"That's 'cause it's cold. I'll take my boat to the Caribbean—you go hang out with moose. Let's see who lasts longer."

Sue scowled.

Normalcy settled over the kitchen like a fleecy blanket. Lou smiled to herself, then stood up straighter as an idea flared.

"Sue, what about a second restaurant?"

Sue's face brightened. "Now you're talking. What are you thinking?"

"Something small, intimate, where the menu changes with the seasons. Maybe even more."

"Lovely." Sue's eyes grew dreamy.

"I'll need to save a lot." Lou paused, then added, "That's what I originally planned for Luella's."

"Why didn't you do that?"

"Devlin suggested a French restaurant would work better. People would be more open to it." Lou shrugged her shoulders.

"Well, he just screws everything up."

Lou smiled. "It was the only advice he gave me about Luella's, so I thought taking it would encourage him to get more involved."

"Thank God that didn't work."

Lou laughed, mending part of her broken heart.

• CHAPTER FIVE •

Al missed seeing his newly printed articles straight off the printer. Pushing Send wasn't quite as satisfying as a crisp, white page emblazoned with perfectly written prose, but it was faster.

He looked at the time on his monitor—2:55 p.m. Time to send it to Hannah. Al read through the review one more time, made two clicks, and done. He looked around the office. Most heads stared at computer screens or out the window. John shopped online.

"Anything good?" Al asked.

John started at the sudden break in silence. He turned his head and said, "Not unless you like strappy neon sandals and wear a size five in ladies' shoes."

"I can't catch a break." Al laughed.

John studied Al, who stood with his jacket in one hand.

"You done?"

"Yeah, I just submitted it." Al smiled.

"You like that, don't you? The power trip."

Al tilted his head to the side and squinted, trying to see the truth in John's question, then shook his head no. "That's not it at all. Someone needs to tell these chefs their food is no good. They need to know so they can cut their losses and move on."

"So, you're doing them a favor?"

"Isn't that how you view telling someone when their outfit isn't flattering? It may not be easy to hear, but they'll dress better as a result of your advice. With so much good food available, subpar dining should be called out. Plus, I owe it to the readers to give honest feedback. If I didn't tell them about my bad experiences, then they might waste money on an awful meal. I'd lose credibility." Al paused, then continued, "I do feel bad, but I believe honesty is more important."

John watched Al as he spoke, judging his words against the resolute Brit standing before him.

"You need to get laid."

"Pardon me?"

John used his palm to make a circular gesture at Al's head.

"Clear up all your negative juju. Then maybe you'll start to enjoy your life a little more."

"I like my life quite a bit. I just don't like where I'm living it."

Al pushed in his chair and left the office, walking out the main doors and heading south toward the Public Market. He didn't notice other people on the street or whether the sun had emerged to warm those around him. Instead, he let John's observations sink in—all of them. As he walked past the newsstand, he couldn't help sniffing the air, searching for hints of bacon, coconut, and vanilla. Combined with John's declaration that he needed to get laid, he couldn't get that smell off his mind, or her adorable freckles, or the broken expression on her face as she blew past him on the sidewalk. Such a marvelous creature deserved someone who understood her talents—someone like him, perhaps.

• • • • •

Four thirty arrived and the restaurant never looked better. With all the help, Lou had time to prepare a special meal for the daily meeting—her way of thanking her staff. The daily meeting always covered the specials, any new wines on the menu, reservations, and any other issues. While Sue ran the meeting, Lou always tried to add a few words of advice or encouragement. After her meltdown yesterday, she wanted everyone to focus on what was important—the customer and her dining experience.

As she looked at the faces of her staff, she warmed with affection. Tyler, who she was so hard on last night, smiled at her as their eyes met, not a hint of lingering anger at her mistreatment of him. Billy sat on the edge of his chair, trying to pick the lint off the back of another waiter, a little agitated by the lack of tidiness. The bussers and dishwashers sat toward the back, whispering in Spanish about a soccer game. The remaining waitstaff enjoyed the last few minutes of rest before the long night ahead.

In such a small restaurant, nothing was private, so Lou knew everyone had heard the abbreviated version of what happened. She teared up a little at her employees' loyalty. Lou stood to get their attention and started to speak.

"Business has been good lately. It was brought to my attention that during my unfortunate meltdown yesterday, everyone was distracted and concerned. While I appreciate the sentiment, our customers may not have gotten the experience they pay so generously for. We have started to build a base of regular diners, so let's not alienate them. If you recognize someone from a previous visit, pay special attention to them. Try to learn their names, their preferences. We need to do everything in our power to make that guest want to come back. Alison, what are reservations for tonight?"

"We have a two-top and two four-tops at six, an eight-top at six thirty, and two more four-tops at seven. The Meyers will also be in at seven. Thursdays usually see a lot of walk-ins, so I expect a steady night," said Alison, the hostess.

"Let me know when Gertrude and Otto arrive; I'd like to visit with them."

If Luella's had a small but loyal following, the Meyers were the flamboyant drum majors. Otto and Gertrude ate there several times a week. They preferred a table in the center of the dining room, where the restaurant bustled around them. Lou tried to make a point of visiting their table often. One, it was a good example to other diners of how regular guests were treated; and two, the Meyers were the most interesting people she had ever met. Lou loved talking to them. Both emigrated from Germany as children, right before World War II. Their parents fled to the United States before things got ugly and came to Milwaukee because of the large German population. The couple traveled often, especially to Germany to visit friends and distant relatives. Lou admired their easy approach to life, how they went where the wind took them. And she was grateful it took them to Luella's at least twice a week.

• • • • •

That night, Luella's hummed with business. Sue's head bobbed to the eighties hair band playing on the radio, dipping and turning while she worked the grill station. Her cooking could double as interpretive dance.

"So, you think we'll get a review soon?" Lou asked.

Sue stopped grooving to give the question her full attention.

"If so, I hope it isn't that Polish asshat from the paper," she said.

"You mean A. W. Wodyski? I don't know. I'd kind of like to hear what he'd come up with. I think we do great food," Lou countered. "And even a mediocre review from him could be good for business."

"Lou, we don't want him anywhere near us. Trust me. We're better off trying to get positive online reviews."

"Did you know the Meyers left one at BrewCityReviews? It's the cutest thing. I can picture them sharing a chair in front of the computer screen, typing together. As of now, it's the only review we have. At least it's a good one."

Sue opened her mouth to respond when Alison sauntered into the kitchen to say a brisk "They're here" before returning to her base, scanning the dining room for any sign that a guest required assistance. *That girl is good*, Lou thought. *She must be due for a raise.*

As Lou pushed open the stainless steel doors separating the kitchen from the restaurant, she caught sight of Otto's shining head reflecting the dining room's dim light next to Gertrude's white hair and beaming face. Gertrude glowed all the time, as if she had a hidden secret waiting to spill into the world. In her eighties, Gertrude probably did have some secrets to life.

"Good evening, Mr. and Mrs. Meyer. It's always so nice to

see you." Lou sat down with them so they didn't have to look up at her when she stopped by their table.

"*Guten Abend*, Lou," said Otto and Gertrude—they even spoke as one.

"Alison mentioned yesterday was difficult," Gertrude said, patting Lou's arm softly with her tiny, pale hands, wrinkled but lively.

"Yes. It's over with Devlin. I feel like I should've known something was up."

"*Liebchen*, how would you have known? You were here almost every day and night. He doesn't deserve you."

"True. But who does?"

Lou's lips curved ever so slightly as she tried to believe her joke was true.

"You will meet someone who appreciates you for you, scars and all." Gertrude rubbed one of the many burn marks on Lou's hands. Lou put her hands in her lap and smiled at Gertrude's kindness, but she felt as if the odds were against her. Under the table, she rubbed one of the larger scars on her left wrist, feeling the smooth, tight bump. Gertrude pulled Lou's arm back above the table and held both her hands.

With her watery blue eyes, she stilled Lou's protests. "Do not hide who you are. These are a nurturer's hands. Cooking is hard and sometimes painful work, but you do it to share your gift with us. Your cooking improves our lives. Don't ever be ashamed of who you are."

Lou's lips rolled inward, as if she were biting them between her teeth; her brows pushed in and her eyes welled with tears. One dripped down her cheek and plopped onto the white tablecloth.

"*Schätzchen*, you will be all right," said Otto, even though he didn't normally speak up other than a "How do you do?" "You have someone special coming for you, someone who deserves you, someone you can laugh with, cook with, and sleep with." Otto's eyebrows waggled and his blue eyes sparkled with his naughty comment.

"You're right. It's got to get better." Lou straightened in her chair and smiled at the Meyers. She still had a great life, full of dear friends and work she was passionate about. One man couldn't take that away from her.

• CHAPTER SIX •

Lou had another crappy day. Two in one week! She pulled the crumpled paper from her back pocket and smeared it smooth on the bar's well-worn surface. Even though she'd nearly committed it to memory, she readied herself for another reading by gulping air and tensing her shoulders.

EAT AT YOUR OWN RISK
By A. W. Wodyski

Has chef Elizabeth Johnson ever met a cliché she hasn't liked? Her basic French restaurant, Luella's, stands as a museum to all French stereotypes—even the service was rude, though I sensed that was from incompetence rather than Francophile superiority. Black-and-white photos of the Eiffel Tower evoked generic Ikea art rather than trendy bistro decor, and bottles sprouting candles seemed to think they were Chianti, not Bordeaux. Too-long white linens draped too-small tables, adding the danger of toppling the table's contents to the dining experience. I caught flashes of a bright kitchen behind silver doors, often eerily still from lack of to and fro.

I arrived on a moderately busy Wednesday, midway through service. The buzzy dining room seemed comforting at first, until I realized the hissing undercurrent was coming from the staff gathered near the coffee machine while their guests shuffled dirty plates and empty glasses around their tables.

Eventually a server found me, took my order, and scuttled away. As per my custom on first visits, I ordered the first item under each category. I believe these should represent the best a restaurant has to offer, showcasing the chef's creativity and execution. My expectations weren't high when their showcase pieces consisted of a seared foie gras topped with a Bordeaux reduction, a toasted-goat-cheese salad, traditional sole meunière, and a lemon soufflé. Little did I know my low expectations gave Luella's too much credit.

It's important to note good French food elevates the ingredients to a higher level. Exceptional French food transcends time and space, taking you on a gastronomical journey to a higher plane. It explores nuances and underdeveloped flavor notes in the ingredients; the final product becomes infinitely more than the sum of its parts. Alas, the only journey you'll take after sampling the French food at Luella's is to the restroom.

My early courses were passable but had a distracted air, as if the chef preparing them was watching the Food Network in the kitchen, hoping for helpful tips. The foie gras, an adequate slab, seared for flavor and topped with a decent wine reduction, would have been much improved with some crusty bread to smear it on, but my basket seemed to have gotten lost in the twenty feet between my table and the swinging silver doors.

The salad was a reasonable re-creation of something I can make in my own kitchen, and often do. The toasted goat cheese, crisply breaded in crumbs and warm through the center, sat atop lightly dressed spring greens, the kind found in clear plastic containers in the organic produce section. The vinaigrette was savory yet pedestrian. I'd expect the same thing from a bottle of Newman's Own.

At this point in my meal, kept company by my dirty appetizer and salad plates, I waited and waited and waited for my entrée to arrive. At last, the sole meunière, a traditionally simple and elegant dish of Dover sole sautéed and topped with a butter sauce made of capers and lemon, arrived after an eternity in restaurant time (about 30 minutes after the salad). The chef somehow managed to serve it both charred and raw, a feat a more talented chef couldn't do on purpose. The capers flecked the sauce like moldy Tic Tacs dropped on the floor, random and grim, lolling about in an underreduced liquid, sharp with uncooked alcohol. When I found a seemingly properly cooked bite, the fish tasted of cindery hate and cheap wine.

After I choked down as much dinner as possible, there was only one way to end the meal with my dignity (and intestines) intact. I requested the check and left the cash on the table rather than wait another interminable second for a waiter working toward the world record in slow service.

> Named after a beloved grandmother (cloyingly noted on the menu), Luella's failed to conjure images of a sweet grandma, passing down hallowed recipes with kindness and love. Instead, I was left with the picture of a wizened wicked stepmother bringing these dishes to a family reunion, still trying to off her beautiful stepdaughter.
>
> You've been warned.

"Brutal" did not sufficiently describe the review's vitriol. Lou took a long swig from her nearly empty pint, the faintly fruity liquid cooling the burning tears. A naked hand clung firmly to the worn glass. Wavy, rumpled brown hair half covered her face; her simple white T-shirt, wrinkled and stained, matched her disheveled hair. Her cheeks glowed red from staring down the shit storm known as her life (and maybe from the drinks). Her shoulders and back slumped, bearing the weight of an invisible globe. She'd hoped for a review, knowing Luella's food and service were impeccable. It was just her luck Wodyski had picked her one off day to visit the restaurant.

When she'd arrived at work today, Sue had handed her the review and fifty dollars followed by a terse "I've got tonight."

Lou had read the review as Sue watched her closely.

More than anything, she was embarrassed she hadn't kept it together enough to work that night. Lou had shaken her head and said, "No. I can work, Sue. I'm not that pathetic. It's one bad review."

“I’m not saying this as an employee; I’m saying this as your best friend. You’ve earned a night off. I’ll join you after we close if you’re still standing.”

Having learned to listen to Sue’s good advice, she caved and left for her favorite pub, sucking down pints of cider—the good stuff. Nice and dry, the kind you’d find in a good English pub with a long, wooden bar worn smooth from centuries of old men in tweed drinking their daily pints—not the sweet crap with the varmint on the label. Her fourth pint would soon need refilling, but her rage and humiliation had started to mellow. Jerry already had her keys with instructions to call her a cab. No use adding a DUI to the smoldering heap her life had become the last few days. Yep, she planned to numb the pain with a cider-based anesthesia.

• • • • •

Al shoved open the pub’s heavy wooden doors and strode through with the confident swagger of a World Cup champion returning to his hometown. He was ready for a celebratory drink. The food section’s Friday edition peeked out from under his arm; a review by A. W. Wodyski headlined “Eat at Your Own Risk” dominated the page.

He removed the black fleece jacket he’d purchased at the bleak downtown mall. It was really too warm outside, quite different from how the day started. His shoes still squished a bit from the torrential downpours earlier. Faint red marks on his arm were the only evidence of the hail and icy rain he walked to work in. By noon, the sun shone. Milwaukee weather needed some form of meteorological Prozac. He didn't mind the damp, chilly weather of London because at least it was consistent. The unexpected shifts in temperature and precipitation caused by the lake drove him mental, but it was Friday and his most scathing review to date had just come out. Al looked down the bar for an open stool and couldn't stop the grin that spread across his face. He walked forward to join the one person in Milwaukee he'd hoped he would see again.

"Oi! Miss Coconut Cake," he said as he tucked his paper into his coat pocket.

She turned to look at Al, a tattered paper on the counter in front of her. He pasted what he hoped was a pleasant smile on his face. She wavered a little on her bar stool and squinted her eyes at him. Recognition lit on her face.

"Oh, you. Don't call me that." Lou turned back to her pint and shoved the paper into her purse as Al slid onto the stool next to her.

The barman walked over as soon as Al sat down.

"What can I get you?"

"I'll have what the lady's having," Al said. The barman went off to pour him a pint of whatever filled her glass.

"Bad day?"

"Youse could say that."

Miss Coconut Cake watched the bubbles rise in her drink, an adorable hiccup escaping her lips.

Al grabbed the pint the barman set in front of him and took a sip, then looked at her with surprise.

"Cider? Quite good cider. In Milwaukee? I thought this was the land of malty goodness."

Annoyed, she scowled. "Yes, you're drinking really good

cider . . . in Milwaukee. Don't be too shocked. We're more than just beer and cheese."

"Right, I hear the sausages are quite good, too." Al gave a little smirk. "You from here?"

"Born 'n' raised. You?"

"Just passing through."

She raised her eyebrow, prompting for more details. Al leaned toward her.

"Work. I have to prove myself here first."

"What do you do?"

Al paused, looked at the two college guys walking through the door, each wearing the local uniform of plaid shirt, jeans, and worn baseball cap.

He took a deep breath and said, "Write."

Al waited for the inevitable follow-up question, but Lou was distracted with her fresh pint from Jerry.

"Oh . . . well, you should give it a chance. It's wonderful here—especially summer."

"You mean it gets warmer? Brilliant." Al breathed a sigh of relief. She rolled her eyes and took a long drink of the cider. He normally avoided discussing work but decided to press his luck.

"So, what do you do?"

"No work talk."

"That bad?"

"Worse. Oh, so much worse."

Al nodded. He could avoid discussing jobs.

She took another long gulp.

"Are you going to be able to walk out of here?" Al asked.

"Not if Jerry fulfills his promise. He's under strict instructions to serve me till I need to be rolled out the door." She gave a saucy wink to Jerry.

"That's your last one if you're going to start flirtin' with me," Jerry said as he washed glasses behind the bar.

"So . . . what's so *wonderful* about your little city?" Al asked.

"Everything." Her eyes stared at the Irish flag hanging on the wall. "Summer's full of festivals, ball games, grilling. In winter you stay cozy when the snow falls . . ." She shook her head to clear the fog and took a deep breath. "Fall walks through crunchy leaves. The spring thaw, everything grows. Yummy restaurants. Lotsa stuff to do for fun. Just go out and do."

Al looked at her from the corner of his eye, a smile on his lips. "I'm new in town. It'd be nice to have someone to show me all these treasures."

She glared at him suspiciously, his baby-blue eyes wide with feigned innocence, his smile making him seem more boyish than he already did. She smiled back.

" 'Kay. I can do Mondays. Deal?"

"Deal."

She fumbled with her bag, searched for a few minutes, then pulled out a pen and paper. She scrawled her name and number and handed it to Al.

"I'm Lou." The charming Lou extended her hand to shake his. Al smiled, turned her hand so the back faced him, and gently brushed his lips across her knuckles, barely touching her skin. He could feel her tense—in a good way.

"I'm Al. It is my very great pleasure to make your acquaintance."

Lou blushed a little, pulled back her hand, then picked up the pint to finish it. When she stood to go to the bathroom, she wobbled and toppled forward. Al caught her in his arms, his body jumping to life as vanilla filled his head. Lou pushed against him to stand on her own. He pulled her in closer for one brief moment, a moment he could savor later, before he let her go.

"I'm dialin'," Jerry said.

Al watched Lou teeter to the bathroom, feeling the folded paper in his hand and the hope it represented. For the first time since getting off the plane and seeing the snow-blasted airfields, he thought Milwaukee might not be so barren. After this last review, he knew his stay would be short—phone lines and in-boxes already beeped with positive feedback. Soon he'd have the numbers to prove he could build a following in any city he chose.

Al sipped his cider. With his exit in view, Al felt more kindly toward the city. It might be nice to get a different perspective on the Milwaukee scene. Maybe he could end his brief tour of duty here on a positive note—find the one lone culinary gem and tout it to national fame.

Maybe he could take John's advice after all, then move on to bigger and better markets. Al's mind wandered toward images of pillow talk and pastries. It had been a long time since he'd had a pillow-talk-worthy partner.

He'd call Lou tomorrow to begin his education on all things Milwaukee. Al finished his cider and set two twenties on the counter, then told Jerry, "One is for her cab home." Jerry nodded, and Al pushed his way back out the doors into the warm evening. With the smack of crisp cider fresh on his lips, he looked at the number scrawled on the lined notepad paper. Lou's wobbly script was like a secret code he could decipher, the missing link between his writing success and a little personal happiness.

. . . . .

In the bathroom, Lou avoided her reflection. The black-and-white tile wavered around her. She rubbed the back of her hand. The hand that felt numb from cider ten minutes ago tingled with sensation. She hadn't tingled in years. Probably just the effect of the day's emotions—and all the cider.

She set her hands on the white porcelain, leaned forward, and banged her head on the smudged mirror. The cool surface provided a focal point for her thoughts.

What am I going to do?

Still leaning into the mirror, she pulled out her phone and dialed the restaurant. Two rings and she heard Alison say, "Bonjour, Luella's. How can I help you?"

"Hey, Alison. It's Lou. Transfer me to Sue, please."

"One second, Lou."

Lou tried to push herself off the mirror before Sue picked up, but couldn't.

"Why are you calling?" Sue asked.

"How bad is it?"

"We can talk tomorrow."

"I need to know."

"How many ciders have you had?"

"Four. No, five. No, four. I don't know."

Sue paused for ten seconds.

"Two canceled, three didn't show. A lot fewer walk-ins than normal. I sent Tyler home early."

"He only came once, Sue."

"I know."

"He said Grandma Luella was the wicked stepmother."

"He's the lowest of the low."

Lou scrunched her face in frustration, smearing the mirror more.

"He's a twat-waffle. A candy-coated asshattery douche bag. The douchiest of all douche bags."

"I know."

Lou moaned into the phone. Sue continued, "We'll figure it out tomorrow."

Lou whimpered. "I gotta go. Thanks for everything."

Lou pushed back from the mirror and looked at herself. The drunk look never worked for her. Her cheeks were red, hair like a haystack after a tornado; even her clothes looked as if she'd slept in them. Was that cheese on her shoulder? Lou took a wet paper towel and vaguely scrubbed at it. Her hand-eye coordination lacked the accuracy necessary to remove the stain. Tears of frustration and humiliation rained fast and furious on her hot cheeks. With her phone still in hand, she pushed the voice mail button and listened again to the message Devlin left earlier that day.

"Lou, I saw the article. I'm so sorry you had to experience such a negative review. Call me and I'll help. I can help you."

Lou held the phone to her mouth and said to the recording, "It's your fault. You aren't a hero—you don't get to help now that it's doomed." Lou punched the Delete button and used her sleeve to sop up the tears. It wasn't fair, but it didn't matter now. Time to focus on reality.

The tiled floor shifted under her feet.

Maybe reality could wait.

She wondered if Al would call. That caused her stomach to do a flip—a drunken, sloppy flip, but a flip nonetheless. She vowed not to discuss work or jobs with him. He'd be her escape from reality. Never mind that her lungs had stopped when he'd caught her and her hands itched to feel what hid under his neat, preppy appearance. She'd always kept her impulses grounded, but tossing her cautions in the air with Al might keep her occupied while life as she knew it blew away.

· CHAPTER SEVEN ·

Al smoothed the wrinkled paper on his desk with his right hand as his left cradled his phone close to his ear, the thud of his heart threatening to drown out the ringing. With each trill, it beat harder. He held his breath as he waited for an answer. The clock on his laptop said 12:15 p.m.—more than enough time for Lou to have slept off her cider.

His throat didn't work properly when the voice mail kicked in, as he scrambled to find the words that wouldn't make him sound like a bumbling fool.

"Hello, Lou. It's Al . . . from the pub . . . and the newsstand line. Anyway, just wanted to set a date for you to reveal Milwaukee's good qualities. My number is 414 . . ."

Click.

"Hold on—I have to turn off the machine." Lou's voice interrupted his message. He heard a click, followed by a beep, followed by a "Crap." Then Lou continued, "Sorry, I was getting out of the shower."

"Excellent. I mean . . . good for you . . . I mean. When would you like to start?"

"Start?" Lou asked.

"My challenge. You promised to prove Milwaukee's greatness last night. Please tell me you remember?"

"No. I do. I just didn't think you were really serious."

"Oh no, I take challenges quite seriously. Reneging will bring shame on you and your city."

"Okay, fine." Lou chuckled. "How about in two weeks? That Monday? That's the earliest I can do it. I'll text the details when I have them."

"Fantastic."

Al hung up the phone and circled the date on his desk calendar.

• • •

Two weeks postreview and Lou still struggled with the bad news.

"You okay?" Sue asked over the flush of the toilet, forehead wrinkled in concern.

Lou wiped her face with a damp brown paper towel, the wet-paper smell nearly sending her back into the stall. She threw it away and tried to get the faucet sensors in the bathroom to acknowledge her existence. She finally managed to splash cool water on her face and gave Sue a weak nod.

"You should go. We aren't even open today."

"I'm not letting you do this on your own." Sue frowned at her.

"Fine, let's get back to the books."

"How about a coffee break?"

"No, I need to know how bad it is."

"Well, Harley and I agreed, we aren't leaving, and Gertrude and Otto promised to be here, too. So at least we'll have one steady table."

Lou smiled, but it melted into a frown. Business had declined more. Lou and Sue worked the numbers every possible way. The restaurant closed on Mondays to give the staff a break, but now they'd close on Sundays, too. While they still had a few regulars and a scattering of new customers who either didn't read the paper or didn't care, it wasn't enough. There were even a few who visited to experience the same awfulness as A. W. Wodyski and seemed disappointed with the considerate service and perfectly prepared French food.

They returned to the desk, papers pushed back to make a work surface for the calculator, and scribbled numbers. Lou's hope disappeared with the bottom line, little by little, until it melted into a lonely black hole. She had to find a way to make this better.

"We barely made black before the review. It was just enough to keep me in green Crocs and polyester chef pants. I don't see how we'll turn a profit now."

Lou stared at the numbers.

"You should close it. Soon. Then take whatever is left and open a new place, like the one you mentioned a few weeks ago. I've checked the websites—the trolls are having a field day on BrewCityReviews."

"Online reviews are a bully's outlet. Smart people know that." Lou waved dismissively.

Sue pointed at the computer screen.

"That says differently. It'll take years to overcome the bad press and troll reviews."

Biting her lip, Lou moved a stack of receipts into a shoe box on the floor and noticed a sparkle under some papers.

"I have some savings. There's a little cushion." She pulled out her engagement ring. "Maybe I could sell this. And I've contacted a few banks for loans. That should get us through. We can stay open. And who knows—a miracle could happen."

She stacked the papers and turned off the computer. Sue leaned back in her chair, watching Lou struggle to keep it together. Lou blinked several times, then stood.

"I guess we can head out."

"Hot date?" asked Sue with a smirk on her face. She always knew what to say to change up Lou's emotions. Lou smiled and wiped away an errant tear.

"You know it isn't a date. I'm merely a tour guide to the many delights of Milwaukee."

"Do they include the ones in your bedroom?"

"No." Lou's face pinkened. "I'm not ready for that."

"But fun to think about."

Lou remembered Al's arms when he caught her at the bar, and his soft, smiling lips.

"Yes, definitely fun to think about."

"Where're you taking him?"

"We're starting with the basics, beer and cheese."

Lou grabbed her coat and keys, leaving Sue to lock up the restaurant and hoping for a few hours of fun and distraction. The preoccupation of planning their outing had helped her through the rough two weeks since she'd seen him last, like the weeks leading up to Christmas as a child: waiting in the glow of Christmas lights for dawn to break, guessing what might be wrapped under the tree, hoping for the mini kitchen she had dreamed of playing with ever since she saw it in the Sears Christmas catalog. Her mom would distract her with Christmas jobs such as draping silver tinsel on the bottom tree branches, frosting cookies shaped like reindeer and snowflakes, and hanging the bright red stocking on the mantel, a promise of goodies to come.

All the dreams and guesses and preparation made the anticipation so sweet, almost better than unwrapping the gifts themselves. That was what this nondate with Al felt like. Would he look as good as she remembered through the cider-fueled fog? Would she want to see him again? Could he appreciate the charms of Milwaukee? She knew she'd get the answer to that final one. She had picked the best custard stand in the city as his test. If he could enjoy the simple but satisfying joys of a classic Wisconsin butterburger and creamy custard, then he might be worth the time.

Lou opened her car door and could smell the restaurant wafting off her clothes. She needed to shower and change. A frivolous afternoon spending time with someone completely unrelated to her work life would be the ideal distraction from the impending war.

• • • • •

Al whistled as he walked toward Lake Michigan where he would meet Lou for their first outing. He whistled? When was the last time he whistled? She had texted him a few days ago. It said:

Lesson 1—The Basics
11:30 am Monday
Northpoint Custard
Meet me at Daisy.

Northpoint Custard was one of the many custard stands in Wisconsin that served burgers, fried sides, and frozen custard. In his short time in Milwaukee, he had heard a lot about frozen custard but hadn't tried it yet. It sounded a lot like ice cream, so his curiosity and anticipation soared. Perhaps his anticipation derived from the who, not just the what. Lou popped up often in his daydreams: her warm eyes, creamy skin, even her scars. Where were those from? Not many women could pull off the drunken-mess look, but Lou had been adorable and charming and a bit intoxicating. And the cake—he couldn't forget the smell of that coconut cake.

The sun almost burned after so many days without it. Al walked on the sidewalk following the shoreline, ignoring the blister forming on his heel from the stiff shoes he wore. He'd never walked the lakefront before, but it seemed the appropriate way to start his time with Lou. The custard stand was a little north of the marina. The area swarmed with kite fliers, walkers with dogs, and adorable elderly couples walking hand in hand. Outside of the breakwater, he could see a handful of brave souls sailing their boats for the first time this season on the chilly spring waters. It might have felt like seventy degrees to him, but it was much colder past the rocks.

While two weeks had passed since he last saw her, but his encounter with Lou had stuck and grown, like his memories of summer camp. As a child, he would forget the awkward moments and bad food once back at home, the memories growing more golden with each passing day. After two weeks, he knew he had inflated the memory of Lou beyond reasonable expectations. Would she still smell like vanilla? Would the freckles on her nose still dance when she smiled? Would his memory implode when faced with the reality?

He saw the custard stand's red awnings up ahead, nestled among several large, old trees. Lou had instructed him to meet her at Daisy. As he crossed the last street and approached the custard stand, her meaning became obvious. Every table and bench was painted to look like a Holstein cow—white with black spots—each with an appropriately bovine name like Bessie or Maisy painted on its surface. Sure enough, Lou waited, fingers tapping and feet dancing, at the table named Daisy.

His feet moved faster as he took in the sight of her. She fit right in with her basic blue jeans, simple V-neck brown T-shirt, and tan Converse sneakers. She dressed casually, but Al couldn't help admiring how the brown T-shirt offset her pale, creamy skin and the sun found bits of red in her long hair. He hadn't seen her with her hair combed before and he liked it. It looked soft, smooth, and free, like she didn't use hair spray or gel—touchable. He stopped in front of her.

"You're late," Lou said. "I'm glad I didn't order when I got here fifteen minutes ago. Our food would be cold." She tried to scowl, but Al could see the corner of her mouth twitch. She looked him up and down and said, "You're a bit dressed up for a custard stand on the lake. You look like Tim Gunn on vacation."

Al looked down at his front-creased khaki dress pants, his tucked-in navy blue polo over a white T-shirt with a matching belt and shoes. True, no one would mistake him for a native Milwaukeean on his way to have a burger and shake at the beach. He even moved with a stiffness from too many hours spent hunched in front of a computer.

He shrugged. "That's why I'm here. So you can show me the fantastic Milwaukee and make me a convert."

Lou's freckles danced and his chest lightened. He had had it all wrong. His memories were dim compared to the reality.

Lou stood and said, "I'll order a little of everything to share so you can get a good cross section. Save our spot. Is there anything you really don't like?"

"Not at all; I'll eat anything," Al said. He was tempted to say cheese but didn't think he could pull it off with a straight face. Al and cheese had a love affair predating puberty. In his opinion, Wisconsin's cheese fanaticism was one positive among the many negatives.

"Good. Before I order, one rule: no work talk. Deal?"

"Are you afraid to discuss your ardent cider evangelism?" Lou laughed, sending a jolt through his heart. He nodded. "And deal."

This arrangement kept getting better.

While Lou ordered half the menu, Al read it. Burgers, fries, some sandwiches, a lot of unique toppings, and a lot of cheese. He had researched the restaurant this morning and knew it was owned by the Bartolotta group, which owned several of the best restaurants in Milwaukee. He had yet to eat at one of their establishments; there didn't seem much point in reviewing the juggernaut. Northpoint Custard had a unique relationship with the city; they rented this prime location from the city as a means of bringing life to the lakefront. And it looked as if it worked brilliantly. For a Monday afternoon in June, the line was long and the lakefront bustled.

Lou returned with a huge tray of food and an explanation to match. "I ordered us one burger to split, but I had them put the toppings on the side. I recommend the cheese spread with fried onions and bacon. I also ordered a lake perch sandwich, onion rings, fries, a strawberry shake, and cheese curds. The curds are the best in Milwaukee, maybe the state, but I'd have to put more time into definitive research. Lastly, here's their homemade cheese sauce. Use it while it's warm 'cause it congeals as it cools—that's how you know it's real."

Al reviewed the golden bounty set before him. The food smelled like home, reminding him of the fish-and-chips shop his family frequented in Windsor; the scent of hot oil, salt, and crispy breading—bliss. He started with the much-hailed cheese curds, hot and oozing a little of the white cheddar; the outside was crispy and salty when he bit. A string of cheese dangled from his mouth to his hand as he pulled the cheese from his lips. He expected something more like a mozzarella stick, but not this. It wasn't just about the gooey and the crispy; he could taste the cheddar and it was good. No, not just good, transcendent.

"Why are they called cheese curds?" asked Al, struggling to stuff the string of cheese into his mouth; it was caught on some whiskers.

"They're the fresh cheese curds from making cheese—you know, curds and whey. They're the curds part. They usually take the curds, press them together to form the block of cheese, but in Wisconsin, we sell them, too. We'll stop for some on the way to the next portion of today's lesson. Then you can experience cheese curds in all their delectable forms."

Al couldn't help smiling, dangling cheese and all. He forced himself to stop shoving cheese curds in his mouth and moved on to the burger. He slathered what Lou had identified as the cheese spread all over his half of the burger, sprinkled it liberally with fried onions, and added a slice of bacon. He wasn't much for burgers, but this one seemed promising. The juices flowed onto the soft, lightly toasted bun; the cheese immediately melted down the sides. This was not a tidy meal. He took a bite. It was almost as good as the cheese curds. The bun was just the right combination of tender and toasted, and the onions and bacon melded with the melting cheese, which dripped down and mingled with the burger's juices, then continued down to his hand. Next up, the chips, which he dipped deeply into the homemade cheese sauce. Lou was right again—definitely homemade and so much better than the canned glop most restaurants served. This was easily the best food he had eaten since arriving in Milwaukee, so he closed his eyes to savor it.

. . . . .

Lou watched Al carefully. She knew a foodgasm when she saw one. He chewed slowly and carefully, eyes closed, senses open. Lou noticed how long and dark his lashes were. They created little smiles sitting on top of his cheeks, matching the one on his mouth. He had the faintest hint of scruff on his jawline, catching the cheese. Lou loved the slightly scruffy look and wondered whether Al ever let it grow beyond today's five-o'clock shadow. She nibbled her food, not wanting to disrupt his experience with idle chatter—and she liked watching people enjoy food.

Devlin never enjoyed food like this. He ate to fuel, not to satisfy the senses. Why wouldn't he leave her alone? She'd found a new KitchenAid mixer sitting on her kitchen counter a couple of days before, the eight-hundred-dollar copper model she'd lusted after for years. Attached was a message on one of his stupid note cards reading, "You need to hear me out.—D." He had used his spare key to enter her apartment as if he belonged there, and now she had to have the locks rekeyed, another expense she couldn't afford.

She was so angry at his hubris, she'd toppled the mixer into the Dumpster, then immediately crawled back in after it. If she wasn't going to keep it, she would make sure it went to a good home. She scrubbed it with bleach and left it for her neighbors across the hall, a young couple who just had a baby. She would show them how to make baby food with it.

Lou loved watching Al savor every bite. She mentally vowed to make him an amazing meal just to see him enjoy it. Maybe her Cuban pork with black beans and cilantro rice. That was a great summer feast—complete with mojitos and mojo sauce. If he savored a burger with such fervor, she knew he'd swoon over her cooking.

Al swallowed his last bite and finished off the strawberry shake.

"Truly and unexpectedly fantastic," he said.

"Are you converted?"

"To what?"

"To the wonders of Milwaukee."

"Deep-fried cheese and tasty burgers do not make a city, but I will definitely eat here again. So what's next?" Al looked around as if their next stop would appear magically out of the parking lot like a mirage.

Lou stood up, tossed the garbage into a cow trash can, and said, "Next is beer." She started walking, expecting Al to follow. He did. Lou heard his footsteps and smiled. They walked to Lou's battered black Honda Civic. One back window didn't roll down anymore, the air system's fan worked only intermittently, and the muffler had surrendered itself to a Wisconsin blizzard years ago. But it worked with minimal upkeep and started every morning, even during the deepest January freezes. Al raised one eyebrow at the large dent on the passenger side.

"I'm supposed to feel safe?"

Lou laughed. "Fear not—it happened in a parking lot. I wasn't even around."

Al got in, made a show of buckling himself securely, and Lou took off in search of beer and the promised fresh cheese curds.

• • • • •

When he returned to work after his adventure with Lou, Al's hair stood in all different directions from the windy afternoon, and he carried a small plastic bag with a white label indicating weight and price per pound. "Do you eat cheese curds?" Al asked as he paused behind John's desk chair. He held out the opened bag to John, who snatched a handful. *Squeak!*

"Mmmm, they're fresh. I love 'em fresh." A cheese crumb fell into his beard. He didn't remove it.

"So you know about the squeak? It's mad."

"Yeah, I know about the squeak—only fresh curds squeak."

"They're so good," Al said through the large curd he had just tossed in his mouth.

"What's going on, and why are you so excited by squeaky cheese?"

"Because I never knew this existed."

"Oh, wait—didn't you ask about Northpoint Custard? You aren't reviewing it, are you?" John squinted his eyes with suspicion.

"Yes and no."

"Why go, then?"

"I met someone there for lunch."

"You met someone? A girl someone? Where did you meet her? Does she have a friend?"

"I am *not* introducing you to any sane woman or her friend. You'd scare the hell out of them with that beard. When are you going to shave that thing?"

"I'm not. It's who I am."

"Ladies don't like men with food in their beards."

"Some do."

"Are there websites for it?"

John laughed, grabbed a few more curds before Al moved out of reach, and returned to his work. Still a little buzzed from the Sprecher Brewery tour, Al set the curds to the left of his keyboard so they wouldn't get in the way of the mouse and sat down slowly.

He had expected they'd take the Miller Brewery tour, with its inoffensive but unremarkable lagers. Sprecher Brewery was something else entirely. Completely local and amazing variety.

Even the sodas surpassed expectations. The root beer was some of the best he'd ever tasted, but the cream soda was perfection.

Sitting at his desk, alone with his squeaky cheese, Al admitted to himself that for the first time since arriving in Milwaukee, he'd had fun. Lou's uninhibited enthusiasm for the local establishments was infectious and soothing at the same time. He hadn't realized how tightly wound he had become. Spending time with Lou felt like putting a soothing agent on a fresh wound—the relief was instant. He couldn't wait to see what they would do next.

• CHAPTER EIGHT •

Al walked across the white, narrow bridge and stepped into the perfect eighties-movie-version of heaven, the Quadracci Pavilion of the Milwaukee Art Museum, often called the Calatrava after the architect who designed it. White surrounded him, reflecting bright, clean sunlight off every surface. The marble floor resembled the purest vanilla ice cream sparingly swirled with the darkest, richest fudge. The walls were a matching pristine white, broken only by the asymmetrical arches leading to long, gleaming hallways and into the museum proper. Above him rose a two-story cathedral ceiling of glass, crosshatched by large white exterior beams that were currently spread like the wings of a bird in flight. At dusk, the wings returned to rest against the main building, but during the day they soared. The comparisons to a bird were apt; he could almost feel the wingbeat poised to happen.

From the outside, the white frame looked skeletal, but not in an eerie way. More like seeing dinosaur bones at a natural history museum. Al scanned the room looking for Lou. He didn't see her waiting. Good. He didn't want her to have to wait for him again like she did a couple of weeks ago at Northpoint Custard. He walked toward the lakeside windows, which came to a V overlooking a sidewalk following the rocky breakwater below—like an infinity bridge. The glass slanted up and out, allowing you to lean forward over the edge, creating the uneasy feeling of falling until you hit the glass. He could see smudges lower on the pane, evidence he wasn't the only one drawn to this view.

A huge mobile of floating red, black, and blue dots hovered over the entrance, an homage to minimalist balance. Displayed between two stories hung a remarkable blown-glass sculpture of bold colors. It reminded Al of exploding confetti and streamers—a celebration frozen forever.

Al kept looking for Lou among the scattered visitors. Nervous energy vibrated through him, amplified by the soaring architecture, leaving him slightly breathless.

• • • • •

Lou watched Al look upward at the Calatrava's wings, reaching toward the sun already high in the sky even though it was only ten in the morning. A smile lit her face as she watched him admire the beautiful building. She'd picked the art museum as their second excursion for two reasons: One, it provided a perfect foil to the beer and cheese. This outing didn't involve any special food, though she had packed a basket of snacks so they could eat on the lakefront. And two, even to a highbrow like Al, the museum was gorgeous. You could always find something new to admire.

"Your first time here?" asked Lou when she stood close enough. Al's head turned quickly to her voice and a smile flashed and disappeared. Her nerves jumped with delight.

"I'm looking for the duct tape. Isn't that how you do things in Milwaukee?"

Lou playfully glared. "We found special white duct tape so you couldn't see it, then covered it with Italian marble."

Both took a long breath. Lou looked around and nodded toward the nearby Chinese exhibit. "Shall we?"

Lou led as they entered into the quiet hall. A wide, winding path led visitors past multicolored silk tapestries, elaborately carved furniture, and enameled decorations that once belonged in the Forbidden City.

"Can you imagine what it must have been like for those first people to view these items after being locked away for more than eighty years? Pretty cool, right?" Lou said.

"Quite amazing."

Lou looked over at Al to decide whether he was serious or sarcastic. He had already wandered off to study an elaborate cloisonné. She could feel the distance as he walked farther away, a bungee cord stretching and stretching until it would fling them back together. With each step, her tension heightened, urging her to close the gap and ease the discomfort, the building panic of being alone. She couldn't tell whether it was her lingering grief from Devlin or Al's unexplored allure, but she wouldn't yield to it.

Lou glanced around. Painted on the wall were a variety of sayings attributed to the Qianlong emperor. One piqued her interest: "Delight is indeed born in the heart. It sometimes also depends on its surroundings." Lou stood and stared at the words, letting them settle into her, burrow into her bones, become part of her. She would find joy again—she knew it now. She felt better here, away from everything and everyone who required something from her.

On most days, delight kept itself hidden from her, so she would go places where it frolicked—like right here, right now. Delight at the beautiful objects, delight with her sometimes stiff companion, and delight at the freedom from immediate responsibility. She would savor her delights where and when she could. Her tension melted away. With a deep, cleansing breath Lou turned to move on to the next object and bumped into Al with an "oof."

"Sorry," she said, the contact sending sparks down her spine.

"Quite all right; feel free to continue bumping into me. That seems to be our thing."

"Ha! Funny English guy."

• • • • •

Al had hoped Lou would bump into him. He stood behind her while she stared at the wall for just that reason. Intrigued by her interest, he started to ponder the quotes on the wall, too. Delight—he couldn't remember the last time he felt delight. Maybe before Eton, when he and his parents took road trips through the English countryside, stopping in little village pubs for lunches, traipsing over hilltops to see what was on the other side, and sharing a hearty meal at the end of the day. Wait—that wasn't quite true. During his last outing with Lou, eating a buttery, cheesy burger and tasting fried cheese curds for the first time, with the sun shining and the world humming, he had felt delight. There had been no cynicism, no pretension, just pure enjoyment. Perhaps it was more about surroundings than the emperor had envisioned.

Al put his hands on Lou's shoulders to steady her and enjoyed the flash of warmth on his fingers and the startled look on her face. He pulled his hands away and turned to the last few items before they entered the obligatory end-of-exhibit gift shop, then went on to the regular museum. Even though he no longer touched her, his fingers retained the heat, which spread through his body. Yes, definitely more to do with the surroundings.

Al and Lou wandered into a new room, where one wall displayed simple squares of red, yellow, and blue. On another wall, a cornflower-blue plastic rectangle leaned like a giant forgotten building block. Clear and orange squares protruded from yet another wall, similar to shelves you might see in a trendy European loft.

"This room insults me," said Al.

Lou smiled at Al's barb.

"Not a fan of minimalism?"

"Not in the least."

"I like its potential. You could turn it into anything. You're only limited by your imagination."

"Show me, don't tell me. Art isn't about what I can do. I know that. I want to see what the artist can do. I look at this and think the artist couldn't be bothered to come up with anything original, so he ripped off Lego. It's lazy."

"So what would you create?"

Al's eyes grew distant.

"If I were an artist, which I'm not, I'd create scenes to celebrate the simple things."

"But you are an artist—you write, don't you?"

Al's stomach twisted as Lou watched him. His mind flipped through all the possible options.

"That's freelance journalism." He shrugged. "Not the same as museum-quality work." He knew a lot of journalists who would smack him for saying that, rightly so.

"What do you write about?"

Al gulped and slipped a sly look onto his face.

"Are we talking work now? Because I have a few questions, too. Like when will you admit you sculpt miniatures out of cheese curds?"

"At the same time you reveal 'freelance journalist' is code for British dog walker to Milwaukee's elite."

Lou gave him a playful hip bump as she strode past him. He followed her over the parquet wood floors to the next room, where she paused to look at a painting of two vases of calla lilies. The colors and bold strokes reminded him of a Van Gogh or Matisse, but when he leaned forward he saw an unfamiliar name.

"This is the kind of painting I'd want. Bright, cheerful. It just makes me happy. It's not making any bold statement."

Al agreed and opened his mouth to say so when a dog started barking from Lou's cleavage. She turned pink and reached into her shirt.

"Sorry—work." Lou answered her phone. "What's up?"

Lou wandered slowly into the next room as she listened on her phone. Al tried to give her a bit of extra space but could still hear the conversation. He knew eavesdropping was rude, but he wanted to know how she spent her time away from him.

"Did you call Joe?"

Pause.

"Tell him if he can get in today, I'll pay an extra ten percent, fifteen if he can finish by two."

Pause.

"I know. Get the file ready to go to Kinko's if he can't do it."

Pause.

"None?" Lou rubbed her forehead with her free hand.

Pause.

"I'll think of something."

Pause.

"Okay." Lou stopped and Al noticed her looking at him. She blushed. He loved her blushes, how they started at her cheeks and spread outward until even her ears had turned pink.

"Good. More later. Bye."

Al smiled, able to fill in the last part of the conversation. Lou shoved the phone back into her bra and caught up with him. He stood in front of a large white canvas with four black stenciled letters on it. *F* and *O* were on top, *O* and *L* were on the bottom.

"Sorry. Work. Never a dull moment," Lou said.

"Everything okay?"

Lou chewed her lip. "I got an awful review, and it's making things difficult. And the freaking copier broke at the worst possible time." She looked up at the canvas and smiled. "There's another painting I wouldn't mind having. A reminder."

"Sorry to hear that and I quite agree." Al nodded.

Questions about Lou piled up in his head. Where did she work? Was her manager's bad review really that bad? Why choose a barking-dog ringtone? Why did she keep her phone down her shirt and could he help answer it? For the first time in a long time, he found he wanted to know the answers to these questions and many more. He wanted to know her better, and he certainly wanted to make her laugh, or at least smile. Lou's smile dimmed the sunlight. These questions inched toward the tip of his tongue.

"Remember when we first met?"

"Yeah?"

Lou looked curious about where his question was headed.

"Where were you taking that coconut cake?"

A frown line appeared on Lou's forehead. Al wanted to take the question back.

"Never mind. Not my business."

"No, it's okay." Lou held up a hand. "It was for my fiancé at the time. I meant to surprise him, but he surprised me by having an unexpected female guest. Ergo, no more fiancé."

"Ouch. I'm sorry."

She shrugged her shoulders.

"It's for the best. In retrospect, I think I was part of a business plan rather than the love of his life." Lou studied the map on a nearby wall. "There's one more thing you need to see; then let's grab a snack outside." She walked through another room to the very end of the hall, where a huge black cube stood. A dark curtain at the top of a few steps marked the entrance. A docent pointed to a basket of blue footies to wear over their shoes. After slipping the footies on, they walked up the steps and slipped around the curtain. Lou confidently stepped into the center of the room, but Al paused. Lou appeared to float among a billion stars. He looked down as he stepped forward. Even though he knew there was a solid surface, and could even see scuff marks on the plexiglass, his body kept waiting to fall into the ether. He stood in the middle of the small, dark room, inches from Lou. They were alone in space, together.

All six sides gave the illusion of endless stars. He looked up and down, enjoying the freaky sensation of being firmly planted on the ground while floating in the universe. Amazing how the mind could play tricks. Al set his hand on Lou's shoulder to get her attention.

"Absolutely brilliant," he said. When his hand touched her shoulder, Lou gave a little shudder and sucked in her breath. His stomach did a little flip at feeling her react to him. Or did she? Perhaps he just surprised her? Yes, that was it—just another trick of the mind. Lou stepped toward the door and Al let his hand return to his side.

"Ready for some snacks? I brought goodies." And she turned and left the Infinity Chamber, almost as if she was eager to return to daylight. Al followed her back out, hungry for something.

• • • • •

Lou pulled the blanket and Sendik's plastic bag from her trunk and walked to where Al sat on the grass. Her skin still zinged from his touch in the Infinity Chamber. It was exactly a month ago that she walked in on Devlin, so it didn't seem quite right to already have the zings with someone new, but she couldn't deny them. Al sat with his back to her, staring out over the gray waters of Lake Michigan, squinting into the sunlight. Seagulls swooped overhead, hoping for a spare scrap of bread or discarded lunch. She tossed the blanket to Al, breaking his reverie.

"Here. Can you spread that out?"

"Putting me to work now?"

"There are no free rides here. You need to earn your goodies."

Al stood and snapped the blanket open, letting it parachute over the grass. They both climbed on, and Al watched as Lou started pulling goodies from the basket.

"And what are the delicious morsels?"

"Nothing fancy."

Lou unwrapped a four-year-old cheddar and set it on a small cutting board with a knife. She pulled out a blue wine bottle and handed it to Al along with two plastic cups.

"Will you do the honors?" she asked.

Al looked down at the bottle and raised an eyebrow when he saw it was a cider, corked like champagne.

"I haven't seen cider in a bottle like this since I was in France. You've got me excited now."

He twisted off the metal wire and popped out the cork as Lou finished cutting crisp red apples, her fingers deftly slicing the fruit into even pieces. She pulled a crusty boule of bread from the bag and a roll of something wrapped in wax paper.

"What's that?" Al said, pointing at the unknown item.

"That's my favorite. It's hand-rolled butter from a local dairy. I could eat it with a spoon." Lou unrolled the butter and tore off a hunk of bread. Rather than use a knife, she scraped the bread across the butter and handed it to Al. He set aside the cider and took a bite.

"Wow," Al said, still chewing. "That's bloody amazing. There is a tang that's brilliant with the creaminess. And on the chewy bread. Fantastic."

He scooped more butter onto the end he hadn't bitten. Lou smiled. She hadn't been wrong about Al's tastes. He knew how to enjoy good food. He handed her a cup of cider and she sipped. This was her favorite cider, too. The bubbles popped with appley bursts, not too sweet, not too dry. She broke off a chunk of cheddar and let it sit on her tongue, mingling with the aftertaste. As she bit, she felt the small cheese crystals crunching as the cider mellowed its bite, a surprisingly good pairing. She might be able to use that at the restaurant. Her musings were interrupted by Al.

"Tuppence for your thoughts?"

Lou sipped her cider to ready them.

"Work."

"Ahhh. Imagining your next diorama of taxidermied rodents?"

Lou chuckled into her red plastic cup.

"So, what about your family? Do you see them much now that you're here?" Lou finally asked.

"Not really. My parents still live in Windsor. Dad teaches at the school there."

"Any brothers or sisters?"

"One brother. Ridiculously successful and charming. I hate him."

"I can tell that's not true."

"No, it isn't. But I'll always be the little brother in his shadow." Al sipped his cider as Lou fit a family into what she knew about him. "What about your family?" he asked.

Lou sucked in her breath and studied Al to decide whether she was ready to share.

"It's just me. My parents died in a huge car crash several years ago. No siblings."

"I'm so sorry." He set down his cup and touched her arm.

Lou wanted to close her eyes and lean into him, but not on a pity touch.

"Thank you. It's been a few years, and I have amazing friends who help fill the gap. I even know an elderly couple who've almost adopted me."

Al squeezed her elbow and they returned to snacking in silence. They both watched the clouds skitter across the lake.

"I really know how to ruin the mood, don't I?" Al said as he laughed at himself. Lou laughed with him and grabbed his hand. She thought his eyes widened, but the moment was gone in a blink. Was he seeing someone?

"You did no such thing." Lou studied her hands. "So, you know about my tragic love life. Any bungled romances in your past?"

"Bungled—good word." Al paused. "There was just one. I thought she was my soul mate until she tried to shag my brother. Her name was Portia—that should have been a clue."

"Harsh." Lou scrunched her face as if she'd just sucked a lemon. "Someone really named—"

"When can I see you again?" Al interrupted, then turned his eyes toward the lake and pulled his hand back to grab an apple slice. "I mean, this is fun. It's nice having you show me what I'm missing, talking to someone about bungled love lives."

Lou watched him, realizing she had wasted so much time on Devlin when she could have found someone who wanted to spend time with her, enjoyed what she wanted to do. Al had it wrong—he was showing her.

• CHAPTER NINE •

The flashing green light was like a screaming toddler who lost his ice cream cone to a gutter; Lou wanted it to disappear but couldn't ignore it. The caller ID already revealed who left the message. She chewed the inside of her lip as she tapped the countertop with her short nails. In a quick motion, much like jumping into a cold lake headfirst or tearing off a Band-Aid, Lou poked the Play button.

"Elizabeth, it's Devlin. I hope you're enjoying the mixer."

"The neighbors are," Lou responded as his message played.

"I'm going to come over at two today. I'll see you then."

"Good luck with that."

Lou pushed the Delete button, picked up her purse and small bag of blue and gold clothes, and left, locking the newly rekeyed door behind her.

• • • • •

Almost three weeks had passed since Al stood in the Infinity Chamber with Lou. His body warmed as he remembered her vanilla scent. He glanced out the window to see if a banged-up black Civic had arrived. But no Civic yet, so he turned away from the window toward his apartment, already envisioning Lou in each room.

He had moved into the two-story condo months ago, but it hadn't changed much since the first day. Al quite liked the open, airy quality of the space. Light yellow Cream City brick comprised the walls. He had liked their color and minimalist style, and found out later the bricks were classic Milwaukee construction. The open, bare brick walls were softened by lightly stained wood beams and pillars. Rosewood covered the floors, ranging from golden yellow to rich, dark reds, and his windows overlooked the busy street below, which made watching for Lou's car easy. The main floor contained an open living room, a kitchen area, a study, and a bathroom for the guests he never had. The loft upstairs was his bedroom and master bath that overlooked the lower level.

Other than one stool next to the kitchen counter and his work desk in front of the two-story windows overlooking the street, Al didn't have much furniture on the first floor. He used the study for storage. Right now it contained his bike and a few boxes of cookbooks.

Up the open stairs to the loft, Al's bedroom had a large king-size bed covered in a soft, gray down comforter and fluffy white pillows. He liked sinking into his bed and letting the comfort surround him. It was his one major purchase in Milwaukee. In the walk-in closet, Al's dress pants and button-down shirts, plus the two suits he rarely wore, hung on hangers, but his socks, T-shirts, and pajamas still sat in the open suitcases, as if he were ready to flee at a moment's notice.

Most nights he worked at his desk, an old farm table he'd found at a rummage sale. It was sturdy enough to safely hold his computer and books but cheap enough for him to leave behind when he moved. He preferred to type his columns at night after he finished a restaurant visit, while it was fresh in his mind. In the quiet after midnight, the window turned into a mirror, reflecting the sparse, bright apartment behind him and blocking out the busy traffic and lights below. Only the sound of running engines and closing doors reminded him of the life on the other side. It was peaceful—his own ivory tower of Cream City brick.

Al walked into his kitchen. He pictured Lou perched on the black granite counters as he whipped up a meal just for her. The counters formed a U shape and small appliances dotted the surface: an electric tea kettle, a KitchenAid stand mixer, and even a yogurt maker. He'd been trying to make a decent Greek yogurt for weeks. The left wall opened into the dining and living area. He usually ate his breakfast on the stool looking into the kitchen, the only room in the condo representing his interests. Hanging on every open wall space shone his beloved collection of French copper cookware—both beautiful and useful. Along one counter he had dozens of cookbooks, some open to a recipe, others battered from frequent use. Al used this space to explore and try to re-create dishes from the restaurants he visited.

Next to a wrapped present, the most colorful object in the kitchen lay on the hard black counter: a magnet of Chihuly's glass sculpture. Al had bought the small kitschy item as a me-

mento of the lovely day he shared with Lou at the museum. Unfortunately, it wouldn't stick to any of his stainless steel appliances, so it lay on the counter where he could see it, never failing to bring a smile to his face when he glanced at it.

Al picked it up and pushed it against a copper pot, hoping it would stick. It plopped to the floor, landing with the black magnetic side up. Picking it up, he opened a nearby cupboard and reached into the dark corner, shifting objects with his other hand. After a few loud clunks, he pulled from the depths a large, heavy, rust-splotched cast-iron skillet that had once belonged to his maternal grandmother. He recalled her frying delicious handmade sausages, bacon, and eggs from the chickens on her farm. Her food was simple but mouthwatering. He knew with certainty that Lou would have loved her.

Al ran his hand over the rust spots, then held the heavy pan to his nose. He could almost smell the sausages. He set it upside down on the counter, hiding most of the rust, and held the magnet an inch above the deep black. He could feel the magnetic pull and knew he had found the perfect spot to display it. Al removed his copper paella pan and hung the skillet in its place. The reds, yellows, and blues of the Chihuly sculpture stood out in stark contrast with the inky-black pan. The melding of these two fond memories brought more homeyness into his apartment than the treasured copper collection surrounding it. Contentedness warmed him like hot tea on a brisk day. But the one magnet looked lonely—he wanted more.

Buzzzzz! Al grabbed the present and bounded from the kitchen to the intercom. He pushed the Talk button, stuffing his keys into his jean's pocket. "I'm on my way down." Al glanced back at the kitchen, where he could see the flash of color on darkness, then walked out the door and locked it before Lou had a chance to respond. When he walked out the front door, Lou smiled.

"Afraid I'll find the severed heads?" she said.

"Something like that." He held out the wrapped gift, about the size of a shirt box.

"What's this?" Lou's crinkled forehead contrasted adorably with her dazzling smile as she took the present.

"A thank-you."

With the unabashed glee of a child on Christmas morning, Lou shredded the wrapping paper to reveal a colorful canvas painting of a calla lily.

"Wow! Is this a real painting?" She ran her hand over the swirls of oil paint, feeling the peaks and valleys under her fingertips.

"I couldn't find a print of the painting you liked at the museum. I saw this one at an art fair, and it reminded me of you."

Al held his breath as he waited for her response. He wanted her to love it, to see it and think of him. Lou wasn't saying anything; she wasn't even moving—just staring at the painting. He had to break the silence.

"I was going to send you flowers, but I couldn't find your address."

Lou looked up, her eyes sparkling with tears—the good kind if her smile was any indicator. She sniffed.

"It's unlisted." She wiped her eyes. "This is the most amazing gift anyone has ever given me."

She hugged the painting to her chest and kissed Al on the cheek. While he barely felt her lips, the effects of them ravaged his senses. She pulled away and used her thumb to wipe away her lip gloss.

"Thank you," she whispered.

Al swallowed and tried to keep his reaction to himself.

"No, thank you."

Lou opened her trunk and pulled out a blue-and-gold fleece blanket. She wrapped the painting and set it in her backseat. Touching it one last time, she turned to Al.

"Before I start crying again, are you ready for some baseball?"

. . . . .

Lou drove her Civic through the teeming parking lot, following the confident arm signals from yellow-vested old men. All around them people fell out of cars, set up grills, tossed baseballs and beanbags. A group of twenty unloaded a small cargo truck containing a full-size gas grill, three large folding tables, and five large coolers. Excitement hung in the air with the smoky fog rising from thousands of hot grills. The Brewers' record had improved steadily since their opening slump, and they'd put together an impressive ten-game winning streak. A few more wins and George Webb's would start handing out free burgers. The local diner chain hadn't done that since 1987, when the Brewers won twelve straight games.

Lou pulled into the parking spot, turned off the car, and looked upward. Warm sunlight hit her face. Today, the sky matched the exact color of Al's eyes, pristine blue. The wind blew softly, the sun warmed without being too hot. Miller Park was the epitome of summer in Milwaukee. The smell of grilled meat over screaming-hot coals, car exhaust, and fresh-cut grass relaxed every muscle in Lou's body. Car doors slammed, gloves snapped shut around flying baseballs, and countless radios blared Bon Jovi, the BoDeans, and Bob Uecker. Lou breathed deeply as she stepped out and popped open the trunk. Al appeared around the rising metal.

"So, why are we here two hours before the game starts?"

"Tailgating." Lou's lips twitched upward.

"Tail-whating?"

"Tailgating. A time-honored pregame tradition involving food, drink, and maybe games. Think of it as a picnic in a parking lot. It can be very elaborate and gourmet, like that group with the cargo truck, but we're going old school. Grilled brats and beer, followed by a game of catch. You can't say you know Milwaukee until you've tailgated at Miller Park. But first we need to do something about your clothes."

Lou eyed him from head to toe. She was looking forward to this.

"What's wrong with my clothes?" Al looked around him and swept his arm to indicate the sea of people, all similarly garbed. "T-shirts and jeans are perfectly acceptable attire."

He looked down at his gray T-shirt and faded blue jeans, a faint crease still visible down the front. Lou smiled and tossed him something blue, similar to the colors flying above the stadium.

"Put that on, and this." A matching blue baseball cap flew at him. Al raised his dark eyebrow.

"If you want to experience Milwaukee, you have to look the part."

Al smiled and pulled his perfectly acceptable but bland gray T-shirt over his tousled dark hair. Lou inhaled—quickly. Her eyes froze on the sculpted body revealed by the missing gray cotton. A dusting of dark chest hair trailed down Al's taut stomach to disappear into jeans that would make Calvin Klein proud. The carved edge of his hips rose just above the top. She loved that. She wanted to trace the path and see where it went. The thought made her toes curl and her face flush. Lou exhaled slowly.

Al pulled the blue T-shirt over the six-pack and set the matching cap on his head, covering his thick hair. The old-school blue Brewers shirt, with the yellow catcher's mitt logo front and center, and cap looked great on him, Lou thought. His blue eyes popped with mirth—he hadn't missed her sudden inhale. Damn.

"Now that I'm properly attired, what's next?" Lou shook her head a little, pinkened, then turned her attention to the depths of her Civic. All business, she lifted out the cooler, a small Weber grill, and two chairs.

"Set up the chairs; I'll get the grill going," Lou said, avoiding direct eye contact with Al.

• • • • •

Al liked Lou. She laughed at his jokes, relished good food, and looked particularly adorable in a baseball cap and number nineteen pin-striped Brewers jersey. He relaxed in her company. But he hadn't expected all the tingles. When he heard Lou gasp—never mind when she kissed his cheek—his entire body felt it. He'd never been so instantly aware of another person's every twitch, every breath.

Al looked to his left to make sure he hadn't lost Lou to the blue and yellow wave moving them toward the entrance. The last ninety minutes had breezed by. Lou had brought the grill from ice-cold to scorching-hot faster than a firestorm; the brats were preboiled in beer and onions and burst with the perfect combination of juicy and smoky, complete with a crunchy outside topped with just a smear of Dijon. Paired with ice-cold Spotted Cows, his new favorite Wisconsin beer, Al got it. He got why people came hours early. It wasn't about good seats or convenient parking. It was a friendly little party with forty thousand of your closest friends.

Lou led Al through the dense crowd, past the turnstiles, up to the second level and to their seats. Once settled, Al looked around. Miller Park was not what he expected. With the roof open, sun flooded the field and stands. They sat in the front row of their level, so no one detracted from his view. He felt like Dorothy awaking to a Technicolor Oz. The emerald grass, the ruby bricks, the golden yellows, and the cobalt blues all buzzed with intensity. On the field, a diamond of sand dotted with white pads at each of the four corners contrasted the vivid green. A few people raked the sand, leaving it with the manicured appearance of a sand trap.

It looked as if each team's bench was underground a little. He and Lou sat one level up from the Brewers' bench, or at least he assumed it was the Brewers', as the name was painted on top of it. The scoreboard showed different spaces for ERA, RBI, and many more acronyms he couldn't decipher. Al's brow furrowed and he looked at Lou, her face raised to the sun like she wasn't often in it.

"I know nothing about baseball. Is it like cricket?" Al asked. Lou didn't open her eyes or move her head to respond to Al's sudden confession. She just laughed.

"I imagine that isn't all you don't know. And I know less about cricket than you know about baseball." She rolled her head to face him, smiled, then leaned forward to pull some folded papers from her back pocket.

"I thought your knowledge of baseball might be a little sketchy, so I put together a crash course. It's mainly definitions, like what each position does, what the acronyms mean. It isn't a fast sport. Everything happens in short spurts of action. In between, there's a lot of standing around, strategizing, racing sausages, singing, and polka." Lou handed Al the notes and resumed her relaxed sunbathing.

After a moment digesting her comment, Al said, "Racing sausages? You're joking."

"They run during the sixth inning. There are five; sometimes the mini sausages race, too. You pick your favorite and cheer along. Maybe make a friendly wager. I'm partial to the brat. He wears the green lederhosen."

"Definitely not like cricket."

"Just another reason Milwaukee rocks. Other teams try to copy, but they're just cheap imitations."

Al began reading the notes, looking up to scan the field, comparing the hand-drawn images with the real field in front of him. Lou's notes were thorough enough that Al knew more about baseball than your average suburban housewife by the time the national anthem finished and the players took their positions. Al leaned forward, matching Lou's eager position as the first pitch flew. Miraculously, the batter hit it. Al couldn't even see the ball because the pitcher threw it so fast. Before he could finish processing where it went, a player in the grassy field picked it up and rocketed it toward first base. The player slowed and returned to his dugout (at least that was what Lou called it in the notes). That was right—he was out because he hadn't beaten the ball to first base.

Al continued to compare the action on the field to the notes in his hand. By the end of the first inning, he tucked the notes into his jeans, confident he could manage the rest of the game without them. He settled into his seat, set his right ankle on his left knee as Lou did the opposite. Their knees brushed ever so lightly, yet he couldn't stop himself from sucking in a quick breath and hoping it happened again. Instead, their legs settled a safe two inches apart—but he could still feel her.

"Nuts?" Lou offered him a bag of peanuts in the shell.

"We just ate."

"Peanuts are an important baseball tradition. No game is complete without them."

Al took a few, cracked one open, and popped the nuts into his mouth. He held the empty husk in one hand and looked around for where to put it.

"What do I do with the shell?"

"Drop it."

Lou tossed her empty shells on the ground.

"You want me to litter?"

"Consider it a sacrifice to the baseball gods. We must appease them for our team to win."

Al laughed and mimicked her.

"I'd hate to incur their wrath. Any other sacrifices I need to know about?"

Al looked her in the eyes and his heart thumped. At that moment, she could have anything she wanted.

• CHAPTER TEN •

John waited, tapping the bar, as Al worked to find words—words that would explain his problem.

"I like her," he finally said, "but I don't think she's quite ready. She can't be ready. Can she?" Al propped his elbows on the smooth, dark wood of The Harp's bar and dropped his forehead into his hands, grasping at his hair. If only he could grasp his words as easily. For the first time since coming to Milwaukee, he had asked John to get a drink. He needed a friend to bounce his erratic thoughts off of, and John seemed willing.

"Ready for what? A car ride? Dessert? A lobotomy?" John chewed a handful of popcorn. Bits of it landed on the bar in front of him and on his already-wrinkled shirt. He didn't seem to notice.

Al gaped at the questions.

"No. Is she ready to date someone?" Al said. "It hasn't been that long since she dumped her fiancé. I like her, but I don't want to be the rebound."

"Does she like you back?"

"How can you tell?"

"You're asking me? You're screwed if you're asking me for lady advice."

"Valid point, but what do you think?"

"You went to the Brewers game on Monday, right? Now it's Friday. You said she doesn't normally call you on the weekends. Huh. I wonder why that is."

"She said she was busy most weekends—that's why we get together early in the week."

"What's she doing, do you think?"

"I don't know; probably working."

"What does she do?"

"I don't know. Never asked. Something in an office."

"Aren't you curious?"

"Quite, but I tend to avoid discussing work for obvious reasons. If I pump her for information about her work, she's bound to ask questions back. It's easier if I don't have to make up lies."

"Oh. Right. I forget you have an alter ego. Too bad he's an asshole food critic rather than an actual superhero. I could be your dashing sidekick."

Al blinked. Was he really an asshole? Did everyone think that? Did Lou?

"So, what do you think? I could still call her, right? Even if she hasn't called me?"

"Dude, calm yourself. Are you having fun? Is she having fun?"

"I think so. But our excursions are about showing me her favorite parts of the city. She doesn't seem to dwell on the ex-boyfriend. That's good, right?"

Al looked around at the bar he and John sat in and took something small out of his trouser pocket. He started tracing his thumb over the raised edges while watching the bubbles rise to the surface of the untouched cider in front of him.

"Are you playing with a bratwurst?" John asked.

Al turned a little red and stuffed the object back into his pocket. "It's just a magnet. I picked it up at the Brewers game. I forgot to take it out."

"You wore khakis to a Brewers game? You need to lighten up. It's called dressing appropriately."

Leave it to John to question his wardrobe choices. At least John believed he wore the khakis to the game rather than the crumpled jeans on his closet floor. He wasn't ready to share his new hobby yet, or explain why he carried the brat magnet with him all week.

"Well. Now I know for next time."

• • • • •

Lou listened to the hold music, a Muzak version of "Money for Nothing." Who knew a bank could have a sense of humor? But as awful as the music was, she didn't want it to end. If she stayed on hold forever, she would never know what the loan officer had to say. Hope could still exist. Hope kept her going. Hope now sounded like Dire Straits.

Alone in the Lair, she'd run the numbers again. If the loan came through, it would give her an extra year to turn things around. A year to pay bills and her employees. Another year to improve their reputation. One year could save Luella's.

The dream of Luella's had started at the local culinary school, where she had met Sue. Sue would whisper inappropriate comments under her breath during classes, forcing Lou to cover up her snorts of laughter with coughs and dropped pans. One teacher almost kicked her out of class for knocking over an empty cast-iron pot.

Sue had recognized immediately that Lou had vision and the talent to back it up but lacked courage. In those early years, they had spent hours in prep fantasizing about all the possibilities. Without Sue's, and eventually Harley's, constant encouragement, Lou never would have saved the money or taken the risk. It was as much their restaurant as it was hers. While Luella's wasn't exactly what they had planned, it was theirs, too, and she wasn't ready to lose it.

She just needed one bank to believe in her and her restaurant. Just one to see the potential. Just one to trust she could make Luella's successful. Three already passed—they didn't believe in her. They all said she would need a third party to guarantee the loan.

The music stopped and Lou's stomach churned.

"Hello, this is Joanne Smith."

"Hi, Joanne, this is Elizabeth Johnson. I'm returning your message. You said you'd finished reviewing my documents." Lou chewed the inside of her cheek.

"Ms. Johnson. Sorry about the wait."

"That's okay."

"Well, I've gone over everything—your business plan, your financials. And while I think you're on the right path, I'm afraid we won't be able to lend you the money without a guarantor—someone who can pay the loan if you can't."

Commercial Lender Joanne Smith might as well have sucker-punched her in the stomach.

"Oh. Okay."

"As soon as you have someone, please call me back so we can finish the paperwork."

"All right. Thanks."

Lou set the phone down as if it were a cracked egg, just one bump away from catastrophe. It was how she felt. Then the bump hit. Lou curled over in her chair, rocking forward and back as the tears fell onto the dated linoleum. She held in her cries, knowing Sue and Harley would hear in the kitchen. The last door had slammed shut, the last glimmer dimmed, the last star wished upon. Her mouth filled with a horrible flavor. Failure tasted like burnt fish and coffee-soaked coconut cake.

Lou pulled herself together, took a deep breath, and entered the kitchen to prep for the evening service. It didn't take long for their normal routine to commence.

"How can you say anything other than *Ratatouille* is Pixar's best movie? You're a chef, for Christ's sake," Sue said.

Lou smiled at Sue's accusatory tone. She needed this distraction.

Harley rolled his eyes and said, "You're letting your biases show, Sue. *Up* uses music better—like a character. The opening fifteen minutes is some of the best filmmaking—*ever*. And who doesn't love a good squirrel joke?"

"But *Ratatouille* brings it all back to food." Sue waved a carrot in the air to emphasize her point. "They made you want to eat food cooked by a rat! I'd eat the food; it looked magnificent. That rat cooked what he loved, what tasted good. Like I've been telling Lou, we should cook food from the heart, not just the rulebook."

"Hey, don't drag me into this," Lou said, looking up from the lamb she was carving into chops, scraping all the meat off the rib to adhere to the strict standards for a Frenched chop.

"It's true. We aren't gaining any new customers. We may as well do what we want," Harley said.

"We could try some venison. Hit the farmers' markets. Otto and Gertrude said we could raid their garden." Sue's face lit with hope.

"I hear you and I'll think about it," Lou said, her stomach clenching again.

"The fish guy had some fabulous Lake Superior whitefish. I know you have a soft spot for it. A friend has a smokehouse. He cou—"

"I'll think about it. Weren't you two discussing movies?"

"I think we settled on me being right." Sue winked at her. Harley snorted over the whirr and snick of his mixers kneading dough. Sue's smile just got bigger, and her red braids shook with silent laughter. "So, you never gave us the details on the Brewers game. How'd it go? Did the Brit figure out baseball?"

"It was fine. A perfect day for baseball—sunny, not too hot. A nice breeze." Lou smiled, pleased with the topic change.

"Bullshit! You know that isn't what we want to know. I see you get all fluttery when he calls. When are you going to invite him in so we can meet him?"

"You act like there's more going on than there is."

"He gave you original artwork."

"From a street fair. I'm merely showing him the city, which does not involve introducing him to you guys. We've been over this. Yes, he's adorable. Yes, I love the accent. Yes, we have a blast together. And yes, he looks great without a shirt."

"What! Why did he have his shirt off?"

Lou bit her lip and smiled.

"I brought a Brewers T-shirt for him to wear, and he changed into it in front of me—that's all."

"Clever. And . . . ?"

"I almost forgot my own name. He has the little side things." Lou gestured at her obliques.

"I love those!"

"You know, he isn't a piece of meat," Harley said, peering through the stainless steel shelves of the pastry area.

"You're just jealous because we don't talk about you like that," Sue ribbed him. "But seriously, why don't you do something about that?"

"A million reasons. Too busy, too soon. He doesn't seem the type to stay here forever. It feels like more of a stepping stone for him. Besides, our agreement is for me to show him the city."

"So, what're you doing next? Since you clearly don't plan to ravage him yet."

"Summerfest seems about right. West of East is playing Sunday night. I thought we'd catch an early dinner at The Good Land, walk the grounds, then watch the show."

"A perfect nondate date."

"Bite me, Sue."

• • • • •

Al checked his back pocket one more time. The notepad didn't stick out too much, but maybe some folded paper would lie better. He stood up next to his desk, slipped a few folded pieces of paper into his other back pocket, and slid a hand over each, trying to determine the less obvious choice.

"Why are you rubbing your own ass? You know, you can pay people to do that for you," said John, who had just walked into the cubicle with a huge grin dividing his facial hair.

"I'm not rubbing my own ass. I'm trying to hide my notes." Al twisted to see his own bum.

"Don't you just type them into your iPad?"

"Normally, but I can't this time. Lou and I are going to The Good Land this Sunday."

"Why not just tell her who you are?"

"If you haven't noticed, I'm a love-him-or-hate-him kind of guy. I'm unsure which side she's on."

"Au contraire. Hannah said your last column received the most feedback yet—and you even liked the restaurant. Proof you don't need to destroy every restaurant in Milwaukee to make a name for yourself. People like you when you're nice, too."

"Ha. Funny you are not. So, which is less obvious?" Al turned around so John could analyze his backside.

"Really, you want me to look at your butt now?" John rolled his eyes, then took the job seriously. "I can't tell there is anything on the left side. Is that helpful?"

"Folded paper it is." Al nodded.

"How is writing on paper less obvious than typing? Unless she's blind and stupid, she'll notice."

"I thought I'd go to the loo before and after dinner to jot down some notes. I'll dine there again, so I really just want my initial impressions."

"Can I go next time?"

"No."

"I'll behave. I promise."

"Will you shave your beard?"

John gasped. "No." His eyes widened in horror, as if Al were wearing acid-washed jeans with black socks and sandals.

"Then no."

"You are a cruel, cruel man."

• CHAPTER ELEVEN •

Al fidgeted, trying to shift the pen in his back pocket. It poked at him in an unseemly manner, a little like his conscience. He didn't know Lou well, at least not well enough to share his secret, but he still felt guilty hiding anything from her. Oh, there—that felt better.

Al and Lou shared a table at The Good Land, a restaurant located in Walker's Point, not far from the lakefront. The restaurant exceeded all his expectations. The service staff attended to their needs without intruding, the wine list would impress the pickiest oenophile, and the menu explored the very best of Wisconsin cuisine in small-batch cheeses, local vegetables, and handmade sausages.

Rather than mask any flaws, the dining room lighting enhanced the beautiful woodwork, muted natural colors, and crisp white linens. Local artists had painted landscapes of Milwaukee that hung on the walls, providing a pictorial history of the area's development, which a note on the menu explained. Inexplicably, he saw stills from the movie *Wayne's*

World decorating the restroom. It must be a private joke with the owner.

Lou looked beautiful in her brightly colored dress, kind of an orangey-pink—John would know the color. Her hair draped past her shoulders, dancing against her bare skin each time she moved. His imagination kept distracting him from their conversation, picturing his lips in place of her tresses. It was a short path from shoulders to neck to lips.

"You okay? You're kind of wiggly," Lou said.

"Just settling in. I think we'll be here a while." Al tried not to choke out the words.

"I hope so. I've been dying to eat here."

While the waiter filled her wineglass, Lou said, "Could you tell Chef Tom I'd like a grilled cheese without cheese?"

The waiter's baffled expression matched Al's.

"Trust me. Just tell him. Feel free to mention how crazy I seem."

"Okay," the waiter said, and rushed toward the kitchen doors, eager to see Chef's reaction.

"What are you doing?" Al looked around to see whether anyone had overheard her request.

"I went to school with Chef Tom ages ago. We worked together before moving on to grown-up jobs. At one restaurant, I washed dishes and he worked the line, and a customer actually ordered that. Grilled cheese with no cheese! It's been a joke ever since."

"Lou!" A booming voice rang over the dining room's quiet bustle. A man roughly the size of a Packers lineman rushed like a freight train across the restaurant with arms wide. Lou hopped out of her chair into those arms.

"How ya doing, kid? I never thought I'd see you here. I didn't think Devlin would allow it." He looked around, searching for the odious man, perhaps to toss him out. Al approved.

"Devlin and I broke up a while ago. I'm here with my good friend Al." Lou gestured toward Al, who felt a little uncomfortable under the large man's firm gaze. Lou sat back down.

"At least he has good taste in restaurants. But what took you so long? It's been months."

"Work's been a little time consuming. I'm sure you understand."

"I heard. You'll be fine. You always are. Let me know if I can help." Chef Tom squeezed her elbow reassuringly.

"Thanks, Tom."

"So, what did you order? Not that it matters, 'cause I'm making you something special."

"We're still trying to decide. You don't make it easy."

Tom laughed loud enough that the customers who weren't already staring now turned to look.

"Well, don't worry. I'll send out the perfect meal with the best the kitchen has today. No plain old meal for you. I'll even make it myself."

"Don't do that. That's not why we came here."

"Bullshit. What's the point of knowing the chef if you don't let him show off for you?"

"Don't overdo it, then."

"Me? Overdo? Of course not." Chef Tom gave a smile that would make the Cheshire Cat jealous and returned to his kitchen.

"I like him," was all Al said, nodding his head toward the swinging kitchen door.

• • • • •

"Bloody hell, I can't remember when I've eaten that much food." Al wiggled, trying to alleviate some of the pressure on his waistband. "Chef Tom has a gift. The way he took simple ingredients like cheddar and mushrooms and made them exciting. Or turning the duck egg and whitefish into a familiar and comforting dish. Thank God we're walking to Summerfest. Even the wine paired brilliantly. I didn't know Milwaukee had restaurants like that."

Al patted his back pocket, checking on his notes. Writing on his leg in the loo had been trickier than expected, and his notes resembled a toddler's scribbles. He kept thinking of details he didn't want to forget. The Good Land ranked as one of the best restaurants he'd ever dined at. Anywhere. His palate still reeled from the decadent braised venison.

"I knew you liked food, but I didn't realize you were so into it."

"My mum's culinary knowledge began and ended with the side of a box, so I appreciate good food after a childhood of deprivation." The half-truth didn't lie easy on his tongue. Al had acquired the cooking duties as soon as he could see the countertop, much to his father's delight. As Al experienced more cuisines with his friends' families, his cooking repertoire expanded. But he couldn't and wouldn't get into his past with Lou—not tonight. With so many little omissions building up, it was no wonder a new one could slide out so easily.

"Ha! My family was the opposite. My grandma could teach Chef Tom a thing or two about cooking." Lou adjusted her bag so it crossed her body. "I'll have to make you dinner sometime."

"I would love that." Al hoped she could hear the truth in those words, at least.

. . . . .

Lou looked around as they walked. She hadn't been in this part of town recently. Several warehouses lined the streets, mingling with bars and boutiques. Over the past decade, Walker's Point and the Third Ward, south of downtown, had evolved as hot spots in the city. Trendy shops, packed bars, bustling restaurants, and pricey riverfront condos brought new life to one of the oldest neighborhoods in the city. Intermingled with the new and updated stood older buildings, still serving the city's industrial backbone.

A soft breeze ruffled Lou's coral summer dress, and her purse's long strap crossed her upper body—ideal for walking. Stars surely sparkled beyond the orange night glow the city emitted—Lou just couldn't see them. The moon still hid beyond the horizon but should rise before midnight. The air lacked summer's usual humidity and promised perfection for the rest of the evening. Being used to the heat in the kitchen, she enjoyed feeling the air whisper over her skin, caressing the goose pimples already there. She didn't want to think about the real reason her skin reacted to every waft of air in the small distance between her and Al. The space between them seemed ten degrees warmer than the air.

This was their fourth outing. If they were dating, she'd be planning to ask him back to her apartment. But they weren't,

Lou reminded herself, and she wouldn't. She frowned, acknowledged the disappointment, and added it to the other disappointments of the past few months.

Lou peered at Al as they walked past Alterra, a local coffee roaster. She closed her eyes to inhale the rich smell of coffee—a nice break from the usual city smells of exhaust, asphalt, and occasional waft of garbage. Devlin had called earlier today, this time at the restaurant. She let voice mail answer it, but her heart still wrenched when she listened to his message.

"Elizabeth, you've made your point. I'll make amends. Now call me so I can help."

Lou had reached for the phone, tempted to let Devlin clean up the mess of her failing business. It would be easy for him to pay vendors, fire employees, and get out of contracts. She could move in with him tomorrow; he'd asked her a million times. It would be so easy to fill the role he had created for her, to sell her dreams for their safe, comfortable routine. Wasn't that what she'd been doing before she found him with Megan? But then she imagined bumping into Al, his expression when he saw her with Devlin. Lou shuddered. He would know she had taken the easy route—and so would she.

"Are you cold?" Al asked, breaking into her thoughts.

They hadn't said much during the last few blocks. Al turned his head to Lou, waiting for her response.

"A little." Lou gave a small smile and put her sweater on. As she stepped off the curb to cross the street, a small car screeched around the corner. Al grabbed her right wrist and hauled her back toward him, using his right arm to wrap around her back and hold her steady against his chest. The car zoomed away, missing them by a wide margin. Lou found Al staring into her face with wide, fiery blue eyes. His hand pressed against her lower back, holding her firmly against him, all of him. His other hand still grasped her wrist. Lou's left hand landed on his chest, spread against the cool cotton of his shirt. She still had yet to breathe after the surprise of finding herself so close to him. Both froze, no breath between them, only the heat where their bodies touched.

She could feel the pulse on her wrist where Al began circling his thumb. Lou's fingers pressed into his shirt, not pushing him away, but trying to grab on to him. Their eyes still locked, he pulled her even closer.

"Get a room!" shouted a voice from a passing car.

Al and Lou stepped apart and took long breaths.

"So sorry. I thought that car was much closer." Al looked at the traffic as it passed. Lou straightened her purse so the bag hung against her front hip.

"No need to apologize. Feel free to save my life anytime. I like to encourage that type of behavior in my friends."

Al's eyes crinkled and he laughed, the tension gone. Lou sent a silent thank-you to the heckler. A moment longer and Lou's resolve to keep their relationship out of the bedroom would have fallen into the nearest hotel room.

Al took Lou's arm and set it on his.

"Since you are clearly not capable of safely crossing the street, I'd best keep a hand on you." Lou chuckled and they walked the last few blocks to Summerfest arm in arm.

• • • • •

Once they were through the gates of Summerfest, the crowds tried to sweep them away. Keeping their arms looped together, Lou navigated the torrent of revelers, guiding them toward the lake, crossing perpendicular to the flow of traffic. Al turned his head in every direction, trying to take it all in. At first glance, one main thoroughfare went parallel to the lake through the center of the grounds. He could hear country music from his left, rock to his right. Was that Meat Loaf?

In front of them, a play fountain materialized between the bodies. Attendees of all ages stood barefoot in the splash zone, cooling their feet after walking the festival in the hot summer sun all day. It was about nine o'clock, the sun long gone behind the nearby overpass, leaving the warmth rising from the blacktop as the only reminder of its earlier blazing. People poured in, ready for a warm night of music and beer at the world's largest music festival. Families, who spent the day when it was less crowded, wandered toward exits, strollers and exhausted children in hand.

Lou pulled Al free of the masses and onto a grassy area beyond the splash fountain. People dotted the grass, resting, snacking, and a few even sleeping.

"Whew. That crowd always makes me question why I come to Summerfest. Thankfully, there are roads less traveled." She led him toward the lake.

They stopped to enjoy the view of the lake; the mishmash of music combined to make a hum in the background. Attendees blanketed the breakwater rocks, resting and absorbing the serenity. Despite the crowd, it was peaceful. Al took a deep breath. He smelled the slight fish odor common on Lake

Michigan's shore, hot grease, and the ever-present vanilla scent of Lou. The breeze fluttered Lou's unbound hair. That combined with the summer dress made her look soft and vulnerable. Her eyes closed and she breathed deeply; Al couldn't look away.

"Mmmm. And this is summer in Milwaukee. Crowded, loud, sometimes a little stinky, and more fun than you can possibly imagine."

"Is that the tagline from the tourism board?"

"Perhaps that's a new career path for me."

"Absolutely—tourists will come in droves."

"It's a gift; I know what the people want." Lou opened her eyes and caught him staring at her.

He snapped his gaze back toward the lake and cleared his throat. "So, where is this band we're seeing?"

"It's on the south end. We'll grab a beer at one of the stands. Usually one of the local breweries sets up down there."

"Who are we seeing again?"

"West of East. They have a folk, country, singer/songwriter vibe. I went to high school with both of them. I like to go to shows when I can, which means not as often as I want."

"Are they good?"

"For shame, Al. Have I ever led you wrong? Not to mention, they wouldn't be performing at Summerfest if they weren't wonderful."

"I think I heard Meat Loaf on the way in. Care to change your opinion?"

"It's a music festival. They need to cover all types of music—even the kinds you don't like. I imagine he's sold more records than you have."

"Everyone has sold more albums than I have."

"Then zip it and enjoy the music."

Al and Lou purchased beers and entered the stage area. Bleachers formed a U shape around several rows of benches, all facing the small stage. The area sat about two hundred people, and almost all the spots were taken. Al took Lou's free hand and led her toward the top row. Two spots appeared between the seated attendees, but not side by side.

"You can sit there, and I'll sit behind you," Al said, pointing to the lower bench.

"Works for me."

Lou settled herself into the spot, then scooted forward to avoid bumping his knees.

Al leaned over. "Feel free to lean back; I promise I won't spill beer on your lovely frock."

"No worries if you do. I make it a point to own all beer-proof clothing."

Lou pulled her hair out of the way so it wouldn't get stuck and gently settled her shoulder blades against Al's knees.

Al leaned over to get closer, a smile flirting on his lips. "We've explored art, beer, custard, baseball, and music. But I'm still not sure I'm convinced Milwaukee is as brilliant as you claimed."

Lou turned. "Really? I think you just like excuses to hang out with delightful little me."

She smiled and set one arm on Al's knees. Al tensed as her hand settled gently on the crisp khaki he always wore. She tucked a lock of hair behind her ear, revealing a stretch of smooth skin. Al wanted to trace a line from her earlobe to her shoulder with his lips, maybe find the source of her alluring scent, but instead took a deep breath to focus on her words.

"Well, since you claim you aren't convinced—we're entering the peak of festival season. For the rest of the summer, there will be a different ethnic fest here each weekend. I have to work, but you should come with someone. This fest, Summerfest, is all about music, whereas the ethnic fests each celebrate a different culture. They're tons of fun, a lot less crowded, and each has its own spin on food and music. You'll probably enjoy Irish Fest—it covers all of the UK—and there's Festa Italiana, Mexican Fiesta, and German Fest. There's usually a tent where you can learn the history of that culture in Milwaukee. It's a great crash course in Milwaukee's past."

"Are you giving me homework?"

"Something like that. You shouldn't miss them because I'm busy. But if you keep getting lippy, I might make you write an essay for me. Perhaps something on the role of multiple ethnic cuisines in Milwaukee's evolving food culture?" Lou said with a smile, but Al liked it.

"That's actually a great idea." Al paused, already mentally plotting out the article.

"Are you going to write it?" Lou asked, her eyes widening.

Al's pulse quickened as an alarm bell clanged in his head.

"What happened to no work talk?" Al took a few slow, even breaths to appear calm. Lou looked even more surprised, then nodded her head.

"You're right—you probably shouldn't discuss your weekend safecracking work for the local criminal masterminds. This is about getting you to love Milwaukee."

Al smiled as the alarm in his head slowed, then stopped. Everything returned to normal; crisis averted. He didn't notice that Lou had started talking again.

". . . State Fair rocks. Great people watching, farm animals, root beer milk, and never-ending deep-fried food on a stick. And you can't forget about the cream puffs. That's our thing."

"When's State Fair?"

"Not until the end of the month."

"So, no plans until then?" Al's brows scrunched a little, struggling with what that meant.

"I hadn't really thought much about what's next. I kind of thought you'd be sick of me by now."

"Never! As you say, I'm just looking for excuses to hang out with little old you." Al could feel his face flush at the truth in his comment. This was getting complicated. His attraction was growing and he loved spending time with Lou, but his plans to leave Milwaukee at the earliest opportunity hadn't changed. The more he wanted to act on his feelings, the more he knew he shouldn't. It would only hurt them both when he left.

"I suppose we could check out the Harley Museum. I'd offer to take you for a ride, but I don't go near them. Though if you really want to try it, I know someone who could take you out. I understand it's different from any other motorcycle."

"That works. You're on such a roll; you don't want to lose momentum."

"We can't let that happen." Lou smiled and winked, then turned to the stage as the first smooth notes of music floated into the evening sky. Lou leaned back against Al's legs before he could straighten up. Her hair spilled over his hands, cool and silky. Hoping she wouldn't notice, he leaned in and sniffed. Vanilla. And not some diluted note buried among other laboratory-born scents, but real vanilla bean. Then Al leaned back, too, and closed his eyes, savoring the sweet smell of Lou, the feel of her hair over his hands, her weight against his legs, and the strumming guitar paired with a soulful voice. Milwaukee summer was more fun than he'd imagined.

• CHAPTER TWELVE •

Sweet silence. Lou heard her footsteps echo on the asbestos-tiled staircase. She unlocked the front door to her apartment and hung the keys on the hook next to the door. A hallway led down the center of her apartment with doorways opening to each room. To the left were her bedroom, bathroom, and living room. The other side housed her kitchen and dining room, linked by an arched opening. Except for the bathroom, all the floors were worn oak, common in older Milwaukee buildings. At the end of the hallway stood a door leading to a private balcony, her favorite apartment feature. More of a rooftop terrace, the balcony had a patio table and chairs, a grill, and a few pots for fresh herbs and veggies. These tended to die since she never watered them, but every summer she tried.

Aside from the stove light in the kitchen, humming and sending a faint glow into the hallway, the apartment's silent darkness soothed her ears after the loud music at Summerfest. She could still feel the bass pumping in her chest but lacked a distraction to occupy her mind. Lou took a deep breath, smelling the lemon air freshener in the hall outlet. She closed the door and let her aloneness wash over her. Lou hadn't spent much time at home in years. If she wasn't at Luella's, then she'd spent her time at Devlin's. She didn't like the echoes of her empty apartment. It emphasized everyone missing from her life. The silence no longer soothed.

Lou clicked the deadbolt and latched the chain. She kicked her shoes into the small pile near the door and began turning on all the lights, starting with the overhead light in the hall. As she walked the hall, dust bunnies raced behind her. She should probably do something about that—everyone knew dust bunnies multiplied faster than their real-life counterparts. She tossed her phone and keys on the kitchen counter, grabbed the Swiffer from the hall closet, and started collecting hair balls, moving into the dining room—she recalled seeing a dust elephant under the old pine table.

Lou groaned when she flicked on the light. What happened to the table? Covered in so many open cookbooks and rumpled notebooks, it looked like a decoupage project gone wrong. She needed to start cleaning up after herself. Time to act like a grown-up instead of chasing dreams like a child. She propped the Swiffer against the wall, setting it against the doorframe so it wouldn't fall—which it did anyway. Twice. She could finish sweeping when she cleaned off the table.

Lou stacked cookbooks, sorting according to topic. She carried one stack into the living room to reshelve and returned for another armload. An old smiling face caught her attention as she walked toward the dining table. A dusty picture of her grandma looked over the room, along with several other family photos. She always liked the idea of working while they watched her. She never felt alone in here.

A favorite picture showed her parents standing in front of the old County Stadium wearing Brewers T-shirts and holding a tiny screaming baby. Her first Brewers game. It was one of the few pictures she had of all three of them. It wasn't fair. Some people had enough family to start a small country and she had no one. No one to call on Mother's Day, no one to suggest she keep her home cleaner, no one to tell her what to do. Looking at her parents' smiling faces, the protective way they held her, she tried to hear their voices and what they would say. But Lou couldn't hear them anymore. She couldn't hear their voices, but her memory of that whole horrific day of the accident remained etched in detail. She could remember what she was wearing, the weather, the shush of sliding down the wall and curling into a ball, where she stayed until Sue had ushered her into bed.

Her mom and dad would have loved Luella's, watching her come alive with fresh ingredients in one hand and a ten-inch chef's knife in the other. Her whole life, they had encouraged her to try new experiences even if they ended in disaster, like when she had skateboarded for the first time and broken her wrist. They had applauded her efforts, asked her what she learned, and held her until she stopped crying. Her fingers brushed the glass over their arms in the photo, wishing they could hold her now. But she was on her own.

Lou looked down at her fingers. Well, she should at least dust. Halfway to the kitchen where she kept the dusting supplies, Lou stopped.

"I'll do that later," she said out loud.

Not looking at the pictures on the walls, she grabbed the

last stack of books, feeling better now that she could see the scuffed wood of her table again, and carried them to the living room. She still needed to put away her notebooks and pens. How did so many accumulate?

In the small, cozy living room, she set the books on the floor next to the first stack. When she'd moved in four years ago, she had painted the walls a cheerful Caribbean blue to offset the white fireplace, mantel, and built-in bookcases. The fireplace worked, but she'd never used it. Instead it contained three dusty blue pillar candles on copper candlesticks. The bookshelves sagged with cookbooks ranging from relics recovered in her grandmother's kitchen to every edition of *Cook's Illustrated*, with a smattering of cookbooks by celebrity chefs, such as Barefoot Contessa and Bobby Flay.

Lou stared at the crammed shelves. She pulled all the books off and stacked them according to cuisine, sneezing twice from all the dust launched into the air. This time she made it to the kitchen to get the Pledge and dust rag she kept under the sink. When she bent down to open the doors, a whiff of spoiled milk from the dirty dishes hit her unsuspecting nose. She only had enough dishes to go a few days without cleaning them, but it had been a while since she ate at home—last week, if she remembered correctly. That milk was at least a week old. Nasty.

Lou turned the water to its hottest setting, which was way past the recommended 120 degrees. She'd convinced the super a few years ago to crank up her water heater because she liked to use really hot water on her dishes. They felt cleaner. When steam rose from the sink, she put on her purple rubber gloves and started rinsing the dishes as she neatly stacked them, emptying the sink so she could fill it with sudsy water.

As the sink filled, she stared out the window overlooking her patio. What should she do about Luella's? She could contact the paper and demand a retraction, maybe bring in a meal to their offices to demonstrate their error. A. W. Wodyski would have to eat his words. That was a delightful thought. His line "When I found a seemingly properly cooked bite, the fish tasted of cindery hate and cheap wine" still stung.

Sigh. But the damage was done. If she had a little more money, she could keep the restaurant open longer, but the four banks she'd contacted had turned down her loan requests. Well, not technically. She needed someone who could pay the loan if she couldn't. She didn't know anyone with extra money lying around. Except . . . Lou glanced at her phone and the text she had received earlier in the night.

Suds rose above the edge of the sink. Lou turned off the faucet and added dishes into the steamy basin. She stared out the window again but continued to wash, rubbing the cups and plates with a washcloth, then setting them on the other side for rinsing.

What about Devlin?

She yanked off a glove, flinging white bubbles into the air like snowflakes, and swiped to read the text.

Elizabeth. Once you close the restaurant, we should think about setting a date. Call me tomorrow.

Lou snorted. He had skipped over needing her forgiveness and now proceeded as if nothing had changed. Lou rolled her eyes. Ass.

Delete.

Her phone whistled with another text. This time, she turned it off. In the morning, she'd block all his numbers.

So the answer wasn't Devlin. If she even asked, he'd use that as leverage. Devlin never gave away anything. He even sold his old suits on Craigslist rather than donate them to Goodwill. Only a miracle would save Luella's, like an amazing review in *Saveur* or winning the lottery. But Lou didn't believe in miracles. The restaurant would close. Accepting that filled her heart with lead.

Lou reached for more dishes but found them all clean. If only more chores got done that way. She rinsed the sudsy dishes and emptied the sink, hung up her gloves and dishcloth to dry, and tried to remember where she'd left off. Dusting—that's right.

She grabbed the dusting supplies and returned to the living room. What a mess. Books covered every flat surface, gravity threatening to bring down some of the larger piles. This was absurd. In large swipes, she removed the worst of the dust, then put the books back on the shelf. She couldn't fix everything in one night.

The lights flickered a little and Lou peered out the window to see lightning flash. She wrapped herself in a cozy robe from the bedroom and went out to the deck; it was the best place to watch a storm roll into the city. The pleasantly warm night stirred from the breeze ahead of the storm, puffing pockets of chilled air. Lou tugged her robe tighter and sat in one of her Adirondack chairs.

Without cleaning to distract her, the loneliness settled on her like dense fog, isolating her. Every sound seemed muffled and distant. Sigh. She had no fiancé to come home to and talk to about her day. Soon she'd have no job where she could share her thoughts, dreams, and jokes. What would she do for money? She'd never made much at Luella's, but she had always been able to pay her bills. She could go back to working the line at someone else's restaurant, but one job rarely covered living expenses, and she was getting too old for double shifts in the trenches.

Lou had really believed she could make her restaurant a success. Never mind the humiliation of failing; now she faced having to get a roommate or move to a cheaper apartment. She curled her legs into her chest and put her head on her knees. She needed to find a solution.

But not tonight. Tonight, she would wallow a little in her misery, letting disappointment fill the empty spaces left by her burst dreams and rocky future. She could blame her misfortune on Devlin for never supporting her business, or A. W. Wodyski for his scathing review. But that didn't sit well with Lou. The fault was hers and hers alone. Taking responsibility gave her control. Taking responsibility gave her hope she would find happiness again.

Judging by the staggering gait of the few pedestrians on the sidewalks below, bar time had come and gone. The air whooshed by with the cool front moving in over the lake. A few more flickers of lightning flashed like a distant pinball machine. Clouds raced, lit by the city below. She crossed her legs and rubbed her sore feet. Working in restaurants, Lou knew constant foot pain, but walking in heels tortured her feet in an entirely different way. But they'd just looked too cute with her dress, and she wanted to look cute for Al.

Al . . . With her time opening up, she could see him more. But should she? She was still dealing with Devlin—granted, mainly by ignoring him, but he was still a presence. Luella's demise and her uncertain financials made her vulnerable. But she was lonely, and a little rebound might be the pick-me-up she needed. They definitely had chemistry. She'd thought they were going to kiss when that car barely almost hit them. Lou touched her lips for a moment, then stuffed her hands in the robe's pockets.

Her heart couldn't take another loss right now. Best to keep it friendly and light, like a frothy meringue for dessert—enough sweet to end the meal on a happy note, without the substance to make you feel stuffed.

There, that was a productive session. She'd cut the restaurant loose, find a new job and maybe a roommate, and keep Al firmly in the friend column. So why didn't she feel settled? Instead, she felt like her apartment—a little tidier on the surface, but still a mess underneath.

• • • • •

Al sipped his morning tea, hoping to jolt his synapses alive. He spread his notes out, turning them different directions to decide which way was up.

"So you suck at nineties movie references," John said. Al swiveled in his chair to see John leaning back in his chair, one leg crossed over the other, his fingers steepled in front of him.

"What?" Al asked.

"I glanced at your notes from the restaurant on Sunday. Nineties movies references. They go right over your head."

"I have no idea what you're talking about."

Al didn't like feeling like an idiot.

"Meel-ee-wah-kay? The Good Land?"

Al stared blankly.

"Dude, we have got to watch some movies together," John said.

"Is this your obnoxious way of asking how this weekend went?"

"Sure. If you insist on talking about it. How did the date go?" John grinned.

"It wasn't a date." Al sighed.

"Was it just the two of you?" John propped his fingers into a tent.

"Yes."

"Did you have dinner?" He added a nod.

"You know I did. I'm reviewing the restaurant." Al sensed a trap.

"So you told her what you do? She knew you were on the clock?"

"No." Al rolled his eyes.

"Then you went to Summerfest to watch a band?"

"Yes."

"Did you meet any other people?"

"No, but it wasn't a . . ." Al sat up straighter.

"Hang on." John held his hand up. "Did you kiss?"

Al paused, remembering the near miss. "No."

"There was a pause—what was the pause for?" John pointed at Al as if catching him with his hand in the cookie jar.

"Nothing. We almost kissed, but it didn't happen. It wasn't a date." He slumped back into the office chair.

"Did you slip her the hot beef—"

"Mate, watch it. I assure you, the answer is no, and even if it wasn't, I'm not about to discuss it like we're in a secondary school locker room."

"I was gonna say sandwich. There are great hot beef sandwiches at Summerfest. Way to go to the gutter."

Al smiled at John's cover-up. The guy was growing on him. Plus, he'd read all John's articles in the paper's archives. Under the sloppy, hairy exterior dwelt an astute critic of all things style and culture. He understood fashion so well, why he continued to break every fashion rule with his own appearance baffled Al, but he'd figure it out soon enough.

"Quite right," Al said. "I need to finish typing my notes from the Good Land visit now. Shh."

Al spun back around to his computer monitor and returned to deciphering his loo-scrawled notes. He could barely read them, but the inconvenience had been well worth it. Dining with Lou beat dining alone any day. She clearly loved food, ate everything, and understood that if you didn't like a food, it didn't mean the dish wasn't successful. If you focused on the flavors and textures, you could break a dish down into definable components. By analyzing the components, you could decide whether the dish worked or didn't.

And sometimes, when a chef understood each ingredient so completely, down to its roots, he or she could create something wholly new and complete, the culinary equivalent of alchemy, and almost as elusive. But when it happened, the diner could taste and feel that chef's love and passion in the food. Al searched for and craved these experiences, and he'd gotten one on Saturday night from Lou's friend Chef Tom.

"Al, come to my office for a minute," Hannah said, interrupting his thoughts.

Al put his computer into sleep mode and followed Hannah to her office. He didn't trust John to not do something in his absence. He'd already changed his desktop twice to lewd Photoshopped pictures of the Queen. Al ran through his last few reviews, trying to imagine why Hannah needed to talk to him. He hadn't libeled any restaurants or chefs. In fact, all the reviews were positive. He'd finally found some good restaurants.

Hannah walked around her desk and picked up a handful of papers to hand to Al.

"These are the latest letters we've received," said Hannah. Al scanned them, picking out a few phrases: "Wodyski really helped me pick the perfect restaurant" and "I learned so much about Thai food, I can't wait to try it." Al looked up at Hannah, his eyebrows scrunched together.

"I don't understand," he said.

"It's hard to believe, but you are getting even more letters. I thought since you've started being less critical, people would get bored. Your writing changed." Hannah looked at him closely, trying to find the difference. "Perhaps you've changed? Whatever is different, keep it up."

Al stood still, shocked by what she'd said. Was he different? He didn't feel different. And if he was different, why? And how?

"Now, out." Hannah shooed him out with a wave of her hand, already looking at her computer monitor and mousing with the other hand.

Al stepped out into the hallway and returned to his desk but couldn't get Hannah's words out of his mind.

• CHAPTER THIRTEEN •

As she briefed the staff on the evening's service, Sue looked at Lou, checking to see whether she'd make a dash for the restroom. She'd told Sue and Harley about her decision earlier, before the rest of the staff arrived. She'd visited the bathroom twice since then. Billy kept peeking at her stomach, searching for a nonexistent baby bump.

Lou looked at each employee, trying to memorize their unsuspecting faces. They didn't know that in a few minutes she'd tell them their jobs would end soon. Billy and his partner had just bought a small house and were hoping to adopt. Tyler's car was in the shop again. Most of the busboys sent money back to family in Mexico, every dollar making a huge difference to little sisters and brothers, parents and grandparents.

She accepted her decision, knew it made sense, but her body rejected it. Thus the vomiting, cold sweats, and wet lashes.

Sue finished the daily specials. It was now or never. Lou stood. Sue sat down, nodding encouragement at her. She sipped her ice water and cleared her throat.

"I'm sure a lot of you have noticed business is slower. I've tried to schedule fewer waiters per shift so your tips wouldn't suffer too much."

Lou took another sip of water and a deep breath.

"I've worked the numbers every possible way, but there's no way I can keep the restaurant open past New Year's. I'll probably close sooner than that."

During the staff's murmured shock and muttered no's, Lou's throat threatened to seal itself shut. More ice water didn't do much to help.

"So, I'd like you all to start finding new jobs. We have a little bit of time, so hold out for a good position. I've written each of you a wonderful recommendation, which I'll hand out after the meeting."

Lou just let the tears fall.

"I want you all to know you've been my family and will always be my family. I can't imagine a day when I don't see your faces, hear your jokes, listen to your stories. I will keep the restaurant open until you all find good, new jobs or until the bank forces me out. Whichever comes first. I'm so sorry I messed up. I've got a few calls in to some friends with good restaurants, like The Good Land. I want you all to know how much your support and friendship mean to me. These past few months have been rough. Without you all, I probably wouldn't be sober most days. So thank you."

Lou turned around to wipe her face dry on her apron. Before she could turn back, arms surrounded her. Voices said, "We love you," "It's not your fault," "Screw Wodyski," and "We aren't going anywhere." She was quite sure this last one was Harley. He and Sue had insisted they would stay with her until the bank knocked down the front door.

Sue broke through the sentimental moment with one brisk "Get to work, people," and the staff scattered to ready their stations for open. Sue handed Lou a clean napkin and pushed her toward the Lair.

Relieved to have the restaurant's fate known to their staff, Lou used the Lair's solitude to calm her tense nerves. As usual, her staff's reaction exceeded her expectations—all love and support, no blame.

Lou sat at the desk, admiring the beautiful painting Al had given her. She had hung it above her desk so she could see it often. It never failed to improve her day. Lou checked her phone, thrilled to see she had a voice mail, then crushed to see the missed call came from Devlin.

Delete.

She opened the top drawer and pulled out the engagement ring he'd given her. She'd had it appraised. Emerald-cut, just under two carats, with a platinum band from Tiffany. A jeweler had offered her fifteen thousand, though it was worth twice that. It would pay rent for a few months.

Lou looked at her painting and smiled.

. . . . .

Seven thirty on a Friday night and the dining room had too many open tables. Lou scanned the sparsley populated room for the glowing white hair and gleaming forehead of her favorite customers. Gertrude and Otto still ate at Luella's at least twice a week, a thought that warmed Lou. She worried about them. Gertrude was moving a little slower than a few months ago. She insisted it was nothing, but Lou had noticed her rouge seemed artificial, as if she was coloring in her face rather than highlighting her features.

But tonight, Gertrude was as cheerful as always. On a selfish level, Lou was happy for a slow night so she could have a long visit with them. Otto, while silent, had a confident presence, implying he had a handle on any situation; nothing took him by surprise. Gertrude merely exuded pure sunshine. As usual, Lou felt better in their presence; they were like guardian angels watching out for her.

"*Gute Nacht,* Otto, Gertrude. I'm so happy to see you." Lou slipped into an empty chair next to the pair. "Seen any of the nieces and nephews lately?"

"Bah, they are too busy with their lives to worry about their old, wrinkled relatives. They have heard all our stories and are looking to make their own."

"Well, that means I get to see more of you. Just the way I like it."

Gertrude looked around at the many empty tables. "How are things, *Liebling*?"

"Wonderful."

"The restaurant is wonderful?"

"Yes . . . well, no, not really. But other things are pretty good."

Gertrude's eyes sparkled with the delight of understanding Lou's words more than Lou herself. "It is this new man, yes?"

"It is. We're just friends, for now. But he's lovely. We both love food, and laughing, and trying new things. It isn't about the next deal, or how many people see him. If anything, he doesn't care about meeting new people. He seems to enjoy my company."

"That is good. Otto and I love spending time with each other. Even when we shop for new tires, it is fun because we do it together." Otto's shiny head bobbed in agreement, flashes of light emphasizing the importance.

"How did you know . . . that Otto was the one?"

Gertrude's eyes glazed, peering through the years at a younger self.

"Ah, *Herzchen*, that is a very good question. I knew love before Otto. My first husband was very handsome, well respected. He sold insurance to everyone. We cared deeply for each other. When he died, I mourned, but I was not bereft. Then I met Otto. Everything made sense. As long as we were together, we could overcome anything. The meanest tasks became pleasurable because we would find the humor together. When one got angry, the other would defuse; when one got lost, the other found the map. We balanced. When we dance, all is at peace. No worries, no insurmountable obstacles. We can handle anything together. You know those dancers from the old movies, the two that danced so beautifully together?"

Lou scrunched her eyebrows in thought. "You mean Fred Astaire and Ginger Rogers?"

"Yes, Fred and Ginger. Otto and I are like Fred and Ginger. Alone, we were good. But together—perfection."

Otto reached a pale, wrinkled hand over Gertrude's matching one and gave a little squeeze of agreement. She shone a little brighter. For once, Lou got it. With Devlin, he never made her shine brighter. He tried to hide her flaws behind fancy clothes, was embarrassed she worked in a kitchen. But when she spent time with Al, she was a more confident, comfortable version of herself. She was Lou, lover of food, friends, and home. A home where she could obsess about her favorite books, giggle at ridiculous movies, and create amazing food from her heart. And with Al, she was all of those things, and he seemed to like her more because of them. She showed him all that meant the most to her, Milwaukee's heart and soul, and he still wanted to spend more time with her. Plus, she could tell his opinion of Milwaukee had softened.

"I think I may have found my Fred Astaire," Lou said half to herself.

"Oh, that is wonderful. When can we meet him?"

Lou's eyes sparkled at the idea of having Al in the restaurant. She had not thought of it before, but she relished the idea of seeing him at one of her tables, enjoying her food. "Soon. We aren't really together yet. I've just been showing him Milwaukee. He may just want to stay friends." Lou's heart sunk a little with that thought.

"*Liebchen*, there is no better place to start than friendship."

• • • • •

Al balanced a flimsy tray of fried zucchini with garlic aioli, a heavy paper plate of warm gnocchi in a tomato cream sauce, an eggplant spiedini, and a plastic glass of Italian red while following John through the undulating crowds around the Miller Stage. He had seen some cannoli and Italian cookies he'd go back for later. He didn't want to risk sacrificing his lunch to the beer-soaked and heavily trodden ground. From behind, John looked even more slovenly than usual. He wore his normal wrinkled blue button-down and stained trousers, but today he'd added ratty black Converse high-tops, his hair so mussed it looked intentional. An open picnic table appeared before him. John looked at him for an opinion on the table options; Al nodded his approval of the seating. He'd been losing his grip on the gnocchi, so he wasn't picky. The smells rising from the plates nearly drove him crazy with anticipation.

Al spread his meal around him, setting the zucchini in between them for sharing. The two ate silently for a few minutes. They had come down to Festa Italiana for lunch under the guise of Al writing a story on the food. Well, that part was true, but he could have come after work or on the weekend. It was too nice a day to stay in the office, so he coerced John into joining him for a little hooky. Al had been to his fair share of festivals, but this town really knew how to throw a party. Most fest food dripped with grease and tasted too salty. While such foods were available, quality alternatives abounded. At Festa, he couldn't decide what to eat; there were so many appealing options. Local restaurants (most of them Italian) set up food booths, serving popular restaurant items and a few unusual ones. The stalls represented a who's who of Milwaukee Italians. The food wasn't just good compared to other festivals—it would stand up to full restaurant menus.

He'd walk home to offset all the carbs. His pants already felt tighter than usual; he'd have to exercise a bit more to keep the weight from ticking up. Lately, food just tasted too good to stop after his first few bites. Perhaps because he dined with more enthusiasm, enthusiasm he could trace directly to Lou. Ever since their chance encounter, Milwaukee was better. Maybe the reluctant arrival of summer cheered him, or maybe it was his blossoming friendship with John. But he knew without a doubt it was mainly Lou. She'd showed him the unique, humble, and delicious side of the town he had refused to acknowledge existed.

He felt happier now, too. He enjoyed the blue-collar work-hard, play-hard attitude of the locals. Last Friday, he had finally gone out for his first Wisconsin fish fry. When he walked in the small corner bar, he thought he'd made a mistake. Ten patrons turned around and stared at the new guy, but the wall of people surrounding the hostess stand made his decision for him: he would eat at the bar. Al took the seat next to a man wearing a gray Packers T-shirt, jeans, and a cap for a local construction company, his gray hair peeking out under the edge.

When he ordered a gin and tonic from the wizened old woman with pale beehive hair, the man chimed in, "You don't want that. Darlene makes a crap gin and tonic. Get a brandy old-fashioned. She makes the best."

"Hard to argue with that recommendation. A brandy old-fashioned, please."

Darlene the bartender made the drink and set it in front of Al. After one sip, Al knew he had found a new favorite drink.

"What do you order for fish?" Al asked.

"The perch with potato pancakes. Best in town." Al followed his advice and wasn't disappointed. During dinner, the two men discussed travel and sports. By the time he scraped the last bite of coleslaw off his plate, half the bar had joined in. He smiled at the memory and what he'd realized while talking with them. It wasn't about who had the fanciest house, or knew more people, or traveled farthest. Many of the people he had met had been no farther than Green Bay for a Packers game. They liked life here and saw no reason to want for more. He had spent his schooling days yearning for what these lucky people had been born to—a life that was enough.

He envied their contentedness but found he felt a little himself, especially around Lou. With Lou, he didn't feel less. He felt like they were equals, no matter whether she'd come from a poor rural farm or a mansion on Lake Drive. When he thought about her background, he realized he wanted to know more. What did she do when they weren't exploring the town? Where did she grow up? Other than her wanker of an ex-fiancé, whom did she spend time with? The journalist in him cringed at his lack of research.

"You going to finish that?" asked John, pointing to Al's half-finished Italian sausage. Al looked down, realizing he'd eaten all of the gnocchi, zucchini, and half of his sandwich without noticing, too caught up in his thoughts of Lou.

"I'm done." Al handed the wrapper across the table and looked at his dining partner. You could barely see his face hidden behind the scruffy beard and long, almost matted hair. You could really only see his prominent eyebrows and grayish-blue eyes. If he didn't know John, Al would assume he spent his evenings under the local bridges.

"I don't get it, mate."

"You don't get that I'm still hungry?"

"No—you're wicked smart; I've read your articles. Your writing is brilliant. About fashion. And you look like this." Al waved his hand at John's clothes. "I don't get it."

"Self-preservation and habit." John shrugged.

"That isn't any clearer."

John held up a finger to indicate he was still chewing. When he finished, he took a long breath, then spoke.

"I grew up in West Allis." The words came out blended so it sounded like "'Stallis." "I've always known I liked two things in life: women and the clothes they wear. What could be a better job than studying beautiful women wearing beautiful clothes? It just made sense to me. Over time, I developed an appreciation for all aspects of style, but it always started with women. But being from 'Stallis, some people aren't always so nice to the young boy who knew how to pronounce 'Givenchy' correctly. Assumptions were made, faces were punched. When I dress like this, people leave me alone."

"You aren't at school anymore; I think it'd be quite safe now."

"Like I said, self-preservation and habit. I did it to hide myself when I was young. Now I'm just used to it. It's easier not to change now."

"I think you'd have better luck with the ladies." Al smirked.

John looked thoughtful. "I know. Christian Louboutin said a good pump is like a beautiful face with no makeup. You can cover a not-so-beautiful face with makeup, but it is just a mask. My mask makes my life less complicated." He took a bite of the sandwich as Al digested the unexpected information. "So, speaking of ladies, how's yours?"

Al ran his hand through his hair and looked around at the passing people, half hoping he would see her welcoming face. "Really good. I think I'm going to tell her."

"Tell her what?"

"Who I am, what I do. I think we could really have something. She should know."

"Well, how are you going to tell her? Just going to spit it out?"

"I've been thinking about this a bit. I'll show her the review of The Good Land. We had so many unique plates, she'll recognize it as our meal and realize I wrote the review. Then . . ."

"Then she'll fall into your arms, convinced of your genius, and beg to spend the rest of her life meeting your every need? Wait . . . that's what I want."

Al laughed. "That would be quite nice. I'm merely hoping she doesn't mind having to keep my identity a secret and agrees that kissing is the best dessert."

"Well, sounds like a fair plan. I'm sure things will go perfectly."

Al picked up his plastic glass of wine, held it out for John to do the same, and said, "Here's hoping."

· CHAPTER FOURTEEN ·

Al felt his stomach drop; the itchy burlap poked at the skin exposed between the top of his sock and jeans leg. A trickle of sweat ran down his back as the yellow slope blinded him in the bright sunlight. He heard Lou's woo-hoos of delight waft past him. How in the bloody hell did she convince him to sit on a burlap sack and race down a giant slide? The children coming off seemed so happy, he now believed it was a complicated scheme to trap fools like himself into parting with the two dollars it cost. Al couldn't believe people actually paid to do this. He wouldn't accept any sum of money to do it again. At last the interminable yellow slope ended and Al opened his welded-shut eyelids to see Lou's glorious smile, hair mussed like she'd just rolled out of bed, and cheeks flushed with the thrill of gravity and speed. And just like that, Al decided he would descend the yellow path of doom as many times as Lou wanted him to. Thank God she seemed happy with one trip for now.

"You okay? You look a little pale," Lou said as Al stood up, clutching the scratchy burlap.

"Yes. It looked a bit smaller from down here."

"I love that slide. I used to ride it with my dad when I was too little to go by myself. Ready for some food, or do you need a little break?"

"Food might not be the smartest. The animals?"

"Cows it is."

August had rolled in hot and steamy. Al and Lou had arrived at the Wisconsin State Fair by nine in the morning for fresh egg omelets in the Agriculture Building and some apple cider donuts. They'd nibbled their donuts and wandered the stalls celebrating various products grown and raised in Wisconsin. You could sample and buy anything, from honey-filled plastic sticks to ostrich steaks to cranberry scones. They followed up their breakfast with a stop at the milk barn, where Lou had forced him to try root beer–flavored milk. While he'd been skeptical, it tasted delicious and precisely like a root beer float.

Now, after the slide, Al didn't think more food would stay put. His stomach roiled, reminding him of those boiling mud pits he'd seen on a public television show about Yellowstone National Park.

As they approached the Cow Barn, Al prepared himself for bovine hell, but once again he was wrong. Instead of piles of manure, muddy cows, and ratty stalls, Al saw row upon row of neatly kept hay piles, clean cows, and hardworking young kids picking up manure before it hit the floor. He smelled fresh hay more than anything else. The cows blinked long lashes over their shoulders at the passing people, tails swishing away flies. At the end of an aisle, a teen boy washed a cow.

"Okay, I'm starving. You'll just have to man up and eat something," Lou said.

"I'm fine now. Where to?" Al said with a smile, realizing it was true.

"Corn on the cob, for sure, then whatever grabs us."

They spent the next hour nibbling their way through the food stalls, sharing spiral-cut potatoes, pork sandwiches, and cream puffs. They found a table in one of the many shaded beer gardens, and Lou retrieved some ice-cold Summer Shandys to go with their food. The beer had a light lemon edge that offset the malt, making it an ideal hot-summer-day drink. The potato spirals, long twirls coated in bright orange cheese, combined the thin crispiness of a potato chip with a French fry. And the cream puffs . . . The size of a hamburger on steroids, the two pâte à choux ends showcased almost two cups of whipped cream—light, fluffy, and fresh. Al had watched the impressive assembly line make it while they waited.

As he watched Lou devour her cream puff, Al's stomach still roiled, but now for different reasons. Today, he would tell Lou about his job. He wanted to ask her on an official date but needed to reveal his secret identity first. He wanted her to know everything about him and A. W. Wodyski.

. . . . .

Lou slid into the chair next to Al, so they sat side by side. She handed Al an already-sweating beer bottle and set the cheesy potatoes between them. She smiled a little at his appearance, his hair out of place and damp around the edges. He wore jeans (thank God he hadn't worn khakis). His light-colored polo showed evidence of butter gone amiss while he was eating corn on the cob.

As favorite annual events go, State Fair topped her list. She always came early for breakfast and to beat the worst of the crowds. Now it was early afternoon and people poured in. The barns crawled with strollers, crying and sticky children, and tired-looking parents. And the people watching didn't get better.

Al sampled their potato spirals, leaving a smudge of cheese on the corner of his mouth. Lou smiled and picked up a napkin.

"Hold still—the cheese is fighting back."

Using her napkin-wrapped thumb, she brushed the cheese away, briskly at first, then slower as she became distracted. His lips were wet from the beer and full from the heat. Using her bare fingers, she grazed his bottom lip. Al's blue eyes ignited. The beer tent and exhausted families disappeared. She only saw him, felt his shallow breath caress her fingertips, shooting desire through her. Every part of her was hot and electric and hungry.

Lou leaned toward him, seeing her hand tremble against his mouth. She licked her lips and saw her hunger reflected in Al's eyes. This was happening. The world seemed to shudder.

"Mommy, why is that lady touching his face?"

A high-pitched voice broke the spell like a snowball to the face. Lou and Al both turned to see a sweaty mom and chocolate-smeared boy sitting across the table from them. A large diaper bag now dominated the table—that explained the shudder. The mom glared at Al and Lou as if they had interrupted her. Lou glared back.

"She is wiping something off his face, Hunter, like Mommy wipes your face."

"Why can't he wipe his own? He's a big boy."

Al and Lou laughed.

"You're right," said Lou to Hunter. "He is a big boy. But sometimes big boys need help. Like you need help to get all that chocolate off your face." She pushed a stack of napkins across the table and smiled at Hunter's mom, who snatched the napkins and set to work.

Lou gave a small smile to Al. He wiped his damp palm on his pant leg and pulled a folded newspaper article from his jeans pocket. He carefully unfolded it, flattened it a little on the sticky picnic table, and passed it to Lou.

"I thought you'd like to read this," he said.

She took the article and looked down to give it her proper attention. The article wasn't long, maybe a column and a half, with a long crease down the middle. But after reading the headline and byline, Lou almost blacked out. She clenched her teeth, dug her nails into fleshy palms, and flared her nostrils to take in the deep breaths she needed. She'd thought she had come to terms with the events of the past four months. She accepted that closing the restaurant made business sense, but seeing the name A. W. Wodyski in print ripped open all the old wounds that had barely healed over. She felt raw, exposed, and cold despite the warm day.

"Why are you giving this to me?" she hissed.

Al looked a little stunned. "I thought you'd like to read it . . . er . . . It's a good review on The Good Land. We had such a lovely meal there. And Chef Tom is your friend." Al widened his eyes at Lou's vehemence.

Lou noticed Al's discomfort and struggled to rein her rampaging emotions back in. Hunter and his mom were watching her, too. She took a deep breath and focused on the gesture.

"You're right—we had a wonderful time there, but I prefer

to make my own opinions about restaurants rather than listen to some overeducated pompous ass." Hunter's mom flinched at the profanity. "Thank you for thinking of me. I shouldn't have blown a gasket like that." Lou crumpled the paper in one hand and shoved it deep into her favorite red purse.

Al's eyebrows scrunched. "Blown a gasket? I'm not sure I get that one."

Lou laughed and the anger subsided. "I'm sorry. It means I got angry, but not at you. You don't have anything to do with it. It's all work related and this article reminded me of it. It's not fair you had to take the brunt of it, especially since our outings have been the ideal escape from my stress. Ready for another beer before we leave?"

Al nodded slowly, his brow still furrowed, and Lou stood to get another beer.

She felt a little guilty for scaring him with her reaction. Too bad she had to work later today; she didn't want today to end. Perhaps she should invite Al to Luella's—then it could continue.

But she cherished their time as a work-free zone. If he knew the wreck her life really was, he'd want nothing to do with her. She didn't want anything to do with herself. And they had been so close to kissing—if it hadn't been for little Hunter. It wasn't all in her head. He seemed to share her feelings. She had wanted to kiss him. She still wanted to kiss him.

• • • • •

"When you asked me to pick you up for work, I thought you'd be ready," said Sue as she followed Lou into her kitchen. Lou saw the flashing green light and pushed Delete.

"Sorry, I got back later than expected," Lou said. She smiled a toothy, sheepish grin at Sue's stern face. She set her red purse on her bed, added the green metal water bottle with her bank's logo on the side, and a stack of fresh bandannas. As she crammed the items into her bag, she felt resistance and heard a crunch of paper. Crap, she'd have to clean that out later.

"Hey, it's not me who Harley will complain about," Sue said.

"No, of course. You don't do anything wrong in Harley's eyes."

Sue's eyes narrowed. "What does that mean?"

Lou finished zippering the purse and lifted the strap over her head. "Seriously?"

"Seriously. What do you mean by that?"

"Everyone knows you and Harley . . . like each other."

"Well, of course we do. So what if we like each other. I like you; what's the deal?"

"I mean 'like' like. You both make googly eyes at each other's backs when you think no one's looking. It's really cute."

"We do not." Sue walked out of the apartment, past Lou.

"If you say so . . ." Lou shrugged her shoulders and headed down the stairs. Sue smiled.

"He makes googly eyes?"

"Just like you do."

Sue absorbed that information, a quiet smile on her lips, then returned her laser eyes to Lou.

"So, what prompted the lateness?"

Lou pursed her lips, then sighed.

"Gah! I don't know. I'm not good at this. I think he wants to kiss me. I know I want to kiss him, but something always interrupts and ruins the moment. Today, it was a chocolate-smeared little kid whose mom acted like we were making out on the beer tent table."

As they stepped onto the street in front of Lou's apartment, Sue nudged her shoulder.

"Just grab him and get it over with."

Lou rolled her eyes.

"Do you not know me at all? I am not the instigator in anything."

"Sweetie, that needs to change if you're ever going to get what you want."

• • • • •

"Do you think she's crazy?" John asked as he spun around in his office chair to face Al's desk.

"What? No," Al said. A little surprised by John's comment, he turned to face him and gestured with his hands for John to speak quietly.

"You sure?"

"Yes, she's not crazy. She has never done anything crazy."

"Until now. That's how the really crazy ones work. You go along, everything's all smiles and sunshine, then bam! You're tied up in a gas station bathroom being fed Cheez Whiz through a funnel."

"Wh-what?"

John nodded knowingly. "She's a crazy. How else do you explain it?"

"She crumpled up a piece of paper. Does that really qualify as mental? I don't think so."

"She crumpled up your article. You said she got all scary, like she gave in to her dark side, then shoved her crazy back in the closet."

"Yeah, that's not quite how I described it. But it definitely revealed a setback. Clearly, she's not too fond of my critiques."

Al grabbed a fistful of hair, leaned back in his chair to stare at the fluorescents. He could still feel her fingertips on his lips. If it weren't for that chocolate-dipped kid, he could have finally escaped the friend zone.

"You act like it's a bad thing if she's crazy," John said.

"Isn't it?"

"Not at all. The crazies are great in bed."

Al let out a sigh, sat up in his chair, and said, "Dare I ask how you know this?"

"Duh, how do you not know that? It's natural law, like gravity." John smiled, or at least his beard moved upward.

Al laughed.

"Now, back to the matter at hand: how do I tell Lou what I do for a living? I'll need to spin it just right."

"You tried. Why do you even need to tell her? Let it go and enjoy her company as long as it lasts."

Al rubbed his hands on his pants and looked at the floor.

"I don't want to leave Milwaukee anymore," he said quickly, stringing the words together into one mashed sentence.

John's mouth quirked.

"What was that? You don't want to leave anymore? Has my fair city grown on you? Or, perhaps, just one fine lady?"

Al smiled, accepting any ribbing as his due.

"It's both. I do really like Lou, but Milwaukee has wormed

its way into my heart. My short-sightedness kept me from seeing it sooner."

John got up and clapped his hand on Al's shoulder.

"Glad you've finally come to your senses. Now, back to your secret-identity reveal. You're not telling her you run a drug cartel. Just spit it out. Get it over with; then you can get to the crazy stuff."

Al rolled his eyes and turned back to his computer. Looking back over his shoulder, he said, "I think you might be right, at least about the spitting-it-out part. Thanks, John."

"That's me, the Dear Abby of smitten men everywhere."

· CHAPTER FIFTEEN ·

A large stage towered in front of the audience, plaid- and green-clad revelers dancing the best they could with a beer in one hand. The loud music gave Al a reason to lean closer to Lou while the partiers gave him an excuse to keep touching her so they wouldn't get separated.

"I can't believe they're here. I loved these guys at university," Al said into Lou's ear so she could hear him above his favorite band from home, his lips touching her hair.

Irish Fest won as his favorite Milwaukee event. While not the homesick type, he missed HobNobs, Cadbury Flake bars, and good tea and he could buy them all here. The fiddle and bodhran called to a part of him he usually ignored.

Lou had surprised him late this morning with a simple text.

Irish Fest? You free?

He'd had a reservation at a new Italian trattoria, but he canceled it. They arrived late afternoon, walked the grounds, argued about their favorite dog breed (he always fancied an Irish wolfhound but he wouldn't hold Lou's preference for

Westies against her), and watched the afternoon parade, complete with bagpipes and dancers.

"Why do I find it so hard to imagine you partying in college?" Lou said.

"That's because I went to university. And we didn't party—we had diversions."

"Complete with picnic baskets and polo, I suppose."

"Precisely."

Lou turned to see whether he was teasing. And he was, only partly. He had attended a lot of polo matches, since Ian was the captain. Those days seemed so far away from the evening's muggy air. After he'd danced in the crowd, sweat dampened his hair. He couldn't hear drums and fiddle without at least tapping his toes. Even back at university he couldn't help patting his hand on his leg under the table. Ian's crowd didn't dance at pubs, even when the music was good. Here, he could dance a jig, sing a song, or slop a little beer.

Lightning flashed behind the overpass looming over the stage. A few cool bursts of air chilled his damp neck. The band played on.

"I think a storm's rolling in. Will the band have to stop?"

"It depends on lightning, I think."

In answer, thunder boomed and the sky dropped its cargo. Before the band could finish announcing their forced break, the crowd scattered. Lou and Al looked for shelter, but every spot filled. Within a minute shelter didn't matter anymore.

Before the downpour, Al had thought Lou looked alluring in her pale pink T-shirt and simple flowered skirt. Her soft brown waves bounced around her shoulders with the humidity. She was simply beautiful. But with the addition of water, she evolved into a siren. Her thin cotton clothes clung to every curve. She slicked her hair away from her face, as if emerging from an enchanted lake. He simply had to touch her.

Without the band playing, Irish music piped through the speakers to fill the dead air until the concert could begin again. Al remembered a dance from festivals back home. The steps were simple and repetitive, and he recalled the basics. Soaked from the warm rain, there seemed no point in finding shelter now. He pulled Lou into his arms.

"Let's dance," Al said.

"Really?" Lou's eyebrows rose, then she nodded.

Al set one of her hands on his shoulder, the other he held. He slid his spare hand down the curve of her hip. What was he thinking, trying to dance? His chest constricted as his hands warmed from the heat of her skin through her wet shirt.

Think about the steps.

"Do you know how to polka?" Al asked.

Lou rolled her eyes.

"Have I taught you nothing about Wisconsin? Any respectable Badgers fan knows how to polka. Honestly."

Lou smiled, her eyes sparkling in the rain, the lashes clumping from the wet.

Al listened to the music to catch the beat, then started moving his feet to the music. Lou watched for a few seconds, then picked up his movements. They stayed in the same spot until he felt that she had the timing.

"Ready to spin?" Al said.

"Spin . . . ?"

But Al had already started turning them in tight circles. Lou's look of surprise almost made him stop; then she laughed.

"Wasn't expecting that."

For the rest of the song, they plunged through the puddles, rain still pouring down, streaming off their faces as they turned. While everyone else huddled to stay dry, he and Lou had the entire area as their personal ballroom. The clean smell of rain washed away the day's dirt and festival scents. The splash of their feet and pounding water muffled the music. They felt the heavy bodhran thumping more than they heard it. When the song ended, he couldn't tell whether he was more out of breath from the fast dancing or the laughter, but he wished for another song as an excuse to keep her in his arms.

Al looked down at Lou. When they first met as he shivered in line at the newsstand, he hadn't imagined her soaking wet, laughing and dancing in a summer thunderstorm with him. All the crowds, all the noise, all the distractions floated away until he saw only Lou standing in front of him. He could smell her, the rain intensifying the scent of vanilla at such a close distance. Her breath warmed the exposed skin on his throat. Everything felt more intense. He was a man tasting life for the first time.

They stood in the slackening rain, gazes locked, brown to blue. He couldn't look away. Her wet hair stuck in strands to her face and a drop of water dangled on the tip of her nose. She licked her lips. He wanted to taste those lips, too, but not yet.

Pull it together, mate.

To break the silence Al said, "You're a brilliant dancer."

"What can I say? I'm a delight."

Lou spread her arms wide. Al, thinking she planned to kiss him, wrapped his arms around her. Her lips formed a surprised

O, arms still spread, as he leaned in for a kiss. In the confusion, he missed her mouth, making contact with her right nostril instead. In hopes of salvaging his romantic attempt, she wrapped her arms around him, too, and tilted her head upward.

"Elizabeth?" a male voice said.

Al jumped away from Lou as her energized body deflated. She turned toward the intruder.

"Devlin."

Al's mouth opened in shock. "This is Devlin?" He studied the well-dressed, dry man in front of him. Al hated him. He wasn't just attractive but great looking. From all the time spent with John, he could see that every item Devlin wore was the best available. This man could clearly give Lou anything she wanted.

Devlin leaned in and kissed Lou on her cheek, but his eyes never left Al's face. As he pulled away, Devlin met Lou's unreadable eyes, then scanned her clinging clothes and dripping hair.

"I need to talk to you."

He reached for her arm, but she pulled it out of reach.

"Why are you here?"

"I'm entertaining clients." He pointed to the VIP area next to the stage. "I saw you dancing in the rain."

Al noticed he didn't mention her dance partner.

The joie de vivre overflowing from Lou just moments ago dried up and drifted away. Her lips remained sealed tight. Al wished she would say something so he could tell how she felt. He'd love an excuse to tell this prat to shove off.

"There are things you don't know. About that morning."

Lou stayed silent, but her eyes looked watery.

"I didn't sleep with her. I didn't even tell her to come over."

Al rolled his eyes. He was really doing this right now.

"Lou, I can take you home." Al took her hand. Devlin glared at him.

"You can leave. This doesn't concern you."

Al took a step forward and Lou pulled him back, squeezed his hand, and let it go.

"It's okay, Al." She turned to Devlin. "Go on."

Devlin looked at Al.

"He stays," Lou said.

Devlin shrugged his shoulders.

"Megan had been working with me. The night before my birthday, I told her I needed a memo first thing in the morning. She took it literally and arrived shortly before you did. I answered the door in my boxers, assuming you were surprising me. I went to the bathroom to get dressed and she found your lingerie. By the time you arrived, I had realized her intention and was collecting her clothes for her."

Lou showed no sign of responding. Devlin took a step closer to her.

"I didn't cheat. I would never risk our plan like that."

Lou took a deep breath and blinked a few times.

"Thank you for telling me." She looked at Al. "I'm ready to leave."

She turned and walked away, neither fast nor slow, weaving through the crowd. Al followed her.

As they left the grounds, he asked, "You okay?"

Lou nodded.

"That was unexpected and answered a few questions," she said.

"You believed him?" Al wanted to gather her back in his

arms, worried that if he didn't keep her close, she would slip back to Devlin. His worry made him breathless.

Lou shrugged. "It's something to think about, anyway."

• • • • •

The sweat followed the path of least resistance down Lou's spine, past the waistband of her shorts, and onward—or perhaps downward was more accurate. It didn't help that she kept recalling the feel of Al's arms around her as they'd danced at Irish Fest a week ago, or the solid wall of his body when he spun her. With those types of thoughts, she was steamy inside and out. If only it were New Year's Day and she could do the Polar Bear Plunge in Lake Michigan. That might cool her off.

She was too pale to be out in this sun. Lou usually did the roasting, not the other way around. But how can you say no when your best customers offer up their vegetable garden if you'll help weed? So that's where Lou and Sue were on a ninety-degree day in late August. Otto and Gertrude supplied cold lemonade and fresh radish sandwiches, thinly sliced radishes with butter and salt on white bread—delicious. Sue and Lou supplied the labor.

She yanked each weed with fervor, imagining it as a hair on Devlin's perfectly coiffed head. How dare he ruin her night with Al and muddle everything with the truth. And it was that. Devlin never lied. Why should he when he could negotiate his way out of any dilemma? So everything that had happened since the coconut cake coincidence could have been avoided if she'd stayed for two more minutes that morning. She and

Devlin would still be affianced. She wouldn't have gone on tilt at the restaurant. A. W. Wodyski never would have written that searing review, and she wouldn't be faced with having to give up on her dream.

But she and Al wouldn't be friends.

And there was the rub. Even with all the heartache, Lou wouldn't change the past few months.

Lou stood up, a handful of weeds in one hand, the other using an already-damp bandanna to smear perspiration around her face. Sweat that had pooled on her flat back while she was bent over sluiced down, putting her already damp underwear into the realm of drenched.

She rounded her shoulders a few times, stretching the tightening muscles. A vision of Al rubbing her lower back flashed and a new warmth flickered. This had to stop! She couldn't keep having flash fantasies about Al. Lou shook her head and returned to the weeding.

The Meyers' garden wasn't large, but weeds threatened to drown the tomatoes, eggplants, and peppers—a summer ratatouille plate formed in her mind. It appeared they hadn't done much weeding at all this summer. She wanted to pull them all so Otto and Gertrude wouldn't try to clear the garden themselves. Lou glanced at the elderly couple.

Otto hovered over Gertrude, adjusting a large umbrella he had attached to her chair, making sure she stayed in the shade. He puffed a little with even that effort. Gertrude smiled at her husband's attentions but still looked a little too pale. They both did. Sue had encouraged Gertrude and Otto to go inside while she and Lou finished, but they refused to leave, insisting they would keep her and Lou fed and watered.

"So Lou, Sue tells us that Devlin interrupted a kiss with a certain English gentleman."

Still folded at the waist, Lou raised her eyebrow at Sue, who didn't even have the decency to look ashamed. Lou straightened so she could look at Gertrude.

"I'm not sure the term 'kiss' is entirely accurate."

"He used his lips? Yes?"

"Yes, but he missed and got my nose. And thanks to Devlin's interruption, we didn't get the chance to work on his aim."

"Aahhh, and you believe Devlin's story?" Gertrude pointed her finger at Lou.

"Does it matter?" Lou shrugged.

"Perhaps, perhaps not. Do you feel like Ginger Rogers? Is he your Fred Astaire?"

Lou nodded.

"Then Devlin's story does not matter." Gertrude paused. "Sue says your young man is handsome."

Lou looked at Sue again, blushed, and tried to cover it by dabbing her face with her limp bandanna.

"He has this amazing rim of golden yellow around his pupil that separates the black from deep blue. It's like a solar eclipse. I can't stop staring." Lou looked up into the sky for a moment, then back at Gertrude. "And a wet shirt looks exceptional on him, too. As my mom would've said, 'I wouldn't kick him out of bed for eating crackers.' "

Gertrude laughed and clapped her hands together. "Aha. The truth is out. We must meet this love." Gertrude's smile revealed how much she enjoyed sharing these little bits of their lives. Lou returned the sentiment. In so many ways, Gertrude and Otto had filled in for her parents this last year. While they'd only known each other a short time, Lou enjoyed having someone to check up on and who checked up on her.

Lou bent to pick a few more leaves and chewed the inside of her cheek. "I could; it might be fun—if Sue and Harley can control themselves. Maybe a barbecue? Would you be up for that, Gertrude? I'd have it on my patio. Something relaxed, where everyone can get to know everyone else."

"Ah, *Liebchen*. We'll leave the late nights to the young." Gertrude's hand trembled as she sipped her lemonade. "Bring your young man into the restaurant sometime—then we'll meet him properly. Besides, then your barbecue can be the double date Sue really wants." Gertrude's lips twitched upward.

Sue stood up suddenly, braids racing to catch up with her head. "What? Why am I getting dragged into this? Clearly I'm not the only one who talks." Sue looked at Lou, then let her suppressed laughter escape. "We are quite the pair. You have the hots for a guy who can't find your mouth, and Harley and I couldn't figure out how to repopulate the planet after Armageddon. Pathetic."

Lou gave Sue a quick side hug.

"We're two bright and creative ladies—I'm confident we'll sort it out." Lou paused. "Should we? Have a barbecue?" Lou said, tilting her head sideways to emphasize the question.

"Absolutely . . . I want to meet this guy. And I can't wait to see what Harley does."

"You don't think Harley will scare him off, do you? He can be a little intimidating when he wants."

"If you like him, Harley would never do that." Sue shook her head, then continued. "When should we do it?"

Lou paused, closed her eyes, and used her fingers to count out dates.

"How about the first Tuesday in September?"

Gertrude looked confused and asked, "But won't you need to work at the restaurant?"

Sue and Lou exchanged a look. Lou said, "Starting in September, we won't be open on Tuesdays anymore. We can't really afford it."

"First Sundays and Mondays. Now Tuesdays? *Liebchen*, why are you keeping it open?"

"We don't need to close it yet. There's still time." Lou tromped to the other side of the garden and began weeding, ripping handfuls of crabgrass and clover from the earth. Flecks of dirt flew high and flurried to the ground.

Gertrude watched Lou's reaction and nodded her head. "I see. She doesn't want to scatter her family to the winds."

"She won't close until we all have jobs lined up. She handed out recommendation letters. The busboys and waitstaff are starting to leave for better-paying jobs." Sue leaned in closer to Gertrude. "And she worries about you two; worries you won't have anywhere to go that will take care of you like she does."

"Bah. Those are excuses. She is afraid. She needs something to nudge her confidence, give her a safety net." Gertrude looked up at Otto, who nodded in agreement at his wife's astute wisdom. The three watched Lou attack the verge.

• • • • •

Al looked down at the text message.

Next Tuesday @ 6, my place. Me, you, & 2 friends. Come hungry.

He looked up at the dark glass in front of him. Moisture beaded on the other side, condensing on the cooled window. He strode to the kitchen to refresh his tea and check the time. Twelve thirty. *Lou's up kind of late*, he thought. *Wonder why*. He felt a twinge thinking she might be on a date, a little jealous other people spent time with her. He poured fresh water into his electric kettle and flipped it on.

An invitation to dinner had to be a good sign, right? He had worried she believed Devlin's story and considered taking him back. If she believed him, why wouldn't she? They had a history, he had a successful career and superhero good looks. But Al was the one with an invitation. Ace!

Al leaned against the counter, his eyes tracing a familiar path to the cast-iron frying pan hanging on the wall. It looked as if a small child had decorated it with stickers. He had added to his magnet collection. His brat and Chihuly now kept company with a State Fair cow, a red Summerfest smiley, a Bernie Brewer, and a cheese wedge. Each magnet a memory, a reminder of everything good about his life in Milwaukee, and each one connected him to Lou.

He should probably reply. Al picked up his phone on the counter, read Lou's text again, then typed a reply.

Still awake? I'll be there. Can't wait.

He watched the text go and waited, hoping for the little beep. Less than a minute passed, and it came.

Go to bed, it's late.

Al laughed and replied.

I'm a night owl. Best time to work. What's your excuse?

Beep.

Me too. Makes AMs rough. Done working, need to shower.

Seeing the word "shower" sent off an explosion of detailed images in his mind. Al's reaction was immediate and a little painful. With a deep exhale he typed.

Need help?

Then erased it.

Then typed,

I'll bring the wine.

And erased that.

With a sigh, he typed,

Sweet dreams.

And hit Send. He needed a shower, too, of the chilly variety.

Beep.

You too.

• CHAPTER SIXTEEN •

Lou gnawed on a fingernail as she watched Al and Harley out the kitchen window while a vase filled with water. They stood on her patio, discussing something, apparently with gusto. Harley could intimidate people without realizing it, and she didn't want Al scared away.

"If you keep eating your nail, you won't want any Cuban pork," Sue said as she stepped next to Lou. "He's nice. I can see why you've kept him to yourself. With an ass like that, all the waitstaff would be after him."

"Especially Billy." Lou smiled, thinking of her best waiter. Billy was so efficient, with business slowing he could work most nights by himself with the help of two busboys. That kept him happy because he earned more tips, and kept her happy because she only had to pay one server.

"Should I go out and save him?" Lou asked.

"From what? Harley?"

Lou nodded, moving on to her next finger.

"Harley loves him."

"How can you tell?"

"Because he's still talking to him. You know that. If Harley didn't like him, he would turn his back and not speak another word to him. Then, if he hurt you, Harley would crush him."

"He never crushed Devlin."

"Devlin would sue. Harley's protective, not stupid. But he'd do it if you asked."

"Honestly, I don't think I care enough anymore. He just doesn't matter, even after he explained about that morning." Lou opened the oven to stir the Cuban black beans, scenting the kitchen with garlic and bacon. Sue finished frying up the plantains and sprinkled them with salt.

"You're really over him? I expected a longer mourning period."

"Yeah, I think I got over him months ago. He was convenient and safe, so I didn't see a reason to change. He sent me tickets for a play downtown." Lou pointed her chin toward the end of the counter where a pristine white envelope lay. "He keeps trying to 'sweeten the deal.' His words, not mine. Honestly, I should send him a thank-you note for the birthday debacle."

"You can only send him a thank-you if I get to hand-deliver it. I want to see his face when he reads it."

Lou turned off the faucet and set the vase on the windowsill. She slipped a bouquet of pristine white calla lilies into the water.

"He did good." Sue nodded at the flowers. Lou smiled, still thrilled Al had remembered her favorite flower.

"Yes—yes, he did."

They grabbed the still-warm plantains and a pitcher of mojitos and left the kitchen for the patio.

• • • • •

Lou's apartment was tiny and cozy, with a brilliant patio—the perfect spot for summer gatherings. Looking to the south, Al could see the tall buildings of downtown Milwaukee against the still blue sky, to the north, trees and swaths of green intermingled with postwar houses. As he had walked through her flat, he caught glimpses into each room, little flashes of Lou. In the dining room he saw several photos with laughing and kind faces. He hoped to hear the stories behind each one. Her kitchen overflowed with food preparation and delicious aromas, while her living room housed an impressive cookbook collection. He spotted a copy of *Modernist Cuisine* and looked forward to seeing where their collections overlapped and deviated.

Al and Harley turned as Sue and Lou stepped onto the patio. Upon first meeting Harley, he had worried they wouldn't have much to discuss. After all, what would a tattoo enthusiast have in common with an Eton-educated food writer? To his surprise and relief, they shared the same passion for quality tea, and he now knew of three stores where he could purchase it in bulk.

Lou stopped next to him and handed him a fresh mojito. He scooped a handful of plantains as Sue walked by with the still-warm-from-the-oil pile. As he chewed, Sue asked the question he dreaded.

"So, Lou tells us you're a writer. What do you write?"

Al swallowed and sipped his drink while perfecting his answer.

"I write freelance pieces. Thanks to Lou, I'm working on an article about the various ethnic influences in Milwaukee's food scene." All true. He'd already spent hours researching the ethnic festivals' origins, the people involved, and their affiliations with local restaurants.

"So you write about food?"

Sue looked thrilled by the idea. Al's heartbeat raced. He needed to change the topic. He liked these people; he didn't want to lie to them. So far, he'd gotten away with revealing so little, even after his failed attempt to show Lou his Good Land article.

"I write about whatever I'm hired to write about, unless I have a story to pitch, like Lou's idea."

"And he's an experienced Irish rain dancer." Lou winked and touched his arm. Sue and Harley exchanged confused looks.

"So," Harley said, "you could write about Lou."

Al's forehead scrunched.

"Now, I'm not sure I follow?" Al said.

"Well, since her review, work's been rough. If you wrote about her, that might help."

Al opened his mouth to get more information.

"Harley." Lou rolled her eyes. "Al doesn't want to write about me. We're here to have fun, not talk about my catastrophe of a career." Lou looped her arm in Al's. "Besides, he wants to see what's on the grill."

Lou pulled him away from Sue and Harley, toward the smell of garlic, citrus, and oregano wafting off the grill. He was curious about their work, but he couldn't ask without the risk of having to answer more questions about his own job.

Lou lifted the hood. He had tried to peek earlier, but Harley had physically blocked him with a terse "No peeking." What was finally revealed went beyond his expectations. A large butt of pork looked blackened with a thick coat of spices, fat melted down the sides adding flavor and moisture to the crust. His mouth drowned in saliva.

"That looks fantastic."

"It tastes even better," Lou said with confidence, "especially with the mojo."

"I'd like to formally offer my services as taster." Al reached toward the roast, going for a juicy dangling bit of meat. Lou slapped his hand.

"You'll have to wait. It needs to rest an hour."

"You're such a pork tease."

"That's why there're plantains and mojitos. You'll live."

Lou lifted the roast onto a cutting board, covered it with foil, and carried it to the kitchen. Al trailed after, opening the door for her. In the kitchen, he noticed the lilies in a place of honor. He smiled. He could see Harley and Sue on the patio. Such a unique pair: Harley with all his tattoos and grumbly voice, and Sue with her sailor's vocabulary and rough edges. Al turned to face Lou.

"How did the three of you meet?"

Lou picked up a washcloth and started wiping the counters and putting dirty dishes in the washer. She smiled.

"It's been so long, I almost can't remember." She paused in her cleaning to give the memory her full attention. "I met Sue in school. We found Harley at our first job. We were so young.

Harley didn't have a beard then. Sue and I would go drinking after work and Harley would follow, but never sit by us, just keep an eye on us. On Sue, really."

Al tilted his head toward the window.

"They've been simmering that long?"

"You have no idea. But I finally think they're about to boil over."

"Nice one." Al laughed.

"I'm all about the food humor." Lou set down her washcloth and headed back out, waving her hand at Al to join her.

. . . . .

An hour later, the four sat at the patio table laden with the sliced pork, mojo sauce, black beans, cilantro lime rice, and grilled peppers and onions.

"Dig in," Lou said.

"About bloody time," Al mumbled, reaching for the end piece before anyone else could grab it and sliding it onto Lou's plate. He then proceeded to load his own plate with a bit of everything on the table. He looked up to see Lou smiling at him. He smiled back, then focused on his plate for the next fifteen minutes. It was some of the best food he had eaten in years; and yes, he included The Good Land in his comparison. Lou's food was that good. Talk focused on silly topics ranging from comic book heroes to politics. Paranoid, Al had steered the conversation anytime it seemed to veer toward work, which wasn't often. No one rushed to eat. They lingered before dessert, picking at stray pieces of pork, tucking them into every available space in their stomachs. Conversation and wine flowed. He looked around the table at the open, relaxed faces. Al had found more friends, more reasons to love his new home.

. . . . .

After coffee and dessert, Lou shooed Sue and Harley out. Al didn't want to leave, but Lou clearly wanted to get the cleaning started. She pulled out her purple rubber gloves and started filling the sink with steaming water. Al brought in some of the empty wineglasses from the patio.

"That was fantastic. I adore your friends, and the food . . . the food. Fantastic." Al placed his hands on his chest and leaned onto the fridge in faux swoon. "You are a goddess in the kitchen."

Lou blushed. "Thanks."

She went to get more dishes, causing an envelope to flutter and drift to the floor in her wake. Al picked it up, noticing Devlin Pontellier's return address on the snow-white paper, postmarked this week. He turned it over to see a thick card and tickets poking out. More than anything, he wanted to know what was on that note card. Why was Devlin sending her tickets? Were they going together? His stomach clenched, worried he had missed his opportunity with Lou.

She walked back into the kitchen, and a line creased her forehead as she saw Al holding Devlin's envelope. He struggled to wipe the disappointment from his face. After all, he had no claim on Lou.

"It dropped when you walked by," Al explained, and set the offending envelope back where it fell from.

She nodded and started setting the dishes on the counter.

"You're seeing him again?" Al asked. Lou looked at the envelope as water dripped off her gloves onto her bare feet.

"What? . . . Um . . . no?" The words came out slowly, as if she had to search for them. Her eyes darted into the hall. Did she want him to go? But Al had to know more.

"Are you considering going back to him?"

Lou looked at Al, the line deepening. This was none of his business. He shouldn't even be asking. He should accept the friendship she was offering.

"I'm trying to do what's best for me."

She licked her lips.

Al opened his mouth, but before he could respond Lou took a step toward him.

"What do you think?"

Al wanted to shout "*Not him.*" But someone like Devlin could always take care of Lou. Al's job depended on the fickleness of newspaper readers. He had to go where the work was. The clock bonged the hour.

"Wow, it's late. I should go." He left the kitchen, picked his light coat off a hook, and opened the door. Lou followed.

"So, Al, you don't have an opinion on what would be best?" she asked.

Al froze in the doorway and turned. Lou was close by, inches away, leaning on the partially opened door. He could feel his coat brushing her arm. Al looked into the warm brown eyes, swallowed, lips pressed together.

"It's not my opinion that matters. Is it?" Al's blue eyes scanned Lou's face, wishing that he could say what he really thought without risking their friendship.

Lou's shoulders sagged a little, and a sigh escaped her lips.

"I should finish my cleaning. Good night, Al." Lou quickly leaned in and kissed Al on the cheek. Lou slowly pulled back, their faces close together, breath mingling. Lou moistened her lips. Al watched her closely, then closed his eyes and backed away. "Good night, Lou." He turned away and walked quickly down the steps. He wanted to haul her into his arms, but he wasn't the best choice for her, was he? He stopped, turned, and looked back up the stairs. He remembered Devlin at Irish Fest. Arrogant, talking of their plan. He didn't want a wife; he wanted a personal chef he could sleep with. Lou deserved adoration, not servitude.

He took the steps back up two at a time.

. . . . .

Lou had closed the door slowly, then leaned against it, eyes shut, and nibbled the inside of her cheek. Damn. She sighed deeply and opened her eyes to look at her newly empty apartment. She could hear cars on the street, doors closing, and the TV on in a neighboring apartment. Her apartment was still, but her heart pounded. She had been so close to telling him how she felt, showing him. She pushed herself off the door and headed to the kitchen to finish cleaning.

Before she reached the kitchen, a soft knock broke the silence. Lou peeked out the hole to see it was Al, cheeks flushed from running back up the steps. Lou opened the door, brow furrowed, wondering what he forgot.

A saucy grin spread across his face. Lou beamed, eyes wide. Al stepped toward her and Lou took a surprised step back. Without taking his hungry eyes off Lou, Al closed the door and dropped his coat to the floor. He grabbed Lou and pulled her tight with one arm, the other hand buried deep into her hair. His blue eyes reminded her of when fire burned too hot.

"I'm best for you, Lou."

Al touched his lips to hers, pulling her even closer. Lou responded with her entire body, kissing back. She wrapped one leg around his legs, tightening to pull him even closer.

Al turned her back to the door and pressed her into it. She groaned as he rubbed himself firmly against her. He kissed her neck, then pulled back so she could yank off his T-shirt. She looked him up and down, bit her lip, then grabbed him by the belt buckle to lead him into her bedroom, kissing him again and bumping into walls along the way. She clumsily unbuckled his belt and began unbuttoning his jeans.

"This is getting uneven rather quickly." Al yanked open Lou's shirt, buttons popping off, to reveal a lacy red bra. Al raised an eyebrow and grinned.

Lou blushed. "I was hopeful."

"Thank God for hope." Al bent his head to kiss along her collarbone, and Lou tilted back her head to give him all the room he needed.

"Mmm, you taste like vanilla ice cream." He pushed her shirt off her shoulder, going to his knees to get it over her hands. His mouth traced tender kisses over her cleavage and onto her shivering stomach.

His agile hands set the shirt on the floor. He touched her ankles, then slid his hands up her legs to her knee. Lou watched him with breathless wonder. His deft hands traced the path up her legs, circling slowly, as if polishing a precious stone. Al nudged her to sit on the bed and kissed her again, slowly and deeply, one hand on her face, the other on her thigh. Lou forgot everything but her racing pulse, the brush of his skin, and the heat of Al's lips on hers.

• • • • •

As far as dreams went, this one was particularly odd. He was an octopus, wrapping his arms around a beautiful mermaid with dark hair and pale skin. No question who that was supposed to be. Every time she moved, he pulled her closer. Even underwater she smelled like vanilla. He pulled her tighter.

"Shit," the mermaid said. Pretty foulmouthed for a mermaid.

"Dammit, let go," she said. This time she pinched one of his tentacles. Grunt. He pulled her tighter. Why wouldn't she just stay still? Then they would be so happy together. He felt a harder pinch.

"Al, I'm late. I have to get up."

Al pried open one heavy lid to see Lou's lovely white backside leave the bed and disappear into her bathroom. He shook his head a little to forget the weird dream and focus on what had happened. He could hear water running in the bathroom, so he took the opportunity to take stock. Last night had been amazing. Sure, they'd had their awkward moments, but all in all, he couldn't remember having had more fun in bed with anyone. And he realized he wanted her back in it—now. He rolled on his side to make his intentions less obvious.

Al started making lists. He'd let Hannah know his long-term plans, then take Lou out on a real date, and maybe get an extra key made for his apartment. But first, he should tell her about his real job—that shouldn't wait one more day, one more second.

Al heard the water turn off and said loudly, "What's the hurry? It's not even seven."

Lou cracked the door a few inches so they wouldn't have to shout. Al could hear her moving about but couldn't see her.

"I have to meet the fish guy at seven thirty. He gets cranky when I'm late. Nobody likes a cranky fish guy."

"Fish guy? Your office has fish?" Al knew that didn't sound right. As he said it, his stomach had already started the slow plummet. Lou emerged from the bathroom wearing a plain white cotton V-neck T-shirt, the kind you buy three packs of in the men's department, and black-and-white checked chef pants. The slow plummet became a bobsled racing down an icy track. She opened her top drawer and began digging. Al quickly sat up, heart racing, his breath coming in shallow pants. All the blood got sucked into the black hole forming in his chest, turning his skin pale and cold. He had to work up some saliva so he could ask his question.

"You're a chef?"

"Yeah, you didn't know that?"

"You never said. We agreed to never talk about work. You had copier problems. I thought you worked in an office."

Lou thought for a moment, balancing on one foot then the other to put on her socks.

"Oh yeah. No, I own my own restaurant. At least for now anyway. And our copier breaks down once a month, but I can't afford to get a new one." Lou looked up at Al. "Are you okay? You look really pale."

He nodded and swallowed, dreading the next question, hoping to any higher being that might be listening that his suspicion wasn't true.

"Which restaurant?"

Lou walked back into the bathroom, pulling her hair into a ponytail as she went.

"Luella's. It's a few blocks away on the corner. Big windows out front. You need to stop by now that you've met Sue and Harley. Sue's the sous chef. Harley does desserts. . . ."

Lou's calm, confident voice kept talking but Al didn't hear anything after "Luella's." He fell back into the pillows, thankful Lou couldn't see him, and stared at the blank white ceiling, searching for answers to questions he didn't know to ask. It couldn't be her. Luella's was owned by an Elizabeth, not a Lou. He pulled himself away from the brink, grasping for his last hope.

"Is Lou short for Luella?" *Please say your first name is anything but Elizabeth. Let it be a different Luella's restaurant, please not the same one, not the same person. Let there be two.* But he knew, even without her answer. Al's heart beat a million times in the second it took Lou to answer.

"Sort of. Luella is my middle name and my grandma's. My real name is Elizabeth, but no one ever uses it. Don't you dare start calling me Lizzy."

He went still—channeling all the emotions into their proper place to be identified and analyzed. Shock would go there, then anger behind that, then sadness blanketed them all. He had to end it. Logically, a person in his job couldn't fraternize with the people he critiqued for a living, and he certainly couldn't make love to them for hours after having a cookout with half their staff. It contradicted his personal code of ethics.

And he felt shame.

He fumbled with the facts—shifting and sorting them into the right order, like Scrabble tiles spelling out words. He lined up the events he knew, then filled in the rest. The last event clicked into place. He knew now what had happened that day, the day he reviewed Luella's. He saw it, saw her sad frosting trail and broken heart the same night he ate at her restaurant. Yes, the food was awful, but he didn't do his job. Any other food critic would have returned, given the restaurant another chance. Not him, no—he had to bury her. Had he gone back, the food would have been perfect. If last night's meal was any indication, Lou understood food and how to coax it into something grander. Shame at a job poorly done caused his eyes to burn with the truth of his situation. He had to leave. She could never know who he was, which meant they could not be together. He sat up, movements stiff and slow, grabbed his pants, and proceeded to get dressed.

Lou came out from the bathroom, a bottle of vanilla in one hand, the other dabbing the extract behind her ears. She saw what he was doing and frowned a little.

"Leaving? You don't have to. You could come with me. Harley usually makes a few fresh pastries for those of us coming in early."

Al looked her in the eyes, building up his courage for the lies he needed to tell.

"I can't. I have to pack."

"You're going on a trip? Where?"

"Work. I have an assignment in California. I'm not sure how long I'll be gone. I leave tomorrow."

"That sucks. You could come over when you finish packing."

"Probably not. I tend to pack last minute, so now I have to spend all my time wrapping up loose ends."

"Of course. I didn't expect last night either." Lou blushed a little, remembering, and Al's guilt surged higher.

"I better be off. I'll call you when I get back?"

"Sounds good."

The radio in the bathroom sounded louder in the silence. "Storms are headed this way. Take shelter and don't go out if you don't need to," said the weatherman.

Al gave her a swift peck on the cheek and left, closing the apartment door quietly.

· CHAPTER SEVENTEEN ·

Thunder rumbled and a cool breeze rushed through the open back door of the restaurant. A waterfall fell over the entrance, the gutters above long since defunct. Other than the rain and thunder, only the whir of Harley's mixer and the snick of knives on cutting boards disturbed the peaceful morning. While Lou loved the raucous music, loud voices, and chaotic movement of a dinner rush, the calm of prep work soothed her soul and gave her time to think. Some people did downward dog, some burned incense in front of a Buddha statue, some prayed the rosary; Lou chopped vegetables into tiny squares, filleted fish, and reduced veal stock. Her meditation smelled better, and even if she didn't find a solution, at least she got to eat.

"I don't know, Sue; it was odd," Lou said, breaking the silence and talking loud enough that Harley could hear in his corner of the kitchen.

"The morning after is always weird," Sue said.

"No, that's not it. He wasn't letting me out of bed. He kept holding me tighter. It was really sweet. Then all of a sudden he couldn't leave fast enough. I half expected him to mention a squash game he forgot about."

"Maybe he really had to pack? You never know. What do you think, Harley?"

"He looks like Harry Potter."

"Just because he's British does not make him Harry Potter." Lou rolled her eyes at Harley's comment.

Sue leaned in close to Lou. "He must really like him if he's comparing him to Potter."

Lou smiled and whispered back, "I know. Not much higher praise than that."

Even with her slightly uneasy feeling, Lou felt joy—giddy joy. She smiled the sloppy grin of the newly besotted.

"You know you're glowing, right?" Sue asked.

Lou blushed. "I can't help it. I'm just so . . ." She searched for the right word.

"Happy," Sue said.

"Yes, happy. And giddy. And nervous. And twittery."

"Twittery?"

"Yes, twittery. I'm twittery. This feels so different from Devlin. I want to know everything about him. Does he always snore when he sleeps? Did he always want to be a writer? Who was his first love? I know so little about him and I can't wait to find it all out."

• • • • •

"Hannah, please," Al said, gripping the faded office chair in front of Hannah's desk.

Hannah studied the muscles tensing in his jaw, restraining the multitude of counterarguments he had ready for any refusals she presented.

"You've never asked for anything before. Why this?"

"I got it wrong."

"Are you telling me you lied?" Hannah sat up in her chair, alarmed at where this seemed to be going.

"No, it happened. I just didn't have all the facts."

"Then, no."

"You have to let me rereview it."

"I don't have to let you do anything other than your job, which is to write entertaining *opinion* pieces about restaurants." She drew out the word "opinion," making her point plain. "If we retracted every *opinion* we published, that's all the paper would be. You didn't lie—you accurately described your meal; the review stands."

"You don't understand—I was wrong."

"I don't really care. Maybe in a year or so you can review it again. If you start retracting your reviews, you'll lose credibility, and so will we. I won't let you do that to yourself or this paper. We have a hard enough time competing with online review sites. At least with print media, we have a modicum of authority. I won't let you undermine that."

"I'll never ask again."

"No, you won't. My word is final. Out."

Hannah turned to her computer and began reading e-mails. Al, recognizing his loss, clenched his fist and returned to his cubicle. But he didn't sit; he stared at the blank computer screen, glared at it as if it had written the cruel review and destroyed a good woman's business. An image flashed of him hoisting the monitor over his head and tossing it through the large windows. But the British never show such emotion. He had to leave, get out of the office, out of the city if he could.

His pocket vibrated and he answered without checking. "Al speaking."

"Hey," said a soft voice. He closed his eyes and sat in his chair, using his free hand to grab fistfuls of hair.

"Hello." He made his voice sound as upbeat as possible, but it sounded more like that of a choirboy sucking helium. He cleared his throat and tried again.

"Hello, Lou."

"You seemed a little off this morning. I wanted to make sure I haven't offended in some way."

"No, no—God, no. You are lovely in every way. I just caught myself off guard, and now I have a lot of catch-up on my end."

"You sure?"

"Quite. Worry not. I'll call you when I get back, right?"

"Okay, talk to you then. Have a good trip."

"Thanks."

Al closed the phone and set it carefully on his desk, as if it might explode. He didn't know what to do. His head clearly knew he should forget her and get out of Milwaukee as soon as possible, just as he originally planned. But his heart acknowledged she'd freed a side of him he didn't realize he had, a side he still didn't understand but wanted to know more about. With Lou, he just fit. And she was worried she had done something. Bollocks.

"You okay?" John asked from behind. "How'd the barbecue go?" Al looked at John and realized he needed to talk to someone, realized John had become his someone. He sighed with relief, knowing he had a friend who cared enough to notice.

"Not really. I need to chat. Can I buy you a coffee?"

John looked shocked, then cleared his face. "Heavy on the cream and sugar."

• • • • •

"Dude, this sucks," John said. Al had just finished telling John everything that happened the night before and this morning. Well, not everything. He was a gentleman, after all. The coffee shop was sparsely populated as the morning rush had finished, leaving the place slightly trashed. The staff worked to tidy it up and get ready for those patrons requiring an afternoon pick-me-up.

John and Al bought their drinks and retreated to the outside tables. John slid on his mirrored sunglasses as Al sipped an Earl Grey tea, too distracted to be bothered with the bright sunshine. Tea normally calmed frazzled nerves, but today it seemed sour on his tongue. Relief would not be found through leaves and hot water.

"Thank you for your astute observation, John. But what do I do?"

"You can't tell her."

"How clever."

"But you could help her. Do another review?"

"Hannah won't publish it—I asked. I have to make this right. It's not fair to her." Al ran his hands through his hair again. He had come straight to the office from Lou's; the combination of a showerless morning and regular mussing had his hair resembling a hedgehog's back.

"What about getting another local critic to do it?"

"I don't think they like me much."

"Yeah, I guess. You've been kind of a douche canoe."

"Again, thanks for the helpful observations. I need advice, not summaries on how much of an arse I've been."

"Are you going to keep seeing her?"

"I shouldn't. It's just not professional, right? The reviewer shouldn't date the reviewee. This can't end well."

"So, you're just going to ignore her. That's cold, but probably the safest."

Al didn't like that idea. Not at all. There was something about Lou, about her kindness, her generosity, her quiet resiliency; he felt drawn to her. He wanted to help her, protect her, show her she had nothing to feel insecure about.

"I don't want to do that."

Under all the scruff, surprise managed to show on John's face. "Well, maybe it's not as bad as we think. Let me make a call."

John pulled out his phone and turned slightly away from Al.

"Hey, Rob, it's John. What do you know about Luella's restaurant. The one on St. Paul."

Pause. Al tapped his foot on the table leg.

"You sure? Okay."

Pause. Al chewed a fingernail.

"That's what I've heard elsewhere. . . . Thanks, Rob. Bye."

John set the phone down and turned to Al. Al could see his reflection in John's glasses. His eyes resembled a meth addict's coming off a high, praying for the next dose but not knowing where it would come from.

"Well?" Al asked.

"Not good. Her vendor orders have decreased—a lot. Most of the staff have left for better jobs. Rumor is she told them to look for new jobs because the restaurant wouldn't make it past the new year."

Al's body slumped with the news.

"Thanks for checking, John. But that doesn't change how I feel."

"I'm not sure you have a choice. How does it end? You like her, right?"

"Of course. That's the bloody problem, isn't it?"

"So, if you continue to let things progress naturally, you'll get to know her better."

"Yes."

"And she'll eventually want to know, maybe even read, the stuff you write."

"I have other things to show her. I do actually write more than reviews. I do freelance work to afford my condo."

"Okay, so you continue seeing her, to what end? Marriage? Are you going to keep all your paychecks from the paper a secret? That sounds like the perfect way to start a marriage. What are you going to tell her when you eat out five nights a week?"

Al looked out at the street, seeing each problem as a brick stacking up quickly between him and Lou. Even Lou's good heart couldn't forgive him for what he did. He cost her her dream.

Al closed his eyes and nodded, then stood up. "Let's go back."

John looked up at his friend, taking in his slumped shoulders and blank eyes. John stood and headed toward the office while Al watched him go, realizing back wasn't where he wanted to go. He wanted to go forward.

. . . . .

Al had been on his work trip for nine days. Lou had counted.

"Can someone call my phone? I don't think it's working," Lou said over the kitchen noise.

"It's working fine. We checked it yesterday, remember?" Sue said, irritation edging into her tone.

"But it's not ringing."

"That's because no one is calling you. Now will you please finish filleting the sole so you can start grilling the chops?"

Lou set the phone on the counter where she could see it, propping it up against the salt pig. She resisted the siren's call of her phone until the fish was done, her hand twitching toward the phone only four times. After putting the fish in the cooler for that night's service, she pulled the chops and hurried back to the grill. She scooped up her phone to check if she'd missed a message in the minute she was gone, but her hand slipped and the phone flew onto the grill.

Lou screamed and grabbed it off, the back of the case melted in neat grill marks. She checked, breath heavy, making sure the phone still worked. With a gasp of relief, she discovered the phone unlocked as normal. Her relief quickly turned to disappointment when she saw that no phone calls or e-mails had arrived from Al.

A firm hand curved around the still-warm phone and

pulled it from her hands, setting it on a shelf between the kosher salt and aged balsamic vinegar.

"Hey!" Lou scowled at Sue.

"iPhone is not on our menu. Come on." She pulled Lou away from the grills. "Harley, we're leaving for a little while. You okay?"

"Yep, get her out of here."

With a wave of Harley's hand, Sue whisked her out of the kitchen and away from her phone.

• • • • •

The fall farmers' market buzzed with wasps swarming the apples stacked high on the wooden plank counters. Children pulled their suburban parents through the crowd while old women scrutinized bunches of spinach like jewelers studying gems. The air hinted of burning leaves with a gentle slap of chill, an overture to the upcoming winter. Shoppers wore sweaters recently pulled from winter storage, and knitted animal hats bobbed atop toddler heads or peeked out from cozy strollers.

Lou took a deep breath, inhaling the scent of just-cut flowers, fresh tamales from the food stands, and sunshine. She preferred the West Allis farmers' market to all others in the area, with its open sides, wide walkways, and rows of stalls. More recently, small tents serving hot sandwiches and fresh Mexican food had popped up outside the brick walls. It all looked so good, she'd learned long ago to come with limited funds or she would buy more produce than she could possibly use. She relished talking to the farmers, learning about what they grew and where. She liked to search for farmers growing something new and interesting she could use at Luella's.

But today's visit was personal, not business. Sue had dragged her out to West Allis for a little lunch and some girl time with fall squash and Honeycrisp apples.

Lou tilted her head into the September sunshine. "It feels good to get outside."

"It was either this or drug you."

Lou looked at Sue, trying to determine whether she was serious. She wasn't sure. "What do you mean?"

"For the past few days you've been a twitchy, nervous wreck. Each day worse than the one before. I figured I'd let you talk about it before forcing Valium down your throat."

Lou picked up an apple and held it under her nose. The sweet scent made her mouth water. "Have I been that bad?"

"Worse. Just call him."

Lou paid for a bag of apples and they moved down the walkway, past tables laden with cucumbers, local honey, and giant stalks of brussels sprouts.

"I want to, but he's on a business trip. He said he'd call when he got back. I don't want to be pushy." Lou stopped and looked at all the stalls around them and added, "Ugh, I can't decide what I want."

Sue smiled and pulled Lou over to a booth full of baskets brimming with root vegetables.

"Yes, you do. How do you think a farmer decided when to harvest these? He couldn't see the size of the potato, or know if the carrot would taste sweet. He used his experience. He studied what he could see aboveground. He learned from the past, but he could still only guess what happened underground.

Eventually, he had to just pull. It was a risk, and sometimes it might backfire, but he'd never make it as a farmer if he didn't chance it. It's time you gave a yank."

Sue nudged Lou with her elbow as they stood staring at the tubers and added, "Call him."

· CHAPTER EIGHTEEN ·

Mum, please," Al said, banging his head silently on his desk. John watched with his arms and legs crossed, enjoying his friend's torment. Every few minutes he would reach for his mug of coffee, lest he become dehydrated watching Al's growing distress. Al had avoided Lou for over a week while working out a solution to the my-review-destroyed-her-dream-but-I-might-love-her problem. He didn't need parents making things more difficult.

"Darling, it's been months. Just come for a weekend."

"I know you want me to come home, but I'm a bit busy here."

"Then perhaps your father and I will visit you."

"I'd really rather you didn't."

"Your articles talk so much about the wonderful places to eat, we want to come."

"You've been reading my articles?"

"Of course. We read everything you publish. At least this time we don't have to subscribe. The Internet makes things ever so much easier."

"It's just not a good ti—"

"Bodkins, it's never a good time when mothers are concerned. That's why we don't wait for invitations. Your father wants to take a trip after fall term. Plus, it's clear you're smitten with her. We want to see why."

"Wh-what? I didn't say anything about her." Al sat up, replaying what he just said in his head. His hand immediately went to his hair as he leaned back in his chair and stretched his legs out in front as if he'd been knocked out.

"Aha, so there is a girl! Alastair, who is she?"

"I've got work to do, Mum."

"I want to hear all about her."

"Bye, Mum."

Al tossed the phone on his desk, closed his eyes, and shook his head.

John, smiling from ear to ear, said, "So the 'rents are coming. Excellent."

"Ugh, I just fell for the oldest mom trick in the book. She's bloody brilliant. I bet she was working on that setup for weeks. Bloody effing hell."

"Where are we taking them?"

"You aren't taking them anywhere. . . ."

"Now wait a sec; I'm an excellent tour guide. Charming. I know all the good bars and stores."

"True. That might not be a bad idea." Al tapped his fingers, thinking about how much his mom would love John, assuming he could deal with her fussing. He could take Dad on a historical tour. Al had started writing a list of all the places to eat with his parents when his phone rang. He picked it up without lifting pen from paper.

"Al speaking."

A soft voice answered his. "Hi, Al. It's Lou."

Al sat up straight. "Lou, sorry I haven't called. Been really busy. How've you been?"

"Pretty good. Where are you now?"

"The office."

"You're back. Wonderful." Lou's voice got much brighter.

Panicked, Al looked at John and held his hands in prayer position in front of him. John fake coughed, exaggerating the motions.

"Yeb. Early this mornig." Al coughed a few times into the phone to bring the point home.

"You okay? You sound awful."

"I feel worse. I picked ub somethig nasty." Al's stomach did feel awful, but from the deception.

"Then you should go home. I'll make something yummy to make you feel better."

"No, too contagious."

"Don't worry about me. I'll bring something over later. Now go to bed!"

Lou hung up and Al stared blankly at the phone.

"She buy it?" John asked.

"That bloody backfired. She wants to cook for me to make me feel better."

"Now that is ironic."

"What do I do now?"

"You go home and pull a Ferris Bueller."

"A who?"

"You know, Ferris Bueller. Eighties movie. High school kid, fakes being sick, has an amazing day playing hooky in Chicago. You know. Bueller . . . Bueller . . . Bueller."

Al spread his hands and shook his head no. "I spent my teenage years trying not to get kicked out of Eton and bring shame on my family. I didn't watch a lot of eighties American cinema."

"We'll fix that. In the meantime, go home, get a hot water bottle, and put it on your forehead so you feel hot. Then climb under all the covers to work up a nice, clammy sweat."

"Done this before, have you?"

"I told you my high school wasn't a real joy for boys who enjoyed haute couture. Now, don't you have a sickbed to occupy?"

Al locked his computer and grabbed his bag. He took ten steps out of the cubicles and backtracked. John had already returned to his latest article on fall fashion trends.

Al said, "Thanks, mate. I appreciate the support."

Without looking up, John waved with one hand.

"Go forth and incubate fake germs."

• • • • •

"I'm really nervous," Lou said. "There should be a law against not seeing a person for ten days after you sleep together the first time." Lou had called Sue to help make some British comfort food. She, in turn, had called Harley. Al would soon be the luckiest sick person in the world. If Lou ever needed proof of their loyalty, this was it. The restaurant wasn't open on Tuesdays, yet all three chefs busily chopped, stirred, and baked a feast fabulous enough to impress the Queen.

"You're bringing food to a sick person; it would be awkward anyway," Sue said.

"He's probably faking it just so you'll cook for him. I would," Harley said from his corner.

"Shut it, Harley. Not everyone thinks with their stomach. Don't listen to him, Lou."

Lou pulled a shepherd's pie from the oven, covered it with a lid, wrapped it in towels to keep it warm and from overheating things around it, and set it at the bottom of a large crate. Next to it, Sue added a container of chicken noodle soup. Harley added a box of still-warm scones, Irish soda bread, and fresh orange marmalade. Sue helped make a batch of fresh clotted cream and poured it into small jars. The three stood around looking at the crate.

"Can tomorrow be my turn to be sick?" Harley said. Sue patted his back.

"I can make you some soup if that will make you feel better," Sue said. Harley smiled a sloppy grin.

"I think I'll be going before it gets awkward here, too," Lou said. She picked up the crate and headed to Al's.

When Al opened his apartment door, Lou's first impulse was to take a step back. He did not look good. Sweat dripped from his face as he clutched a tattered blanket around his sloped shoulders, looking as if he could crumple into a ball at any moment.

"Oh my God. You shouldn't be out of bed," Lou said. He had sounded awful on the phone, but she wasn't expecting the sweaty, pathetic figure who opened the door. How could he be pale and flushed at the same time? All business, she walked past him into the kitchen to set the overflowing crate down. She came back out and placed a gentle hand on Al's sweaty forehead. Her lips pursed and she looked him sternly in the eye. "Get back to bed. You shouldn't be out."

"But—"

"Go. I'll bring up some soup." She pointed toward the stairs and waved her hand, indicating he'd been dismissed.

Lou walked back into the kitchen. She stopped in the middle to assess the facilities. Clean, nice copper, quite a lot of cookbooks—always a good sign. She saw the electric kettle and teapot. She filled the kettle and plugged it in. While waiting for the water to reach near boiling, she unloaded the crate and rummaged around the kitchen for supplies with the efficiency and comfort level of someone used to a well-stocked kitchen. By the time steam began leaking out, Lou had put the shepherd's pie in the oven to stay warm and filled a tray with food to bring upstairs. Once she poured the hot water over the waiting tea leaves, she climbed upstairs to her waiting patient.

As she crested the top step, Lou looked at Al propped up in the center of his comfy-looking bed. His bed stand held a pile of scrunched tissues and a scattering of Walgreens cold medicines. Poking out from his closet was an open suitcase overflowing with rumpled clothes. She'd help him get that in order.

Lou set the tray across his lap and settled on the edge of his bed. He coughed a few times—it looked as if it hurt.

Al sat up a little and said, "You didn't have to do this."

"Of course I didn't, but what's the point of sleeping with a chef if you don't get some of the perks?"

Al winced a little.

"You okay? What is it? Are you achy?"

Al shrugged.

"Can I get you some medicine?"

"I took some right before you came." His voice sounded a little scratchy. Lou touched his forehead, and Al closed his eyes as if enjoying the sensation.

"It must be starting to work. You feel cooler."

Lou brushed her fingers down Al's temple and cupped the side of his cheek. His blue eyes seemed to plead with hers, begging for an answer to a question he didn't ask.

"Eat. You'll feel better," Lou said.

Al looked down at the laden tray and cleared his throat.

"This looks amazing. Is that clotted cream? And marmalade?" He picked up a scone gently, then cupped it between both hands. He looked up at Lou, eyes wide.

"It's still warm." He split it open, spread a generous amount of jam over one half, and topped it with a glob of cream.

. . . . .

Al chewed slowly, retreating to his childhood. If he closed his eyes, he could smell his grandma's house. On Sundays after church, his family would visit and have tea and scones fresh from the oven. After, he and Ian would chase her chickens and play jousting where their parents couldn't see.

"These are amazing. Did you make them?"

"Harley made the scones and jam, and a loaf of soda bread downstairs. Sue made the clotted cream and helped with the soup and shepherd's pie."

"There's shepherd's pie? Where?" Al scanned the tray as if it were hiding between the tea and soup.

Lou chuckled. "It's staying warm in the oven. If you're still hungry after this, I'll go get you a plate."

"I don't deserve this."

"Everyone deserves a little pampering when they're sick. I'm sure you'd do the same."

"Of course. I'd bring you mountains of cheese and frozen custard and coffee with too much cream and sugar."

"And stacks of eighties teen movies?"

"The very best ones."

"See? You'd spoil me, too." Lou ran a hand through his hair. Al leaned into her gentle touch. "I'll leave you to it. Let me know when you're done and I'll take the tray away." Lou retreated back into the kitchen.

Somewhere between anxiety and guilt, Al fell in love. Lou had descended into his false den of airborne disease to coddle him back to health with a basket filled in heaven. It wasn't just her spoiling him. With her business struggling, she couldn't afford to get sick, yet here she was tidying his home and starting his laundry.

He could hear her emptying the dishwasher. This had to stop. He moved the tray so he could roll out of bed, picked it up, and carried it downstairs. When he entered the kitchen, Lou was no longer emptying the dishwasher. She stared at the wall next to the entrance, just a few feet from where he stood. Briefly worrying she'd had a seizure of some sort, he recalled what hung on the wall and blushed.

Lou noticed Al's pinkening. "You probably don't want to hear this, but this may be the sweetest thing I've ever seen." Al took his place next to her so he could admire the collection with her. Now that at least one secret was out, he wanted to share the moment.

"It started out as a random impulse buy at the museum, and now it's a nice bit of our history. These are all the best times I've had in Milwaukee. They've all been with you."

She turned to him, eyes shinier than usual, then leaned in to softly kiss his lips. Her lips were warm and dry.

"I'm sick." Al tried to sound like he meant it.

"I don't care." Lou took a step closer to wrap her arms around his neck. Al responded immediately and eagerly, pulling her so tight that her breath whooshed out.

"You're sick. You shouldn't be tiring yourself," Lou mumbled between kisses.

"If this is what sick feels like, I don't ever want to feel better." Al lifted her, wrapping her strong legs around his waist, and carried her upstairs.

• • • • •

"I think we've discovered a miracle cure," Al whispered.

Al and Lou were buried deep beneath his soft, cozy covers, savoring the lazy freedom of afternoon sex. They lay on their sides, he behind her, arms wrapped around her rib cage.

"Perfect timing. I need a new career."

"Mmmm, I don't think so. I'm not sharing." Al nuzzled her neck, trailing kisses from her shoulder to her ear, then back down. Lou giggled. She could feel it releasing all the tension, the uncertainty. The afternoon sun filtered through the tinted glass; a warm breeze whispered from somewhere.

"Bit selfish, don't you think?"

"Absolutely. But you are my miracle."

Lou bathed in the compliment. Maybe it was all just teasing, but his words warmed her more than a thousand extravagant gifts.

"Hey, what's with all the cookbooks? I didn't know you were so into cooking." Al twitched a little. Had she pried too much? Lou rolled over to look Al in the eyes, laying one leg over his waist and resting her hands on his chest, running her fingers through his hair. “I didn’t mean to be nosy—I thought it might be fun to cook dinner together sometime.”

Al’s normally cool eyes heated and his voice choked a little when he said, “Sure.”

“You feeling okay?”

Al nudged her with his hips. Lou’s eyes widened and she leaned her head back to laugh. Al took the opportunity to trail hot kisses down her throat.

“I think I’m starting to feel ill again.”

Lou pulled his chin back up to her mouth in response. Right now, she couldn’t be happier that her restaurant was failing.

• CHAPTER NINETEEN •

Al checked his watch, grabbed a cup of tea to go, and walked out the door. He stepped onto Water Street, where the sky was a pristine blue. A crisp fall breeze ruffled his hair while the sun warmed his face and birds chirped. Snow White had never experienced a day as spectacular as this. He half expected pigeons to swoop down and airlift him to work. Except for that ominous black cloud of guilt spreading on the horizon.

He loved Lou. He loved her warm brown eyes, her freckled nose, her quick smile. He loved her gentle, slightly callused and scarred hands, the hands of an artist. Every aspect of his life had improved since meeting Lou, yet he couldn't enjoy any of it.

His hands shook at the thought of her discovering his secret identity, spilling hot tea onto his wrist, an inadequate penance. His insides clenched with guilt over the pain he had caused her and the additional pain he would cause her if she ever learned the truth. Without a solution, that cloud threatened everything Lou had helped him discover. He couldn't be the cause of more heartache in her life. He needed to stop that cloud from taking over her life, too.

. . . . .

"Lou got lucky last night," Sue's voice said in a singsong tone.

Lou propped the back restaurant door open to let in the refreshing fall breeze. After months of sweltering kitchens, the chilly air lifted her spirits. Or maybe it was waking up in Al's arms; he really did seem miraculously recovered. She pulled on her chef's jacket and joined Sue at the prep station.

"How could you possibly know that? I just got here."

"You look like a white shirt under a black light—all glowy. Couldn't wait to rub it in my face, could you?"

"I can't help that you and Harley haven't figured it out. Do you need a diagram? I can draw one up for you."

"Bite me."

Both women started laughing. It felt good after so many months of stress and uncertainty. Sue elbowed Lou and said, "Seriously, all good?"

Lou's face softened, then softened some more, followed by a dreamy sigh. She looked at Sue. "Real good."

"Barf . . . if you got any sappier it'd smell like a Pine-Sol commercial in here." Harley's voice broke Lou's dreamy mood.

"Oh, Harley, let her enjoy the honeymoon phase. It's not often Lou has a lucky night."

Cough. "Morning." Cough. Lou batted her eyes at Sue.

"You wench." Sue hugged her tight. "I'm so happy for you."

Lou gave Sue a scrunched-nose smile. "How's prep coming?"

Sue's face fell like a soufflé taken out of the oven too soon. Harley emerged from his corner to stand beside her.

"Okay, now I'm concerned. What happened?"

"Two bussers called to quit today, Alison gave her two-week notice, and only the Meyers have reservations."

"Well, it's only a Wednesday. It's never a busy night. I'll help bus tables if needed. Who's scheduled to wait?"

"Billy. He's the only waiter left."

"So it's just us now."

Lou sighed, not because employees had quit, but because she knew they had to. Business just wasn't there at Luella's anymore. The restaurant industry ran on tips—preferably cash, thank you very much. No customers, no tips, no employees.

"That's right. Sam quit last week—he got a job at the new steak house. He should make some good money there. What about you two? Where have you applied?" Lou asked.

Harley looked down to study the floor mats, but Sue looked directly into Lou's eyes.

"You know damn well we aren't looking. We're here till you close the doors. Harley volunteered to wait tables if needed."

Harley's head snapped up. "I did not."

Lou smiled at Sue's ribbing. She always knew where to poke him. "The horror. I don't think we've come to that yet. But can you imagine a customer's face with Harley thundering up to them?"

"I don't thunder."

"Of course not. You're a vision of grace and delicacy in an ink-stained wrapper," said Sue.

Harley studied his tattoos. "I like my ink."

Sue gave him a soft smile and slipped her hand into his. "So do I."

Lou had never seen any form of affection between the two before. It was about time! It felt right that they would make a connection. Big, burly Harley with the heart of an angel, soul of a teddy bear, and Sue with her backbone of titanium, spiked with rusty nails, ready to take on any threat to those close to her.

She needed them to find work soon. She couldn't afford to pay them much longer, never mind paying herself. She'd lost ten pounds because she only ate one meal a day and walked everywhere to avoid spending money on gas. At least she had it to lose.

"Seriously, you two, you need to find jobs. Soon."

"Are you firing us?" Sue asked.

"I don't want it to come to that. Just start looking, please."

. . . . .

"I can't do it, mate. I love her," Al said to John in a hushed voice so their coworkers couldn't hear.

"Whoa." John put his hands out to stop Al's insane ramblings. "Six months ago you couldn't wait to get out of town. The women were ugly, the men stupid, and don't get me started on what you said about the food. Now you're in love and want to live here forever?"

"Right, right. I was a douche canoe, as you so eloquently said once. I know better now." Al picked up his pen and started shaking it, creating the illusion of a rubber pen.

"You're glossing over the fundamental flaw in the plan, dude. You sunk her restaurant. I don't care if you make Fabio look like a crude Neanderthal and she forgives more sins than the Pope, she ain't forgiving you for this."

Al sat back in his chair, defeated.

"You're right. This will crush her. I can't do it. John, I'm going to lose her." Al looked at John, eyes begging him for rescue, a way to protect Lou's heart from his thoughtless, arrogant words so many months ago.

"Well, maybe you can keep it from her, like a CIA job."

"Be serious. I like my job; I'm proud of my writing. I need to share that with her." He started tapping his pen on his forehead, as if hoping to dislodge a brilliant solution.

"Maybe you can get a job somewhere else as a food critic."

"No. This is the job I want." Al sat up. "Wait, maybe . . . you might have it. I need to talk to Hannah." Al got up and rushed toward Hannah's office.

John leaned back in his chair. "Happy to help."

• • • • •

Al paused outside Hannah's office to catch his breath and organize his idea. He looked in the door to see Hannah talking on her phone, feet up on the desk, and at least three pencils stuck in her bun. She held up a finger to let him know she saw him there and to wait.

He leaned his back against the doorframe, which provided support so he could channel his energy inward. He couldn't stop tapping on his legs. The idea could work. Lou knew he wrote, knew he appreciated food. With a few strategic comments, an article or two, he wouldn't have to live a lie anymore. Hannah hung up the phone and focused her attention on the twitchy man in her office.

"What can I do for you, Al?"

Al strode to stand directly in front of Hannah, set his hands on her desk, and leaned forward. He spoke precisely and clearly. He didn't want any confusion.

"I want to kill A. W. Wodyski."

Hannah blinked at him, but her features didn't betray her disappointment.

"Is this your two weeks, then?"

"What? No. Why would you think that?"

"Now I'm confused. Why would you want to destroy your alias? You don't have a column without him. A. W. Wodyski writes the food articles. You are A. W. Wodyski."

"Hear me out. If A. W. dies, then you need a new critic. Perhaps you hire a freelancer you've used a few times named Al Waters. He's young, British, and has a unique take on Milwaukee's restaurant scene. Having him on staff adds an international flair to the food section, and maybe the paper as a whole?"

Hannah's eyes narrowed as if she could see him clearer through a more focused window. "Is this about that chef you like?"

"Is it a problem if it is?"

"You can't review her. And you'll lose your anonymity if you use your real name. The Internet makes it too easy for people to find pictures of you. So, are you doing it for her?"

Al's gut response flew to his tongue. Of course he wanted to make these changes because of Lou, but it wasn't just that. It was more than protecting her from the hurt of discovering he was A. W. He'd been living a lie since he arrived. He'd pretended to be a local, yet had loathed everything about Milwaukee. Now Al knew differently. He didn't want to be anything else but himself: a cheese curd–loving, festival-going, Brew

Crew fan who adored the most incredible chef in the city. He couldn't really be himself if he hid behind a pseudonym.

"It's quite a bit more than that. I don't want to hide behind A. W. anymore."

Hannah assessed his sincere eyes, his pleading posture. His heart stood bare to her in his face.

"I need to think about it. What you're suggesting hasn't been done here. There could be some serious repercussions if the truth surfaced. There's more to your plan than A. W.'s existence."

"I'll take that for now." Al turned to leave, then stopped. "Thank you, Hannah—for at least considering it."

• CHAPTER TWENTY •

He's here," Lou said after peeking out the pickup window. "I'll come back if we get any more customers." Sue nodded and continued scrubbing the oven. During downtime, which they had a lot of, they worked to get the equipment shiny and bright for the inevitable auction. It was just a matter of time before the bank pulled the plug on her cash flow. She could only skip payments for so long. Lou pushed through the swinging doors and walked to greet Al in the quiet dining room.

Al stopped by the bar and surveyed the restaurant, taking in the mostly empty tables, subtle decor, and single waiter working the entire restaurant. He paused when he saw Lou approaching him with a smile engaging her entire body. Lou kissed him quick on the lips and stepped back. She hadn't felt nervous until he walked in the door, and now every nerve danced the jitterbug. She looked down and bit her lip.

"You came. I didn't know if you would make it."

Al looked surprised.

"Nonsense. Luella's is your baby. I have to visit."

Lou grabbed his hand and squeezed.

"Thanks."

"The pleasure is all mine. Besides, I recall the promise of a free meal."

"You'll get your food. First you need to meet some people, then I'll give you the nickel tour."

Al looked around for the people Lou planned to introduce him to. He already knew Harley and Sue in the kitchen. She led him to the center table, where Otto and Gertrude sat holding hands. They both seemed to be losing weight. She'd bring them both a dessert on the house tonight, since they'd already finished their dinners.

"Al, I'd like to introduce you to my very best customers and good friends Gertrude and Otto Meyer. Gertrude and Otto, this is my . . . Al." Lou stumbled over what to call Al.

"*Herzchen*, this is your gentleman friend, yes? The one that makes you smile so much?"

Lou smiled and blushed.

The door jangled and new customers entered the restaurant.

"Excuse me; I'll be right back." Lou hurried off to assist the new customers. A full house at this stage wouldn't save Luella's, but every new customer meant a few extra dollars she didn't have to earn before she could open her new restaurant. As she left, she heard Gertrude tell Al, "Sit. I don't like looking up when I talk to people."

• • • • •

Al sat. He already didn't want to disappoint this lovely, small woman. His phone beeped.

"Excuse me while I check this," Al said.

"You young ones with your gadgets. When do you get a break?" Gertrude said.

"I guess the theory is if we're always available, then we don't have to be in the office as much," Al explained as he searched his phone.

A text had arrived from Hannah.

RIP AW. Need obit asap.

Al absorbed the words, let them swish about in his gray matter and funnel into every cell. He'd done it—well, almost. The news energized him. Phase one of cover-his-tracks completed. He tried to ignore the niggling fact that he was still hiding the whole truth from Lou.

Now that he had Hannah's response, he powered off his phone.

"My apologies. My attention is all yours," Al said.

Gertrude waved his apology away.

"Is everything okay? Not bad news, I hope," Gertrude asked.

"No, not at all. The very best news actually."

"Delightful," Gertrude said. The three paused in conversation, deciding where to go next.

"Lou tells me you come here quite frequently?" Al asked.

"Oh yes. She makes the very best food. Her servers are always attentive. We've never had a bad meal, have we, Otto?" Otto nodded his head in agreement.

"She's only cooked for me a few times. What I've had ranks among some of the best ever. I can see why you come here often."

"It's really a shame she has to close. I can't believe that horrible man wrote such awful things about her cooking, our *Liebling*'s cooking. He is a *Dummkopf*."

"Quite right." Al nodded in absolute agreement.

"Lou fancies you."

Gertrude leaned in as if sharing a top secret, a smile brightening her pale face. Al tilted toward her to respond.

"I should hope so. If not, she should stop snogging me so much."

"Are you saying you don't like it?" Lou swooped down from behind and kissed him on the cheek. Otto's eyes crinkled at the affection, and Gertrude clapped her hands.

"Haha. They are in love, Otto. You remind me of when I first met him. We couldn't stop touching. At our age, people seemed to think we should keep our hands to ourselves. I say bah to such silliness. When people are in love, they should show it." She leaned over and planted a wavering kiss on Otto's wan cheek, then wiped the smudged pink lipstick off.

"You should see the mess when she wears the red lipstick," said Otto.

"Otto, they don't need to know such things." She gave him a sly wink.

"So how did you first meet each other? In Germany?" Al asked.

"Hasn't Lou told you?" Gertrude responded.

"You tell it so much better," Lou said. "I couldn't do it justice."

"All right. We were both married, you know. Our parents came to Milwaukee before World War Two. They were smart, our parents. They came here because other friends and family already moved. People spoke the old language, made the old food, supported each other in this very different place.

"Otto and I grew up here but never met. There were so many Germans—we didn't know everyone. We married our high school sweethearts, then we each buried them after many years of marriage. I had settled into widowhood, content with my friends, my nieces, my nephews. One summer, when German Fest was still new, I waited in line for *Spanferkel*." She saw the confusion in Al's eyes.

"Do you know what this is?" Gertrude asked. Al shook his head no.

"The *Spanferkel* is a young piglet. They roast it slowly and the juices leak, making crispy skin and moist meat. In Germany, we make this for celebrations. It is not something a widow would make to eat by herself. At German Fest, they had a stand selling *Spanferkel*. When I made my order and pulled out my money to pay, the most handsome man stepped forward to set his money on the counter.

"At first I grew quite angry, thinking him pushy. But then another order was added and he paid for both. And then he said, ach, I'll never forget his words. He said, 'If I may?' "

"That was it? Just 'If I may?' " Al said.

"My Otto uses few words. His polite question gave me shivers I still feel now. I nodded; he carried our orders to a nearby table, waited until I sat; then we ate. After a cold beer, he asked me to polka. We danced all night to every song. I remember his sparkling eyes under these same bushy brows. They were darker then. He danced with springs on his toes. By the end of the night, I danced on springs, too."

While Gertrude told her story, Al and Lou looked at each other, remembering their spontaneous dance at Irish Fest. Lou gave a gentle squeeze to the back of Al's neck and continued to play with his hair. She swirled soft circles across the bare skin. The gentle touch went directly to his soul, soothing any lingering tension from his meeting with Hannah and uncertainty about their future.

"It is so fun to watch young love," Gertrude said. "Now, this young man is hungry. Aren't you a chef?"

Lou looked a little startled at Gertrude's obvious dismissal. Al was sad she took her hands away, but the rumble in his stomach agreed with Gertrude's suggestion.

"I suppose she's right. I did promise you food. What would you like?"

"Surprise me. If you make it, I know I'll love it." Lou nodded and headed back to the kitchen. Gertrude watched her leave.

"Good, I never thought she'd go." Al didn't expect to hear that from the sweet little lady. "She'll be back too soon, but I wanted to chat with you about your intentions with our girl. As you can see, she has become family to us. While you seem a nice gentleman, I want to know what you plan."

Otto, his bald pate bobbing in agreement, actually cracked a knuckle under the table. Al wanted to dismiss it as coincidence, but the stern look on Otto's face reminded him of his first girlfriend's father when he'd picked her up for a date. That particular man had polished his hunting rifle on the dining room table as Al waited for his date to make her entrance.

Al sat up straight, taking Gertrude and Otto's concerns seriously. He paused before he spoke, wanting to make sure his words reflected the certainty he felt.

"First, Lou is quite lucky to have so many people around her who care for her so deeply. I hope that caring someday extends to me. When I arrived, I knew no one other than the few people I worked with. I wasn't particularly fond of the city. I arrived in the depths of winter to a blizzard and below-zero temperatures. It seemed an omen of things to come.

"Then it warmed, sort of. And Lou fell into my life. She showed me where to find the heart of Milwaukee. I didn't know it when I came here, but I've been searching for a place like this. Lou represents everything I love about this city: the past, the present, and I hope the future. I fell in love. This is my home now."

"Good," Otto said, nodding his shiny head again in approval.

"Be good to her, *Liebchen*. She is a treasure," Gertrude added.

"I will do anything to make her happy. She is in good hands."

"I hope your thoughts lean toward a permanent change for our Lou." She tapped her ring finger with her other hand. "Otto and I met and married within a few months. When you have found your match, you know, right?"

Al blinked at Gertrude's suggestion. He hadn't thought about marriage. It seemed too quick, but he still found himself nodding along with Gertrude; when you knew, you knew.

"We are done now; she comes," Gertrude said, interrupting his thoughts.

Lou appeared at his side with four plates, two containing entrées and two containing apple tarts with large scoops of ice cream.

She set the desserts in front of Otto and Gertrude.

"Harley sent these out for you. He's topped them with the salted caramel ice cream you like so much."

"That man spoils us too much. He will make us fat," Gertrude said, but the two eagerly scooped up bites.

Lou set the remaining two plates in front of Al and herself.

"It looked so good when I made yours, I realized I haven't eaten today."

Al looked down to see a plate of sole meunière. He couldn't help remembering the last time he consumed this dish in this restaurant. But this was different. She was different. He was different.

He cut off a large piece of fish and shoved it in his mouth with an inward flinch. He chewed. Then sighed. Perfection. How could he have expected anything less? Further evidence of his past arrogance. Al devoured the delicate fish, hoping to smother the guilt stomping about in his stomach.

• CHAPTER TWENTY-ONE •

Al sat alone at the bar sipping a cup of tea. It had been almost three weeks since he'd first entered her restaurant, and he had since become a fixture. She loved the way he looked sitting at her bar.

Miniature pumpkins dotted the surface, most with kooky painted faces. Harley had painted them whenever it was slow. Looking around the restaurant, she could see that each pumpkin had a different expression. It had been slower than slow.

Lou could see Al each time she passed the pickup window. She refused to let him help, insisting he'd only get in her way. Every Sunday morning she came in to clean out the fridge of items that wouldn't last until the next open. Finding food past its prime prodded her latent OCD. Lou could let a lot of things slide, but reaching into a box and pulling out a moldy lemon or slimy head of lettuce triggered the gag reflex. Normally she tossed anything approaching its expiration date, but today she planned to bring home anything usable, and perhaps a few things in no danger of expiring. What was the point of owning a restaurant if you couldn't use the good stuff occasionally? Today she had plans to make dinner with Al, so no reason to waste perfectly good food.

Lou recovered some foie gras, duck confit, and assorted veggies and herbs. As she grabbed the items, a menu started bubbling to the surface: foie gras ravioli with a cherry-sage cream sauce, crispy goat cheese medallions on mixed greens with a simple vinaigrette, pan-fried duck confit, and duck-fat-roasted new potatoes with more of the cherry-sage cream sauce. For dessert, a chocolate soufflé with coconut crisps. She grabbed a few more ingredients off the shelf to avoid a stop at the grocery store.

"Hey, Al, why don't you grab a few bottles of wine from the bar? Pick something for foie gras, duck, and chocolate," Lou shouted through the pickup window.

"On it. Don't forget the truffles." Lou could hear him hop off the bar stool and start searching for the wine. She packed all the items into a few bags and her small cooler, then pushed open the doors to join Al.

"I like you a lot, but not enough to use up my truffles."

"You wound me. Not even a shaving or two?" Al dramatically set a hand across his chest.

"Shameless. How about this? If I still have any by the time I close the restaurant, I'll make you a truffle-themed meal."

Al took the bags from Lou's hands, set them on the bar, then pulled her into his arms.

"That's all I'm asking." He set his lips on hers in the faintest of kisses, just a whisper to start. Lou moved to tighten her arms around his neck to settle in for a thorough kiss, but Al ducked his head out of her embrace and retrieved some of the bags from the counter.

"Well, best be off. I'm getting hungry," he said.

Lou squinted her eyes, hoping to discern his intentions. He was up to something. She grabbed the remaining bags and followed him out.

• • • • •

Smells of frying onion and sizzling duck fat hung thick enough that Al wanted to lick the air. His stomach rumbled but his mind couldn't stop focusing on Lou's bare shoulders, the way her dress clung to her hips and swished around her bare legs, the waft of vanilla every time she got too close. He wanted to trail his fingers from her ankle until they disappeared under the hem of her dress.

They had all night together without any interruptions, any responsibilities other than to enjoy themselves, and he would make sure of the latter. He planned to add to the growing list of reasons he loved her—the newest reason being the foie gras ravioli she'd planned.

"Are you going to help, or just keep staring at my behind?"

Lou interrupted his daydream that involved strategically dripped Baileys and her neck. Al shook his head. That helped a little. Lou flicked on the radio and returned to her cooking.

". . . thunderstorm rolling. The air is sizzling with electricity, so watch out for the lightning," the weatherman said.

He had no idea.

Al enjoyed watching Lou cook. She moved with precision and grace, each move intentional. Any indecision or lack of confidence disappeared when the knives came out—and that confidence was remarkably sexy. She'd been cooking for fifteen minutes. In that time, he'd unearthed the bottle opener, dusted off two wineglasses, and poured them each a glass to sip while they cooked. He thought that was quite efficient. She had unpacked all the food, pulled out sauté and saucepans, heated the oven, chopped and started cooking onions, chopped shallots for the sauce, and heated duck fat for the potatoes. She had lined up ingredients according to the dish with such efficiency it seemed absentminded. Al could have watched her for hours.

Thunder rumbled, indicating the promised thunderstorm was approaching. A cold breeze broke through the heat in the kitchen, a hint of the warring fronts above that seemed to isolate them from the world outside. The increasing winds and electrically charged air added an element of reckless energy to his growing tension. Al picked up Lou's wineglass, stepped directly behind her, then leaned into her so he could set the glass in front of her. Lou straightened, then melted against him. He leaned over, close enough that the tiny invisible hairs on her ear tickled his lips, and whispered, "Where should I start?"

• • • • •

By kissing me senseless, Lou thought. But Al just set the glass down and stepped away. Maybe he didn't realize the effect he had on her.

Lou cleared her throat and spoke.

"Think you can handle the salad?"

"You're giving me salad duty? You must think I'm useless."

"Prove me wrong. If you do a good job, I'll let you make dessert."

Al went to the salad station to organize the ingredients but knocked a shallot off the counter that rolled near Lou.

When he crouched to pick it up, one hand closed around the small bulb; the other grazed her ankle. As he stood, his hand traced a barely perceptible path up her leg until her dress started to bunch. When he took his hand away, Lou turned to react but Al already had his back to her and was chopping the escapee vegetable into minute pieces. She took a deep breath and paused to admire his correct knife-hold and even dicing, just as a professional writer would admire a well-written sentence.

Lou turned back to her ravioli filling, her skin still tingling. She sautéed the foie gras with shallots. Off heat she'd add in finely diced sweet cherries, sage, and a little goat cheese.

Al finished assembling a vinaigrette and put his breaded goat cheese rounds in the freezer so they wouldn't melt when cooked. He did know more about cooking than she thought he did. He joined her at the stove, standing close enough that she could feel his clothes brushing hers. The strap on her dress had slipped, and Al pushed it all the way off her shoulder so he could brush his lips over its former location.

Between caresses Al asked, "Should I start the soufflé?"

"Uh-huh." Lou slanted her head to the side, giving him more room to work, expecting him to continue his playful kisses. Instead he stepped away and put ingredients into a pan for the soufflé.

"Hmph." *Two can play at this game.* Lou scanned her tasks—no use burning dinner. She just finished stuffing the ravioli and the potatoes cooked in the oven. The duck would wait until right before that course, as would boiling the ravioli. She just needed to start the sauce. Plenty of time for a distraction. She picked up her wine and walked to check on Al's work. Too bad she tripped on nothing and spilled her red wine all over Al's back.

"Oops."

"No worries." Al smiled. "There are worse things than a wine stain."

Lou looked over his shoulder as he unbuttoned the stained shirt, inhaling the aroma of red wine and Al's spicy scent of black pepper and cinnamon.

"It looks like you're ready to whip the egg whites." Lou smiled innocently. She handed Al a whisk and returned to her station. She began the sauce, sautéing the onions in duck fat, deglazing the pan with a little stock and port wine. Creating sauces always seemed magical to her, like alchemy. With the right steps and proportions, mundane ingredients could change into liquid gold.

While she scraped up the browned bits of deliciousness, Al crossed the room with a spoonful of chocolate base he made.

"I added in some orange zest. Let me know how it tastes before I mix it with the egg whites."

As he moved the spoon toward her mouth, she could swear he tilted it so chocolate drizzled down her dress. He popped the remaining chocolate into her mouth.

"Damn. Now your dress is stained, too. Let me help clean that up."

He leaned in to kiss the warm chocolate off her skin, adding to the considerable heat already in the kitchen.

Al pulled back, licking the last bit of chocolate off his lips.

"Now you can finish off that sauce."

Lou sighed and thought she heard Al chuckle when she returned to her task. Every cool breeze, flash of lightning, and growl of thunder added to the electricity in the air. Her bare skin thrummed with leashed energy. She worked in silence, adding the last few pats of butter to the sauce.

"Al, can you come here? I want you to taste the sauce. Let me know if it's done."

Inches away from him, she dipped her finger in the creamy sauce and lifted it between them. Looking into Al's eyes, she slowly smoothed the sauce onto his lower lip. Neither breathed. She lifted her mouth to kiss the sauce off, tasting the rich cream balancing the layered flavors of onion and duck.

Their stained clothing fell to the floor. Lightning seared the night sky, thunder shook the building, and rain pounded against the window glass.

• • • • •

The sauce burned.

"That smells awful." Lou giggled from the kitchen floor. She lay partially atop Al, her head propped up so she could see his face. Her free hand played with his thick hair as he traced squiggles on her bare back.

"I can't believe a chef would let her sauce burn. How unprofessional." Al shook his head in mock disgust.

"Mmm, I'd choose burnt sauce over professionalism any day." Lou's stomach rumbled.

"It seems we worked up an appetite. We should probably eat so we have energy for the rest of the night," Al said.

Lou got up and tossed Al an apron that said "Wisconsin Cheddar Does It Better."

"Here's an apron. We don't want you to get burned." Lou put

on hers. They finished making dinner, both enjoying their memorable meal wearing nothing more than their aprons.

. . . . .

Lou woke to the smell of fresh coffee and something delicious baking. She reached over to find Al's side of the bed cool and empty. She could hear him knocking about in the kitchen, a room she'd never look at quite the same.

Lou rolled onto her back and spread her limbs wide to take up most of the bed, enjoying the sensation of lazing about fully awake. Warm sheets gave way to cool ones as she reached onto Al's side of the bed. Hmmm, Al's side. She now thought of them as having sides, having a future.

A loud crash echoed down the hall.

Before Lou could get enough momentum to swing her pleasantly tired body out of bed, Al's voice said, "Don't get up. Nothing's broken. I'll be there in a minute."

Good enough for her. Lou settled back into the pillows, enjoying the smell of breakfast prepared by someone else. She loved to cook, but she still liked having other people cook for her. When you're a chef, most nonprofessionals are too intimidated to cook for you. You get used to preparing all the meals when you have dinner parties with friends. The long hours, late nights, and weekends whittled away at any non-restaurant-based friendships. Eventually, most of your friends came from the industry. Al cooking for her was a special treat.

And here she was, lying in bed with a handsome man making her breakfast. When she heard his footsteps coming down the hall, she sat up in anticipation. Al walked in carrying a full tray including a plate piled with scones. He settled it between them on the bed.

"You can bake?" Lou asked.

"Any proper Englishman can make a scone."

Lou rolled her eyes at him.

"Okay, that's not true. My grandma taught me. It's saved me more than once. It's difficult to find a proper scone here—Harley's excluded, of course." Lou grabbed one and took a bite. "These are wonderful. And coffee. I don't deserve you."

Al concentrated on fixing his tea, then said, "I don't think that's true."

They munched scones and drank their hot drinks in comfortable silence. Finally, Al looked at the alarm clock on the bedside table and said, "Would you mind if we turned on the telly? I feel like I've been out of touch with the world."

"It's been less than twelve hours. Are you implying time with me seems like forever?"

Al was struggling to find the words to get himself out of this quandary when Lou laughed.

"Don't worry. I'm just teasing. Here's the remote."

Lou started on her second scone as Al flipped on the TV. The local morning news had just begun. The young weatherman promised an Indian summer for the next week, then temperatures would drop below forty. Given the time of year, they would probably not see forty again until March. Where would her life be by then? Would she have a job? Money for rent? Would she and Al still spend lazy mornings in bed together? She looked over at him, admiring his scruffy jaw, thinking about setting aside her scone to nibble on his neck instead. He was a wonderful distraction. Over her daydream, she heard,

"Restaurant critic A. W. Wodyski died this weekend of a heart attack. His tenure in Milwaukee, while short, was full of controversial and popular reviews."

Lou's coffee cup hovered inches from her mouth. Her emotions swirled. She wanted to be happy with the news, but even after his crap criticism, she couldn't muster enough energy to truly care. Because of Al's presence in her life, she'd found an unlikely path out of that pit. Now on the other side, she was okay. Better than okay at the moment. She looked over at Al, who was watching her from the corner of his eye.

"What?" Lou asked.

"Nothing, I guess. You looked upset for a moment."

"Just gauging how I felt about the news." Al looked confused, as if he needed more information. "Did I never tell you? His review of my restaurant destroyed any chance of growing my customer base. Since his negative review, only our most loyal clients still come. I wish they had posted a picture. I would love to know what he looked like. Not that I'd remember. The night he ate at Luella's was the same day I found Devlin with Megan. The day we met, actually. I don't remember much except doing a lot of dishes. I'm surprised my hands aren't still wrinkly."

She wiggled her fingers in front of her face.

"Lou." Al looked uncomfortable. "You should know—"

"I'm sorry," Lou interrupted. "I shouldn't be talking about him. That's not fair to you."

"That's not it. You—"

Lou interrupted him again.

"Seriously. It feels like ancient history to me, so I didn't think how mentioning Devlin might bug you. Let's not talk about it."

Al sighed.

"I assure you, it doesn't bother me. We can talk about anything you like." Al touched her face, cupping her cheek in one hand. She tilted toward it and closed her eyes to really enjoy the sensation of his touch.

"I love you," he said.

Al whispered it. But a whisper with the power of a spring thunderstorm—the power to cleanse, to excite, and to calm. And the power to destroy. Lou felt safe and vulnerable, whole and scattered. With open eyes, the last bastion of resistance in her heart disintegrated in his shower of affection.

Saying "I love you" changed everything.

Lou managed a breathy "Me, too."

· CHAPTER TWENTY-TWO ·

How long do you think I need to wait before I tell her?" Al asked.

He tapped his fingers on the bar, waiting for John's reply.

"Tell her what? . . . Oh, you mean tell her you're taking the job of the man who destroyed her livelihood who was really you but you've created a fictional death and obit because you would never hurt her 'cause you love her so much."

"That's about right, but I probably won't add in all the extra bits. What's up your bum?" Al prodded John with his elbow. When Al wasn't dining out—he sometimes took John now, who had a surprising eye for detail and refined palate—they often went for drinks while he waited for Lou to finish at the restaurant.

John turned toward him and chewed his lip. Al had never seen him so rattled. John always acted sure of himself and his surroundings.

"The paper wants to send me to Paris."

"That's fantastic. Why so crabby?"

"Hannah wants me to meet with different fashion houses. They want to actually have coverage rather than relying on Associated Press for the details. Hannah seems to think I have a good eye and they want to make it more prominent in the paper."

"Mate, that's brilliant. I'm not understanding your bad mood."

"I can't go looking like this." He gestured to himself. "They'd never let me in. No one would take me seriously."

"You've done all right thus far. Maybe you don't need to change."

"Ha—I may be a boy from 'Stallis, but I'm not an idiot. I get away with this here because I do most of my shopping online. Any local shopping I do I act like I'm an errand boy. They accept that and I get what I need."

"You name-drop yourself?"

John gave Al a stony look.

"No one in fashion would respect me if they knew what I looked like."

"Then cut your hair and shave the beard. It's not like you don't know how to dress well."

"I haven't been beardless since my freshman year in high school."

"You could grow a full beard in high school?"

"My family's hairy." John shrugged his shoulders. "I shaved in sixth grade."

"Oh." Al looked around the bar. "I still don't think I'm grasping the entire issue."

"Look, I don't expect you to understand; I was just hoping you'd listen."

"Mate, I'm listening. But I can't offer any advice if I don't get it."

"I know it doesn't make sense, but I like this look for me. People avoid me. In high school, that was a benefit. Now I'm used to it. People don't talk to me, they don't stare at me."

"What do you mean they don't stare? Half this room can't keep their eyes off you."

"But they're gawking because I look homeless."

"As someone who doesn't look homeless, may I suggest people would probably stare less if you were shaven and had clean clothes."

"People used to stare—that's why I grew the beard and hair out. They still look, but at least now they see what I want them to."

What was he hiding? Birthmarks, scars from a rabid squirrel attack? Al wanted to know, but the politeness his mother had drilled into him had finally taken effect.

"So what are you going to do?"

"I have to get a shave and haircut. I don't see any way around it."

"What if you just trimmed it up a little neater? You still wouldn't see a ton of skin, but it would give a little definition to your face."

"Nah. If I'm doing it, I'll do it right." John sighed in submission. "I can't believe we're sitting in a bar full of lovely ladies and we're talking about my beard."

"Pathetic, really. And I've got your back should you need it." Al put his hand on John's shoulder. "At least I have a lovely lady to go home to. Which brings us full circle. Thoughts?"

"It's all about you, isn't it?" John's smile told Al he teased. "Okay, it's been two weeks since the obit. I'd say in the next week or so tell her you got the job. That works out. A week for the paper to mourn, a week accepting résumés, a week for interviews. Heck, you could even push it back more with the holidays. If Hannah really was hiring you, she'd tell you the week of Thanksgiving so you'd have the long weekend to get ready. Plus, you'd be hired in time for all the holiday food columns."

"Thanksgiving. That might be perfect. Once again, John, you've saved my pasty white arse."

• • • • •

Al twitched as he watched the clock and listened for Lou's arrival. Today was his first Thanksgiving. Lou planned to cook the two of them her family's traditional meal. The turkey sat in a cooler of salted ice water, happily brining since last night. So far, it didn't differ much from Christmas dinner back home, except Lou hadn't mentioned anything about pigs in a blanket. But any holiday centered around food was his kind of holiday. The only possible negative was that he'd planned to tell Lou about his fake new job today.

Since waking, he had changed his mind four times. He didn't want to ruin a perfect day with Lou, but he couldn't bear not sharing this part of his life with her. He didn't want to lie or evade anymore when she asked about his writing. He had his freelance articles to show her, but Hannah planned to use his real byline next week so he had to tell Lou now. With all the grief A. W. Wodyski had brought her, Al fretted that Lou couldn't accept his new job, that she'd be crushed he wanted to work for the paper that ruined her restaurant. He took a deep breath to calm himself.

Lou had said she'd arrive at eight in the morning to start cooking. She'd given him strict instructions to have coffee waiting, the bird brining, and something for breakfast. He made scones again, this time with pumpkin pie spices to fit the occasion. They had the entire day ahead of them to fill with cooking, talking, and making love. He wouldn't get a better opportunity.

Buzzzz! Finally. He pushed the button to let her in but thought better of it. He ran to open the door in person. Thank God he did. She had two large bags full of food and supplies stacked on top of a rolling cooler. When he opened the door, her face split into a glowing smile.

"You saved me. I didn't know how I would carry this up. I've got the bags if you can grab the cooler."

With a peck on the cheek she scooted past him to prop the door open while he carried the cooler. Back in the kitchen, she unpacked using one hand while the other held a disappearing scone.

Between bites she said, "Happy Thanksgiving, handsome."

"You, too. But it feels a little wrong to celebrate people having to leave England."

"It's the perfect holiday for you, too. You left England looking for something better, just like the pilgrims did."

Al hugged her from behind and kissed her neck.

"But I found so much more than Native Americans and pumpkins." Lou turned and kissed him. When he tried to continue, she briskly broke it off. "Not today, love. This is serious cooking. No time for messing about. We have a bird requiring stuffing, rolls to start, and pies to bake."

"You are a cruel mistress."

Lou winked.

"Trust me—it will all be worth it. This is the best holiday!

It's like a chef created it. Thanksgiving is the only holiday we have contingent on the food. That's all you have to do—eat. Best. Holiday. Ever."

"What can I do to help?" Al said with a dramatic sigh, which Lou chose to ignore with a smile.

"Rinse the brine off the bird, dry it off, then rub it with this." Lou handed him two sticks of soft butter. "Salt and pepper it, too. Don't forget the inside."

Lou started browning sausage and ground beef, adding the mirepoix, and tossing it all with seasoned croutons made from the restaurant's bread scraps. In minutes the kitchen felt like home. Now was his time to tell her, while she was busy but not chopping anything.

"So, I have a new job. A full-time one."

Lou turned to look at him.

"That's amazing. Where is it? What are you writing about?"

"Well, you know how I love food, right? I applied for the job to replace the food critic who just died, and I got it. I'm the new food critic for the paper." While Al spoke, his fingers continued to rub butter into the same spot on the turkey. Lou stopped stirring the meat; her shoulders dipped, and a line grew between her eyebrows.

"You applied for the critic job? Why would you do that?"

"It's something I've wanted to do for a long time. I just never had an opportunity before now." He hated the lies. *Get through today and I'll be done,* he thought. *All honesty from now on.*

"You didn't mention you wanted to apply." Lou's eyes shone a little more, her face scrunched as if she were sucking on a lemon.

"I didn't know how you'd react. And what if they didn't hire me? I didn't want to have this conversation if I wasn't getting the job."

"I see. Why upset the apple cart if the cow isn't going to hit it?"

"I'm sorry I didn't tell you. I should have." Al waited for a response.

Lou stood still for a moment.

Unable to stand the silence and not knowing what she thought, Al asked, "Lou?"

"Give me a moment, please; I need to think about this." Lou turned back to the stove, finished the stuffing, and shoved it into the turkey. She set it in the roasting pan and added some turkey stock. The entire pan went in the oven. She washed her hands, set the timer, and turned to face Al. He never wanted to hurt her. That was the whole point of the plan.

"Lou—" Al stepped toward her and she put up a hand to stop him.

"I'm not thrilled you'll be the new critic. I have some unresolved feelings I need to work through on that. Like how can they criticize a restaurant after one visit and not give a chef the chance to, I don't know, try again." Lou's shoulders slumped and she dropped her chin to her chest. "Oh God, it still hurts so much."

Al pulled her into his arms as her body quivered with each sob and whispered, "I'm sorry. I'm sorry. I'm sorry." Lou quieted after a few moments and stepped out of Al's arms, wiping tears away from her red eyes with the edge of her apron.

With a sniff she said, "Clearly, I still have some wounds left to heal, but I would never ask you to not take a job you wanted. I've been on the other end of that and it sucks. I'm happy you have a job you want. Not many people can say that. I am a bit disappointed you didn't tell me about it sooner, but I guess I understand why you didn't."

Lou stepped closer to Al so she could hold his hands and look closely in his eyes.

"I love you. You say you love me. Spending time with you brought me back from a really ugly place. In hindsight, I believe I'm better off now. I lost my restaurant, but I'm also rid of Devlin and I found you. I want a future with you. Don't ever be afraid to tell me about your life. If you want to share it, I want to know it. Can you do that? Tell me things even if you think I'll be upset and end up a mess like I am right now?" She gave him a little smile as she finished.

Al soaked in her words, let them seep into his worry lines. She didn't care about the new job. She only wanted to know him more. He could do that. Al smiled in relief. He really didn't deserve her.

"Lou, full disclosure from this moment on." He lifted one of her hands to his mouth and kissed it. He could see Lou take a quick breath, just like she did when they first met at the pub so many months ago.

"One last thing," Lou said. "Promise you won't be anything like the last guy."

"I can absolutely promise that."

He pulled Lou in tight, enjoying the feel of her in his arms, the vanilla smell always right behind her ears, her soft hair against his cheek. He didn't realize how terrified he was of losing her until just now. He took a deep breath.

"Feel better?" Lou asked.

"Quite, you?"

"Much better. Now, back to work. We have a feast to prepare."

"Lou, who is going to eat all this?"

"Silly man, Thanksgiving isn't about the meal. It's about the leftovers. Turkey-and-cranberry sandwiches, stuffing on toast, and gravy fries. Thanksgiving is great, but the day after is even better."

Yes, Thanksgiving was his holiday. Today was good, but tomorrow would be better.

. . . . .

"Isn't it pretty? An entire day's accomplishments spread out for consumption," Lou said.

"Like a fat man's fantasy."

Al and Lou sat at the table with the feast in front of them. Lou's arteries congealed as she recalled the pounds of butter that went into the meal and the two pies cooling in the kitchen. But you couldn't skimp on butter on a holiday, and any substitute would feel wrong to a girl born and raised in the Dairy State. At least she'd resisted putting cheese in half the dishes.

"Do you want to carve the bird? Or should I?"

"I'd love to, if you trust me."

"Butcher away—it all goes to the same place. Use these."

Lou handed him the carving knife and fork. Al tilted his head. The blade was typical, long and thin, not particularly sturdy. The fork had two tines attached to the handle. What caused Al to pause and what endeared them to Lou were the handles, covered in haphazard paint splotches of every hue. No sign of the original wood appeared under the rainbow handles.

Noticing his pause, Lou explained, "My family has used these since I can remember. One year, when I was about five, my dad explained how they were special utensils for holidays. I decided the plain wood wasn't good enough. I took the box when my parents didn't notice and hid it in my room. I spent months painting it just so. When I completed my masterpiece, I put it back in the hutch with the fancy plates and silver. At the next Thanksgiving, my father took them out to carve the turkey. He knew immediately what had happened."

"What did he do?"

"He asked my mother where she'd purchased such fine carving tools, because they were surely meant for royalty. My mom was so confused; then she saw my handiwork and played along. We pretended we were eating at a royal feast. I played princess and hostess. It was our best Thanksgiving."

"Rest assured, the Queen would be green with envy if she knew such a fine carving set existed."

Al set to carving the turkey, neatly removing the wings and legs, impressing Lou with his deftness. He removed the breasts and set them on a cutting board, then turned the bird to get at the thighs.

"This isn't your first bird," Lou said.

"We do eat turkey in England, just with slightly different trimmings."

While Al finished cutting the turkey to manageable pieces, Lou filled their plates with a little of everything. She still struggled with Al's new job. The hurt had surprised her. She had thought she was over Wodyski's bad review.

While they chewed, Lou examined the hurt, turned it around in her mind to see it from every side. He'd known she wouldn't like it—that was why he waited until he got the job. She could accept that as a thoughtful gesture. But why apply to begin with? He knew about the review; she was kidding herself if she thought he hadn't looked it up online to read it. He also knew how wrong that smug son of a bitch was. She'd served Al the very same meal Wodyski received and he'd raved about the perfectly cooked fish, delicate sauce—said Julia Child would be proud.

Lou thought about what she'd told Al in the kitchen, verifying she meant every word. She did understand wanting a job your partner didn't support. How long had Devlin begged her to quit the restaurant, never listening to her dreams? From what she knew about Al, he loved food as much as she did, but he also loved writing. Now he could marry the two—a perfect job. She could never deny him that. Yes, she did mean every word. She would support his job, be excited for him, and look forward to a few nice meals on the paper's dime; it was the least they owed her.

"So how is this going to work?" Lou said, bringing Al back from his happy place with the food.

He chewed and swallowed.

"Funny you should mention that. I could start by reviewing Luella's. Maybe that could help it out. Maybe even start a section in my column where I revisit Wodyski's bad reviews and refute the ones he got wrong."

Lou smiled at the gesture.

"No, you can't do that. At least not with Luella's. There would be too much bias, and it's too late. The closing date is coming like a cheek-pinching great-aunt."

Al nodded. "Okay then, so I won't review any restaurant you work at or own. But at least I can still visit."

"Aren't you worried people will find out what you look like?"

"Not really. Frankly, I think it would take the pressure off."

Lou's head bobbed and her eyes narrowed in thought.

"So, will you need any dining companions? I'd like to volunteer my services. I'll have some time opening up soon."

Al smiled. "You must be reading my mind. I can't think of anyone else more qualified. Plus, date nights on the paper sounds about right. Have you set a date?"

"Harley and Sue finally agreed to get new jobs, but I already know chefs who will hire them whenever they can start. I'm closing December twenty-second. We'll have one last party on the twenty-third, and everything will be ready for the auctioneers after the New Year." Lou took a few more bites and stared at her half-empty wineglass.

"I'm so sorry, Lou."

"Don't be sorry. It's not your fault. I thought I accepted it months ago, but now that it's less than one month away . . . it's really hard." The table clouded over as if she were looking at it through a fishbowl. Some of her face muscles started to cramp from holding in the tears.

"I don't mean to cry again; it's just . . . I worked so hard and I was so close. I keep wishing I could do it over, do it better. Now I just hope I don't owe money after the auction. If I could do it again, I'd . . . do things different. But I don't think I have the heart to try again."

Al got up, knelt before her, and grabbed her hands. She couldn't stop her heart from doing a little unexpected flip-flop.

"Don't say that. I'll help you do anything. Don't give up on your dream. It's not fair I get mine and you don't."

Lou took a shuddering breath and dried her eyes.

"Enough serious for today. Today is for giving thanks." Lou looked into Al's upturned face. "And I am so thankful you've finally started wearing jeans instead of khakis every day."

Al laughed.

"And I'm thankful you introduced me to squeaky cheese and frozen custard."

Al kissed the back of her hand, soothing her with his gentle touch. He still believed in her. Lou leaned forward and kissed the top of his head. She would find a new dream.

• CHAPTER TWENTY-THREE •

Lou sat at the center table, her empty restaurant still and peaceful. She usually liked the pristine solitude of an empty restaurant right before open, when the silverware lay ready for use, the bread warmed in drawers, prep cooks smoked their cigarettes behind the Dumpster having finished their mise-en-place for the night, the entire restaurant waiting for action. Today was different.

Dishes lay wrapped in boxes and the last few bottles of wine sat along the counter, ready to go home as gifts for her guests. Blank walls studded with nails bespoke the decorations that once hung. The tables sat bare, all the tablecloths sent back to the rental company. Most of the pots and pans sat on a counter in the kitchen, recently scrubbed and ready for auction. All the cupboards and shelves echoed with emptiness, their contents packed in boxes or set out to be used for tonight's feast. Yes, today was definitely different.

Open cookbooks and a scribbled-upon notebook covered the table. Lou had searched for a few ideas to add to Luella's last meal. Tonight she'd hold a dinner for the restaurant's remaining staff, Otto and Gertrude, and Al. Yesterday had been the last official day. Today, she'd use the last of her supplies before packing it up. Sue and Harley were starting new jobs after the New Year.

She should probably find some work, too. She picked up the phone, took a deep breath, and swallowed her pride.

After a few rings, Chef Tom's booming voice said, "Are you finally coming to work with me?"

Lou laughed, feeling better already.

"Get out of my head. Yes, I'm calling to beg for a job."

"It's me who's begging."

Lou's eyes began to tear up.

"This means a lot, Tom."

"You'd do the same."

"I owe you one."

Her voice cracked.

She hung up the phone, one more step away from her past and toward her new future. The bells jangled on the front door, a reminder to pack them before she forgot. She quickly wiped her tears away.

"Hey, love, I didn't expect you until later. I thought your parents were getting the grand tour," Lou said as she turned around to greet Al. But instead of Al's warm British accent, she heard a familiar voice, colder than she remembered.

"It's time we had our discussion, Elizabeth." Devlin's eyes reflected the chill in his voice. Lou inhaled as she stood up.

"We have nothing to discuss. Leave, please. You never came here when we were together, and I don't want you here now."

Devlin took his time walking toward her, observing all the packed boxes, empty walls, and clear tabletops like a general studying the enemy's weaknesses.

"I won't be long."

"Get out before—"

"Before what? You call the police?" A corner of Devlin's mouth turned up. "Really, you're going that route?"

"Fine." Lou waved her hand, indicating he should get on with it.

Devlin stopped to stand in front of Lou, and his eyes softened as he took in her appearance: her hair piled on top of her head, her clean but tired face and white chef's coat.

"We had a good plan together. We could still get back on track." He reached up to brush a strand of hair away from her face. Lou swatted it aside.

"Don't."

Devlin's eyes hardened like those of a hawk spotting its prey, and his lips pressed firmly together.

"I see. So, what does my replacement do for work?"

"That's none of your business."

"I think it is. I still want you in my life, even after all this time. I need to know he can take care of you better than I can."

Lou huffed, but she realized the sooner she played his game, the sooner he would go.

"He writes."

"Ah yes, a writer. Sounds almost as stable as a restaurant owner. What does he write?"

"He's a freelancer. And he just started as food critic for the paper."

"Just started? Huh. It took him a while to find a regular job."

Lou sensed Devlin building his argument, setting up his points as he would in front of a judge and jury.

"Quit the grandstanding. This isn't court."

"Isn't it? I think there'll be some judging needed after I tell you what Wonder Boy did."

"Are you so petty you'll try to ruin the one good thing in my life right now? That's below you, Devlin."

"I'm only thinking of you. I want to make sure you know who you sleep with at night." Devlin picked up a pen and flipped it between his fingers. "I have to admit, I'm surprised you're so committed to the man who destroyed your business."

Lou's face scrunched. "What are you talking about?"

"A. W. Wodyski." Devlin tilted his head, studying her reaction. "Haven't you ever wondered who he really was? You had to know that wasn't his real name."

Lou stilled.

"I did some research after I saw you at Irish Fest. I wanted to know who my future bride was spending time with." Devlin paused and looked Lou in the eye. "I really do care for you, Lou. You'll realize soon I know what's best for you."

He looked as if he meant it, every word. Lou's spine shuddered.

"You're making a lot of assumptions you have no business making."

Devlin leaned in toward Lou, but she took a step back. He inhaled and nodded.

"Imagine my surprise when I found out your toiling young writer's big secret. When you think about it, it starts to make sense. Wodyski started about the time Al moved here. Wodyski died, then your Al happened to get the open position. What if

Wodyski never died? What if he just started using his real name?"

Lou's stomach twisted as she sucked in all the awful words. She wanted them to bounce off, to not stick.

"You . . . you know nothing," Lou whispered, then found her voice. "That's all circumstantial."

"You don't have to believe me now. I know the truth. Now you do, too."

"You're lying."

It hurt to fight back the tears, but she would not cry in front of him.

"I don't lie, Lou. I may shape and bend the facts in my favor or make tactful omissions, but I don't lie. You know that." He paused, studying her clenched jaw and fists. "For when you're ready to accept the truth."

Devlin tossed a thick red-and-white paperback book on the crowded table and left, leaving behind echoes of doubt and disbelief. Lou read the title; it was a Polish-English dictionary. He had tucked one of his expensive personal note cards into it. She could see his slate-blue initials, DP, in the corner of the snow-white, thick stock.

She stared at the book, afraid of its contents. Her fingers twitched toward it. No. She shook her head to reinforce the sentiment. No.

Lou knew Al. He laughed at her silly jokes, savored good food, respected his parents, and showed kindness to Otto and Gertrude. A. W. Wodyski could not, could never be the same person she loved. They were not compatible.

With trembling hands, Lou stacked her cookbooks and the offending tome to carry into the Lair. She should know better than to let anything Devlin said distract her. She had a meal to cook, guests to entertain, and a man to love. Tomorrow, she'd finish packing up this life so she could begin her new one. Screw Devlin.

. . . . .

Al watched the delays flash across the airport monitors as he played with the square box in his pocket. It thrilled him to think about what it contained. How could a tiny thing hold so much hope and happiness? As Gertrude had said a few months ago, when you knew, you knew. Tonight, Lou would leave one path alone and start another path with him. Tomorrow, she could meet his parents, but they had to land first.

The first hard blizzard of the season charged toward them, forcing flights to delay their arrival and land in different airports. His parents' flight was due to land any minute. It was a race to see which would arrive first, the storm or the airplane.

"Dude, if you want to play pocket pool, choose a nice quiet bathroom stall, not the middle of the airport," John said.

"What?" Al looked down and realized what it looked like. "What do you expect? I haven't seen Lou since yesterday morning."

He chuckled at John's shock that he played along with his joke rather than act embarrassed as usual. That's what the Al of ten months ago would have done. That Al would also never be at the airport waiting for his parents. He wore jeans and a gray T-shirt under a plaid button-down. He'd thought about wearing the Brewers cap Lou had given him at his first game, but that might prove too much for his parents to take in at one time. He no longer stuck out when they went to bars. Milwaukeeans just didn't dress up for most nights out. Sure, they had the occasional bar or restaurant where the clientele wore trousers or dresses, but most places were casual. And he liked it.

Al started pacing to calm his nerves.

"You're starting to make me nervous. Is there something I need to know about your parents before they arrive?"

"No, sorry. I haven't seen them in over a year. I didn't realize how much I missed them until they bought their tickets. But a lot has changed since I left. They weren't thrilled with me leaving the country. I want them to see I'm happy. Does that make sense?"

"Give me a squish then and tell Mum all about it," a feminine voice said from behind him.

Al spun, grabbed his mum, and hugged her tight.

"Now that is a proper way to greet me. Step back so I can look at you."

The tiny woman dressed in black pants and a jacket, with a splash of color from a scarf, gave Al a once-over.

"Tsk, I expected you to dress up a bit more. But I have to say, it seems to suit you."

"Where's Dad?" Al said, looking around.

"Oh, he told me to come ahead and find you. He's getting the carry-ons down. He knew I couldn't wait to see my boy. Ah, here he comes."

A short man, looking like a slightly older version of Al, walked toward them wearing tan trousers, a white oxford shirt, and a tweed jacket complete with patches on the elbows. He pulled two small suitcases and carried another across his body.

Al went to take them, but before he could grab the suitcases, his dad pulled him into a tight hug.

"It's good to see you. Take these—I'm positively knackered." He handed Al the bag and a suitcase. They joined his mom, who was eyeing John with curiosity.

"Mum, Dad—this is my friend John. He's one of the finest writers I've ever met. John, my parents, Katherine and James." John grasped Katherine's hand and bowed over it.

"Pleasure to meet you. And may I add, that scarf is stunning. Vintage Hermès?"

"Yes, how did you know?" She looked pleased at the greeting, quickly forgetting his unusual appearance.

"John's the style editor for the paper. Look closely and you'll notice he's wearing couture from head to toe. He works very hard to make it look like he dresses out of the laundry bin."

"Yes, yes, we can focus on my deficiencies later. But now that they've landed, let's get back downtown before the worst of the snow hits," John said. The small group headed toward the parking garage, where John had his car.

Katherine looked around, then asked, "Al, where is your lady friend? I had hoped to meet her."

"You'll meet her in a day or two. She closed her restaurant yesterday and tonight is the farewell party, with only close friends." Lou didn't need strangers around on such an emotional evening, even if they were his parents. "That's why you'll be hanging out with John. I imagine you'll want to rest. Then tomorrow we can start seeing the city. I've picked up some movies and takeout menus."

"But you can't go out in this weather. The pilot said the storm coming was quite nasty," James said.

"Ha, welcome to Wisconsin. We don't let the weather stop us. We just drive slower and dress warmer," John added.

"It's true. Her restaurant is close enough to walk and I finally have boots and a coat warm enough. I'll be fine. And they won't cancel—not tonight."

"Well, I can't wait to meet her. From what you've mentioned on the phone, I may have a daughter-in-law soon."

"One can hope," Al said with a smile. The wind whipped around them in the small parking garage, but Al could only think of the warm kitchen where the center of his universe prepared a feast. With luck, they would find plenty to celebrate tonight.

• • • • •

Cooking always cleared Lou's mind. Planning a menu was the mentally taxing part; making food soothed her with the repetition of chopping, the simplicity of following a recipe, even if it was in her head. In her kitchen, everything was so familiar, she could almost close her eyes and prepare a full meal. Three steps to the fridge, bend down to get the limes, plates were in the warmer next to the stove, exactly as they should be.

After Devlin's visit, she needed the calm to soothe her rattled nerves, stop her shaking hands. While chopping, sautéing, and blending, Devlin's words replayed in her mind, pinging off her exposed heartstrings while her faith fought them off. She refused to believe what Devlin'd said was true.

She could hear the wind whoosh around the buildings, sending sheets of white snow across the front window like a thick curtain, blocking out the buildings across the street. She'd thought about postponing the dinner, but she didn't have any options for rescheduling. She called Harley to see whether he could pick up the Meyers. They shouldn't be coming out in this weather, but Lou knew they didn't want to miss it. He assured her he'd already called and made plans to pick them up in his large truck.

She'd finished all the prep. The rest of the cooking would wait until right before serving. Time to get ready. As she entered the Lair, her eyes passed over the Polish-English dictionary she'd thrown at her desk—the red-and-white cover contrasting with the scattered paperwork. She picked up the dictionary and turned it over in her hands, trying to feel the truth it might contain. If she looked, then she could set the issue aside, prove Devlin wanted to cause doubt. But looking would be a testament to her doubt. If she looked, that meant she didn't trust Al.

Lou tossed the dictionary in the garbage. Done—now she'd shower and get ready for the party. Grabbing the dress hanging on a nail in the wall, she ducked into the bathroom. By the time she dried her hair, put on a smattering of makeup, and slipped into her dress she felt better, more put together, even though her work life had completely imploded. Today she ended one life and began another, one in which Devlin held no sway.

Lou looked at the clock; she still had a half hour before people would start to arrive. The mountain of papers, bags, and random objects on her desk threatened to topple. Now seemed a good time to at least remove the top level. Lou moved a stack of old menus and tossed them in the garbage can. Underneath she found her favorite red purse. She'd been looking for it at the apartment but must have forgotten she had left it here months ago.

She sat in the desk chair to go through the contents, hoping to find a forgotten twenty. Old receipts and State Fair ticket stubs went straight into the garbage. Lou pulled out another handful to discover a wadded piece of newspaper. She flattened it on her desk to see A. W. Wodyski's review of The Good Land. Now she remembered—Al had given this to her last summer at the State Fair. She'd been so angry she'd crammed it in the bottom of her bag and forgotten it.

Her stomach twitched, signaling something important was about to happen. Before she could second-guess herself, Lou read the article. At first, reading Wodyski's article calmed her worries and she enjoyed the well-written description of a delicious meal. The same delicious meal she and Al had shared, down to the special items Chef Tom had sent out. Lou paused her eyes on the page. Those dishes wouldn't have been served to a normal customer; he had created them for her.

Lou's body knew the truth before her mind did. It thrummed with numbing energy, making her limbs move sluggishly. The article trembled in her hands. She lifted and dumped the garbage can. Menus fluttered around her, covering the ground in white; the red dictionary lay amidst them—a fresh cut on new snow. Moving as if she were in taffy, she bent to pick it up; it felt as if the hand closing around the book were someone else's. She drew out the note card, written in Devlin's hand:

A = Al

W = Waters

Look up Waters in dictionary.

Shaking, Lou paged through the English side to "water." It read "woda, plural = wody."

Wody. Waters. Wodyski. A. W. Wodyski.

Lou's legs wobbled, then folded, and the dictionary thumped to the floor. Devlin hadn't lied, but it was she who had the real proof—the article. Everything else was ash on the already burnt fish. A. W. Wodyski and Al Waters were the same person. Wodyski never died; instead, he made love to her every night. Her heart burst into flame.

Al knew the entire time. Lou shivered, holding her knees close, grappling with the trickery. She recalled meeting him that day with the coconut cake, the day her engagement ended, the day he reviewed her. The day that review appeared, he seemed jubilant at the bar. He had just crushed her restaurant. And the days at Northpoint Custard, the art museum, Irish Fest. All those days he watched her restaurant fail and did nothing; no retraction, no remorse, no feelings.

Her hand still clutched the wrinkled article. Why would he give it to her? Did he intend to show her how clever he was? That didn't ring true. It would be easier if it did. Then she could be angry and anger could protect a broken heart while it mended.

This time she couldn't climb out of the pit to get to the anger. The hurt was too much, the deception too clear. Tears finally loosed themselves, washing away her minimal makeup, leaving mascara tracks. She remembered his words on Thanksgiving: *I'll help you do anything. Don't give up on your dream. It's not fair that I get mine and you don't.* Was that guilt or guile?

He had promised to be honest.

The fire in her chest fizzled into cold ash. Lou crumpled onto her side, letting the pit swallow her whole. When Sue opened the door, she found Lou curled on the floor, surrounded by white papers.

"Oh my God, Lou. Are you okay? Do you need to go to the hospital?"

Lou held up the article for Sue and tried to sit up.

"I don't understand. Almost everyone's here." She took the article from Lou. "Are you sick?"

Sue's presence reminded Lou she did have people who cared about her, believed in her. It bolstered her enough to sit up and shake her head that she wasn't sick.

"Is Al here?" Lou whispered.

Sue looked baffled.

"No, he's the only one not here yet."

Lou looked up at Sue, her destroyed heart visible on her tear-soaked face.

"Al is A. W. Wodyski." Lou's voice cracked as she said it, as if she didn't want to say it out loud because that would make it real. Sue laughed.

"Don't be absurd. How could he be? He just got the job at the paper. His reviews are nothing like Wodyski's."

"Read that."

Sue quickly read the review, then looked up, more confused.

"It sounds like he really enjoyed the meal."

"That is the meal Al and I shared at The Good Land. Chef Tom sent out some special dishes for me. You know how he likes to spoil other chefs. A normal customer would never have gotten those."

"I'm sure there's a million explan—"

"Yes, I've already thought of them. The simplest explanation is often the right one. 'Wodyski' derives from the Polish word for 'waters.' It's right there in the goddamn name." Lou got up off the floor and handed Sue the dictionary and note card with a shaky hand. She breathed deeply. The anger trickled in her, burying the pain a little, helping her continue.

"Why do you have a Polish-English dictionary and this?" Sue asked, waving the card.

"I got it from Devlin."

"Devlin gave you this? I think you have your answer right there. You know—"

"I'm not wrong about this. Al is A. W. Wodyski," Lou shouted. "I've looked at it from every angle. It's true. Regardless of Devlin's intentions, he didn't lie." Lou could tell when Sue accepted the truth. If she had been a dog, her hackles would have risen. That was one of the things Lou loved most about Sue—she always protected with ferocity and determination. Al better hope Lou got to him before Sue did.

After she wiped the tears from her face, removing the worst of the raccoon eyes, Sue and Lou left the Lair to join the party. As they entered the kitchen, Harley's voice boomed.

"We're all here. We're waiting for the guest of honor."

Lou looked out the pickup window to see Harley standing next to Otto and Gertrude at their favorite table. Both looked happy, but shaky and pale from their adventure out in the blizzard. The large front window looked covered in Styrofoam from all the snow sticking to it. Al walked around the bar, snow clinging to his hair. He shook the snow off, set his coat over the back of a chair to dry, and dried his face with a napkin while chatting with Harley and Gertrude.

Lou's face paled and her breath came fast and shallow.

"You can do this," Sue said in her ear.

She blinked several times, as if she were trying to move a grain of sand out. With a deep breath and clenched jaw, Lou tightened her grip on the article and grabbed her favorite chef's knife from the counter. Sue raised her eyebrow at her, but grasping the blade comforted her, brought things back into perspective. Sue carried the book and card, like a soldier carrying extra ammunition into battle.

When she emerged, Al sat with Otto and Gertrude. Though her attention focused more on Al, she registered that Gertrude looked even thinner and Otto had worry lines on his previously smooth forehead. When Al saw her, he paled and looked fidgety, but a bright smile crossed his face. Lou's heart panged.

He looked so believable, and part of her still wanted to be with him, forget this awful mistake. Lou strode across the empty dining room, each step adding to her anger at him for making her feel betrayed, humiliated, hurt. It was his fault she had to close her restaurant, shutter her dream. Her nostrils flared. Al noticed and the smile melted off his face, like the snow on his hair: slowly at first, but faster as the heat of her anger became more palpable. Lou's lips were thin and tight; red anger tinged her cheeks.

"Lou?" Al asked as she stopped in front of the table. Four faces looked up at her with confusion, Sue standing behind her like a proper lieutenant. Lou banged her fist on the tabletop, causing the water glasses and silverware to knock together.

From behind clenched teeth, she said, "Out."

Her body vibrated with the anger racing through her system along with the blood flushing her cheeks.

"What the hell, Lou?" Harley said, starting to stand.

Al sat still, resolved as her anger slapped at him. Lou slapped the review on the table in front of him, then stabbed her knife into the review. The handle quivered when she removed her hand.

"Get! Out!"

Her hands shook; her whole body twitched. Tears singed her eyes, nearly sizzling as they slid down her heated cheeks. Sue set the dictionary and note card next to the article.

Al's eyes went to the note card and a look of confusion crossed his face. Then he squeezed his eyes shut, clenched his jaw, and nodded with a deep breath, understanding the full story. As Lou towered over him, he rose, put his still-damp winter coat back on, then reached into his inner coat pocket to pull out something. He moved his hand over the review and opened it. Al looked into Lou's stony face, hoping for some softening. Instead, she turned her face from him. She would give him no break. When he pulled his hand away, a small, square, red leather box with gold trim sat next to the knife, still wobbling from being thrust into the table. With another nod, Al turned and walked to the door.

Before pushing it open, Al turned and said, "I'm so sorry, Lou . . . about everything."

Then he walked out into the blizzard. Lou watched him disappear into the whiteness and wind, a shadow figure, then gone. Gertrude and Otto raised their faces to Lou. She couldn't tear her eyes away from the little box, staring as if it were a rat in her kitchen.

"What in the hell just happened?" Harley said.

Sue grabbed his arm, then pulled him aside to explain.

“What’s in it?” Gertrude asked with her soft voice.

Lou looked at her blankly; her lungs stopped working. As if it might bite her, she picked up the box. She hesitated, not sure she really wanted to know. If she never opened it, she could pretend it contained a pair of earrings. Gertrude interrupted her thoughts.

“Open the box, Lou. You know what it is. He loves you.”

Using her thumb as if she were opening a mussel, Lou popped the box open. Her eyes widened and Gertrude leaned over to see the contents. A brilliant round diamond hung suspended in a platinum band. The simple band emphasized the modest gem. It was simple, romantic, and elegant. Lou slumped in the chair, head in her hands, and wept. Gertrude rubbed her back with a delicate hand and whispered soothing yet ineffective words.

What could she say?

Lou thought she knew loss after ending it with Devlin and her restaurant failing, but that seemed pleasant compared to right now—watching the beautiful ring sparkle, taunting her with its promise of a perfect future. Instead, she had to watch it disappear into the snow. Lou put her head on the table as Gertrude rubbed her back, wishing she could disappear into the storm, too.

• CHAPTER TWENTY-FOUR •

The frying pan made a spectacular sound as it hit the brick, a solid *thwunk* followed by a pattering, magnets flying off like firework sparks, carving out a chunk of wall from the impact site. Al threw the empty whiskey bottle at the same spot, missing it by three feet. Glass rained down, adding glittering specks to the rainbow-hued detritus. He staggered across the room to admire the effect. The destruction felt good, but it didn't lighten the chains hanging around his conscience.

Karma had found him, and he'd paid the price for his arrogance. He walked back to the kitchen to search for another bottle. Behind his wineglasses, he found a half-empty bottle of vodka. That'd work. While unscrewing the cap, he leaned against the counter. Al didn't think he could stand straight and tilt back the bottle at the same time. Better be safe than sorry. Before drinking, he listed his head to the side and studied a trail of red marks on the floor, difficult to see against the rosewood. Huh, it looked like blood. He dropped his head to see his feet, which were smeared with scarlet streaks.

"Bloody hell. Ha, bloody," Al said to himself.

Al sank to the floor, the counter supporting his back, sliding his feet until his bum hit the wood, leaving a long stripe of red. He reached for a towel hanging on the oven door and started wiping the blood off his foot, smearing more than removing. Must have stepped on some glass. Probably not too bright to be barefoot. He took a long swig from the bottle. This should be enough to knock him into oblivion.

He leaned his head against the counter, closing his eyes. He needed to get new lights; these were much too bright. Everything blurred anyway. The whiskey and vodka were almost doing their job. But Lou's face, red with anger, wet with tears, was still displayed crystal clear on the back of his lids. He would never forget her face, the hurt so plain. He could have tried to explain, but he didn't deserve it. He didn't deserve her.

He pulled a slightly bent white note card from his shirt pocket, the note card he'd received months ago from an anonymous source. It suggested he review Luella's. He had held it in his hands when he first encountered Lou at the newsstand. It was an unexpected gut punch when Sue set its twin next to the Polish dictionary. When he sobered, he'd give some thought to who wrote them.

He took another swig, staring at the white spot where the frying pan had hung, and waited for the liquor to knock him out.

He heard footsteps in the hallway. A tiny part of him, buried deep, hoped Lou had come to talk, to forgive him. Instead of her pale face framed in soft brown hair and kissable lips, he saw his parents. Bugger. He had forgotten about them sleeping off their jet lag in the guest bedroom.

"Alastair, what are you doing on the floor, I thought you were at a party, is that blood?"

His mom said it as one long question, her pitch rising as the interrogation morphed into panicked inquisition. This did not help the situation. His dad walked past the progressively hysterical woman. She was decidedly un-British when it came to her children. James stood in front of Al, sizing up the situation.

"He's pissed. Best get him cleaned up and to bed," James said.

"But why is he bleeding? Why is my baby bleeding?"

"Calm down, Katherine. He's fine. Can you get a bowl of water and some clean towels to clean up his feet?"

Katherine began digging through cupboards, searching for the requested supplies.

"Has he been burgled? Should we call the police?" Katherine continued her stream of questions.

"He's sloshed, drunk, arseholed. He's done this quite on his own. No one's attacked him."

Al's brain whirled like a Sit'n Spin in his head from moving it back and forth, trying to follow his parents' conversation.

"Why would he do this? He's never done this," said Katherine.

That wasn't entirely true, and his dad knew it. He did it once before, during university. He'd fallen hard for a daughter of a minor royal—Portia. They went to pubs, checked out movies, cheered at polo matches for his brother, Ian, and appeared at all the right parties. He thought about proposing, even took Ian ring shopping with him. He knew he couldn't afford the kind of ring a girl like that expected, but she loved him and he loved her. He'd buy her a better one when he could afford it.

During a weekend party at a friend's country estate, he'd overheard her trying to seduce Ian. When Ian refused, as she was his brother's girl, she'd explained she was only dating Al to get to know Ian. He'd promptly kicked her out and apologized to Al, but the damage was done. Al had spent the next week drinking until Ian called their dad.

Al had expected his dad to lecture him about never turning to drink to solve problems. Instead, he'd commiserated that sometimes you need to get really pissed so your body feels as bad as your heart does. Once every fiber in your being feels like bloody hell, you can start mending the broken bits one day at a time. It helped him find the first bits to mend: his family.

"Sweetums, we won't get any answers today. I'm guessing the cuts came from stepping on the broken bottle all over the other room. If you can, why don't you sweep it up," Al's father said. "And I'll call John. I think we could use his help."

Katherine rushed off to find a broom.

Al had tried to explain, but it came out only as mumbles. It appeared he drank enough that his mouth no longer functioned. Someone took his bottle away—he couldn't tell who. Black crept in from the sides until all he could see was his father's face, mouthing words he couldn't understand. Then sweet oblivion.

. . . . .

Consciousness came back the reverse of how it went: first a circle of light framing his father's face, then growing to reveal his worried mum and a serious-looking John. Wait, one difference: instead of his not feeling anything, everything screamed. His mouth tasted like cheap whiskey used to disinfect a toilet, then stored in a dirty ashtray. His stomach agreed. Before he could fall out of bed in the direction of the bathroom, he felt a bucket land in front of him and his father said, "About time. Better out than in." His mother left the room.

Al heaved until he saw stars, then fell back into the pillows feeling much better. He took stock of all his body parts: stomach woozy but better, head contained a thousand sharp-toothed chipmunks intent on gnawing their way out, feet stung, everything hurt. His father and John shared concerned looks, and Al figured he should explain. He cleared his throat.

"Lesson learned—don't try to replace blood with whiskey."

His lips tried to twist into a smile but failed.

"This is not funny, Alastair. Your mother and I—"

"And me," John added.

"Quite right, and John, were very worried. We came in last night to you barely conscious, sprawled in the kitchen with bloody feet."

Oh yeah, Al remembered, the glass. That explained the stinging feet. He lifted the covers to see stocking-covered puffy feet.

"We bandaged them and put socks over to keep everything in place. They'll be fine in a day or two," said James.

"Thanks," replied Al.

"That's it? Thanks?" John said. "I think you owe us more than that."

Al looked behind his father at John.

"She found out. I went to propose, and she'd found out. I cocked up."

Al could feel the tears starting to burn behind his eyes again. The whiskey should have dried those up.

"Language, Alastair. And what did she find out?"

Al's mother came up the stairs carrying a tray full of tea and scones, the same tray Lou had used when he had faked sick. The sight almost sent him reaching for another bottle. Mum made him a cup with just a little tea and handed it to him.

"Now tell us what she—I'm assuming you mean your lady friend—found out," said Katherine.

Al sipped the hot tea. It helped. It bolstered him enough to admit what he had done. The arrogance, the unprofessionalism, the lies, and the breakup. The last part was new to John, too. They let him finish without interruption.

"You're lucky she didn't stick that knife in you. You quite deserved it," Katherine said when he finished. "That poor girl. Everything she's been through because of you."

"I'm not responsible for all of it. She dated that arse all on her own." Al paused, having put a few things together. "And he may be more involved than I thought." Al told them about the note card he had received suggesting he review Luella's several months ago, and the matching card he saw with the Polish dictionary yesterday. He realized now that the *DP* were initials, Devlin Pontellier's initials.

Katherine handed out tea to the rest of the group. John sniffed it, then dipped a finger in to taste. Satisfied, he took a drink.

"So you're just going to let her go?" John asked.

Al looked as if he'd been hit by a train.

"What am I to do? I wouldn't forgive me. How can I ask her to?"

"She doesn't know the entire story; from what you said, she thinks you knew the entire time, that this was one big joke on her."

"You're right. She should know the entire truth. I can't let her think I used her," Al said. Hope blossomed a little in his eyes. "You think she might listen?"

"Don't be all talk and no trousers. And you can't tell her anything moping about in bed," James said, pointing at some fresh clothes on the end of his bed.

"Make her listen. She has an answering machine. Leave a message on that," John said.

Al nodded, thinking about what he wanted his darling Lou to know most. When his mum and dad went down to the kitchen, John snickered.

"Your name is Alastair."

"Bugger off."

"Merry Christmas to you, too."

Then he trotted down the stairs, leaving Al alone with his delicate stomach, tender feet, and a scrap of hope.

• CHAPTER TWENTY-FIVE •

She didn't remember getting home after the dinner. Sue had settled her on the couch with a blanket, some tea, and a promise to call her in the morning. Sometime after Al had disappeared, her emotions shut down. Too much data and too many crashes, and now she was the human equivalent of the Blue Screen of Death. She had sat on the couch all night, staring at the calla lily painting propped on her mantel.

When the sun rose, she put on her coat and walked to the nearby Sendik's, stopping at the ATM on the way. The balance on the screen said $63.39. She took out sixty dollars.

The grocery store was full of harried people finishing their Christmas food shopping. Lou ignored them all. Weaving through carts and shoppers, not deviating from her precise shopping list, she collected her items and paid for them, leaving her with $2.45. She bought a two-dollar scratch-off lottery ticket and dropped the forty-five cents into the Salvation Army bucket by the exit.

Back in her apartment, she unpacked the items (the scratch-off was a loser). She planned to make a roast beef, a pile of mashed potatoes, corn—then mound it into a bowl and drown it in gravy. Some people ate ice cream or pie when depressed; she went for the warm comfort food she learned to make in her grandma's kitchen.

While the beef roasted, Lou slipped into her pajamas, complete with a ratty bathrobe and bear-claw slippers. When it finished, she took a big bowl, mixed the beef, corn, potatoes, and gravy all together like her dad used to do, and sat cross-legged in the center of her bed. A little eating in bed seemed warranted.

With each bite, her emotions rebooted. Her heart ached, her anger simmered; she had lost her restaurant, didn't have any money . . . and Al. Al. Al was the fifty-ton straw that broke the camel's back. Her tears fell to season her food.

Her phone rang and she let it go to voice mail. When the phone chirped, indicating there was a message, she played it. Even though she knew who had left it, hearing the voice yanked at her insides.

"Lou, I know you don't want to talk to me, but I want you to know everything so you hate me for the right reasons. I did write that review; I didn't follow up. It was the most unprofessional thing I've ever done, and it was a mistake. When I first met you, I was a very different person. I will never regret anything more than that review, except if I didn't tell you the entire story now. I tried to get a retraction, or even write a new review, but my editor wouldn't let me. That doesn't make it right. I'm sure I could have done something.

"I didn't know you were a chef until the morning after the barbecue. After our first night together. It never occurred to me you were the Lou of Luella's—I knew the owner as Elizabeth. It was too late. I already loved you. I tried to stay away. I faked the trip to California and being sick to give me time. But I couldn't stay away. You were so amazing, so wonderful, and I was selfish and greedy for you. I came up with the crazy plan to kill off Wodyski so then I could get hired as the new critic. I tried to protect you, but I know that was a mistake, too. That's the story, the whole story. I've lied to you in so many ways, but you still know me better than anyone ever has. You know the real Al Waters, the Al Waters who loves you. I'm so sorry."

Lou sat still, absorbing the long message. The onslaught of information came at her like a bear attack. She curled herself into a ball, tucking her head into her hands. Each loss was another clawed swipe. Her restaurant. Her family. Al. She was alone. Just she and the onslaught. She wasn't brave enough to fight back or strong enough to run away—she could only take each brutal blow. She stayed curled tight, praying she'd survive.

• • • • •

The ringing phone pulled Lou out of her bed. It was a local number she didn't recognize. She cleared her throat before answering so it wouldn't sound like she had just woken up.

"Hello." The throat clearing didn't work.

"Ms. Johnson?"

"Yes?"

"This is Pam with the St. Boniface Hospice. I'm calling because Otto and Gertrude Meyer requested we contact you."

Lou was awake now.

"Okay. Are they all right?"

"We've admitted them both. They asked that we let you know."

Lou looked around her dark bedroom. Clothes lay scattered. Dirty dishes threatened to topple off her nightstand. There was a definite funk in the air.

"Can I visit today?"

Pam with St. Boniface Hospice paused.

"I think that would be a very good idea."

"I'm on my way. Thanks."

Lou hung up the phone.

Five days after Luella's last supper and five days since her last shower, worry about Gertrude and Otto had her moving again. Life continued, and there were people who still needed her. She pulled on the nearest clothes and darted out of her apartment.

• • • • •

Lou rushed past fake presents stacked under an artificial Christmas tree to the hospice's front desk. Paper snowflakes cut out by children hung from the ceiling and each door had red stockings with the patients' names. The fluorescent lights made the decorations appear garish next to the boxes of gloves and hand sanitizer hanging every few feet. The staff tried to create a festive air, but you couldn't hide illness and death under sparkly garlands and Santa window clings.

The woman at the desk wore reindeer scrubs and a name tag reading "Pam." She had a Santa hat with a pin that read "All I want for Christmas is a narwhal."

"Hi, I think I spoke with you earlier," Lou said. "I'm here to see the Meyers."

Pam looked up and raised an eyebrow at Lou. Lou looked down at her clothes. She wore hot pink sweatpants, a red "Teach me how to Bucky" sweatshirt, and her green Crocs. Covering her messy hair was a knitted cupcake hat. Pam blinked.

"Yes, that was me. Are you family?"

"No, a good friend."

She nodded.

"They're in one-seventeen, fourth door on the left."

Lou hurried down the hall. As she approached the door, a nurse came out of the Meyers' room. Lou pulled her hat off her head and smoothed her hair. The nurse saw Lou and stopped.

"Are you here to visit Gertrude and Otto?"

Lou nodded.

"You must be Lou. I'm Val. I'm their afternoon nurse today. They've mentioned you."

"How are they?"

"They're extraordinary, as I'm sure you know. Healthwise, not well."

"I just saw them a few days ago."

"At their age, things can change very quickly. Bottom line—Gertrude has had stage-four breast cancer for a while. They've chosen not to treat it and instead to manage the pain. Otto seems to be deteriorating along with Gertrude. It isn't unheard of in a couple this close."

"That's it? They just die?" Lou's knees wobbled.

"This is what they want. They've been very clear about their wishes—that's why they're here instead of the hospital. We'll make them comfortable."

Lou just blinked at her. It felt as if a dump truck full of sand had just landed on her.

"Are you going to be okay?"

She shook her head and tried to speak, but her mouth twisted itself like a Slinky mangled by a toddler. "Mmph," was all she could manage.

Nurse Val opened her mouth to speak, then closed it. Then opened it again.

"You know you have mashed potatoes in your hair, right?"

She pointed to a spot near Lou's shoulder. Lou ran a hand through her hair, feeling the dry, crusty chunks. That explained a lot.

"Ugh. Long story."

Val smiled and nodded.

"I think you should go in and talk with them. You'll feel better."

Nurse Val squeezed her arm and left while Lou tried to scrape the potatoes out of her hair with her fingers. Sadness hung in the air, floating down the hallways, seeping under closed doors. People spoke in whispers to not draw Death's attention too soon.

Lou entered the room, expecting the same sorrow and distress. Instead, thin and pale versions of Otto and Gertrude lay in twin beds, turned toward each other, both smiling. Their love sent out a beacon of calm, their shared memories a bulwark against despair. A few IVs dripped from their hooks, administering the pain medications needed, but serenity reigned in room 117.

Lou studied Gertrude. The hospital bed nearly swallowed her. Lou frowned at seeing her good friend so weak.

"Ach, *Liebchen*, don't make that face," Gertrude said as Lou stood in the doorway. "Come here."

Lou squeezed Otto's cold hand in greeting, then slipped into the chair between the hospital beds so Gertrude could see her face. She reached out to hold Gertrude's hand, noticing the blue fingertips and chilled skin. She had never been around death. Her parents had died so quickly she'd only had coffins to comfort her.

"This face better not be for us. We have lived good, long lives."

She looked at Otto, who had drifted off to sleep, then back to Gertrude.

"Does it hurt?"

"Nothing a tough woman like me can't handle." Lou chuckled. "It hurts more to see those we love sad about something inevitable. We are born, we live, if we are lucky we love, then we die. That is the way, not something to mourn. Only mourn those who haven't lived, who haven't found love. They deserve your sadness, not us."

Lou held her hand, wanting to savor the powdery softness of it, the smell of ivory soap and tea, the comfortable sweat suit she wore, so unlike her normal crisp attire.

"I don't know what to say," Lou said.

Gertrude smiled at her honesty and reached up to touch her cheek.

"Say you will forgive your young man."

Lou's face turned stony; only her respect for Gertrude kept her from pulling back from the touch.

"I can't do that, Gertrude. He betrayed me too deeply. He destroyed my life."

"You love him, yes?" Lou nodded. "I saw his face. He didn't defend himself; he didn't try to talk his way out of your accusations. That is not how a bad person would act."

"The Al I thought I knew couldn't have written that article."

Gertrude took several short breaths and pointed to her water. Lou gave her a sip. Seeing her dear friend struggle with a simple task frightened Lou. It seemed another bit of joy was getting sucked out of the world. She took a deep breath and returned the cup to the table.

"Maybe you didn't know the Al who wrote it. Maybe you knew a different Al, one who knew and loved you. People change. You are worth changing for." Gertrude pointed her finger at Lou.

"It's too soon. I can't even think about him without getting so angry I want to . . . pry his teeth out with a dinner fork."

Gertrude's eyes crinkled and her shoulders moved a little, trying to express the laugh she didn't have energy to make.

"Little savage. Just don't let your heart get too hard. He made you happy. That was not an act. Try to forgive him—promise me."

Lou looked into Gertrude's watery eyes and pale face, her wispy hair floating away, the first part of her escaping toward heaven. She couldn't deny Gertrude.

"I promise."

"Good, now where is my Otto? I need to rest."

Lou stood and moved the chair so she could push Otto's bed closer to Gertrude's. Gertrude's eyes still sparkled in response. Lou bent over to kiss Gertrude on the cheek, then did the same to Otto.

"I'll be in the chair if you need anything."

Gertrude's lips twitched, but her eyes were already closed, her breathing slow and sleepy.

Lou settled into the chair to watch over her favorite customers and think about Gertrude's request. She had been happy, even amid her restaurant failing, but with her emotions rubbed raw from too many assaults, Lou needed a distraction. Being trapped in the hospice bubble isolated her, leaving her in close quarters with her troubles and amplifying the solitude. The more time alone, the more she worried about Otto and Gertrude, her stalled career, and whether her heart would ever heal.

The subdued quiet was only broken when nurses came in and out, checking vital signs and replacing IV bags. One suggested she take a shower, handing her a towel and soap. Afterward, she scrounged up a notepad and pen from the nurses' station.

Over the next day, Lou sat vigil as Gertrude's breathing became more labored, her skin more purple. She scribbled ideas in the notepad. New recipes, table settings, and a plan. Sometime in the night a nurse brought her some bland chicken noodle soup and stale crackers. Lou kept writing. A new restaurant was being born even as Gertrude's breathing became more ragged.

Action in the hospice picked up as the sun rose, and visitors came and went. Midmorning Gertrude opened her eyes and beckoned Lou over. She bent close to Gertrude so she could hear her whisper.

"What are you writing?"

"A business plan. For a new restaurant."

"Good. Second chances are good."

Lou tilted her head in confusion. Gertrude waved at the notepad.

"You deserve a second chance at your dreams. Otto was my second chance at love."

"It will take some work, but I have a plan. Do you want to hear about it?"

Gertrude nodded and listened as Lou poured out all her ideas.

"It is a good plan." Her breathing became short and quick. "*Liebchen*, you must take my advice and find your happiness."

"I will."

Lou rubbed Gertrude's icy hand, more purple than not.

"Keep my Otto company until he is ready?"

Lou nodded.

"Of course."

Gertrude took a deep, wet breath, patted Lou's hand, and closed her eyes again, reaching for Otto's hand. Lou helped her find it, linking the two together, as it should be. She walked to the coffee station, trying to control her breath. The nurses she passed nodded and let her have some privacy.

When Lou returned to Otto and Gertrude's room, Otto's breathing was loud and heavy, but the two still held hands. Gertrude's covers had slipped off her legs. Lou pulled them up and noticed Gertrude wasn't breathing. She watched for a few minutes to make sure, as a mother would watch her newborn baby, then sigh in relief as the chest rose and fell. But Gertrude's chest did not rise and fall. A tear plopped on the blankets. Lou covered Gertrude up, made sure Otto still slept, and went to tell the nurses.

• • • • •

Otto stayed unconscious while Gertrude's body was wheeled away. Lou knew because she held his hand the entire time, feeling it grow colder. She pulled the chair next to his bed and continued to plan. It kept her mind from dwelling on the remarkable people the world was losing.

Otto moved his sheets and opened his eyes.

Lou's stomach twisted. She had to tell him. She reached for his hand and looked into his shiny blue eyes.

"Otto, Gertrude passed earlier today."

Otto smiled and nodded his head. Of course, he knew already. He tilted his head toward the door.

"I'm not leaving you alone. I promised Gertrude."

He worked his mouth until he could manage a crackled whisper.

"When you love someone, *Schätzchen*, you are never alone."

Lou kissed his forehead.

"Thank you for everything." Lou's voice choked. "Give Gertrude a hug when you see her."

Lou picked up her notebook and settled into her chair. She looked back at Otto's shining head and peaceful face, thinking about second chances.

Otto died in the early morning, Lou keeping vigil.

• CHAPTER TWENTY-SIX •

Lou swirled a spoonful of browned butter on a plate, set a preserved lemon in the center, then topped it with a small piece of sautéed Lake Michigan whitefish. She sprinkled parsley over the top like confetti and stepped back to admire the new dish. Otto and Gertrude would have loved it.

Since she'd started at The Good Land a few days ago, Chef Tom had been letting her play with new ideas before her shift. She enjoyed working in a busy restaurant, feeling the heat of a dinner rush and the rhythm of a well-run kitchen. While his restaurant was much bigger than Luella's, it didn't take long for her to fit in. She would enjoy the steady income, too. But these weren't her recipes, they weren't her ideas feeding the hungry diners. That's why the few hours when she got to play in Chef Tom's sandbox were her favorite of the day.

"When's the funeral?" said Chef Tom as he walked up beside her.

Lou gave him a small smile.

"Wednesday."

Tom put his arm around her and squeezed. Lou sniffed and slid the plate toward him.

"What's today's invention?" He already had a fork in hand.

"Deconstructed Lake Michigan whitefish meunière."

"Bit tiny, isn't it?" Tom winked.

"It's meant to be a small plate." Lou rolled her eyes.

"May I?" Chef pointed his fork at the dish.

"You're the boss."

"Yes. I am." He sliced into the fish, making sure to get some of the lemon and butter. He set it on his tongue and chewed thoughtfully. If she'd done it right, he would experience the browned butter first; then it would be cut with the tart and tangy lemon, followed by the barely crisp, flaky fish. As he chewed, the flavors would meld together to replicate the classic dish, but in an entirely new way. Lou held her breath as Tom swallowed, then grinned.

"That is the best one yet, Lou." He studied her as he took another bite. "While I love having you here, you're wasting your talent on my line."

"You could always let me add some dishes to the menu."

"Ha! This is my kitchen. I make the menu. Get your own kitchen."

Lou gnawed her lip.

"Speaking of my own kitchen, I've been thinking about that."

"As you should."

Tom took another bite.

"Some of us don't have buckets of money being thrown at us by abundant customers."

"Yes, yes, your point."

"I have my business plan written for a new restaurant. Could you read it? Give me your thoughts?"

"Of course. Bring it in tomorrow."

Lou's lips twitched.

"It's already on your desk."

Chef Tom sighed dramatically.

"Oh, fine—I'll go read it. And get that dish ready as the small-plate special tonight."

Lou glowed. Tom really was a great friend. She started breaking down whitefish into small pieces and making sample plates for the waitstaff to try, then worked on her regular prep. She cleaned up her station, putting the final touches on her mise-en-place. She turned to see Tom standing behind her with the business plan in hand. He was rifling through the pages.

"So?"

He looked up at her, his face serious. Lou was used to the jovial Chef Tom, not this one—the one reserved for his vendors and accountants.

"That bad?" she asked.

"No, this is really good. Great, actually. Are your numbers accurate?"

"I think so. That represents the money I owe and that one is the value of the equipment." Lou pointed to a spot on the page. "I'm looking at a less expensive property, and my start-up costs will have to be smaller than with Luella's, but those numbers should be right. If the bank gives me the loan I'm asking for, I can start a very small kitchen—just me, a waiter, and a dishwasher. Only four or five tables. Very intimate."

"What if you had an investor?"

Lou's face got dreamy, then frowned.

"I'd love the extra money, but not having to keep them happy. I'd rather do it my way."

"What if that investor gave you one hundred percent control of his share because your idea is so great he just wants to be a part of it?"

She grinned, understanding Tom's meaning.

"Don't get too excited. It wouldn't be a lot, but I've had a good year," Tom added.

"It would be more than enough. I'll call the bank."

Lou bounced as she dialed, buoyant at the thought she could soon climb back into her own sandbox.

• • • • •

Snow floated down in big, fluffy flakes, creating white car and tree silhouettes, muffling sounds, and converting the city dirt to a heavenly white. The ethereal weather brought those who mourned them closer to Gertrude and Otto, lending their joy and serenity to the solemn occasion. Lou had no idea what to expect at their funeral. The two had paid for and made all the plans in advance. They even had arranged for a *Spanferkel* roast afterward.

Almost two weeks had passed since she had spent those few days in hospice. During that time, she'd worked at The Good Land, gotten her life back in order, and learned the Meyers had left their house to her—while not enough to open a new restaurant, the surprise inheritance brought her plans that much closer to reality.

Lou had unearthed her one dark suit from the back of her

closet, ironed it the best she could, and walked the few blocks to the funeral home. She intended to be there from beginning to end. She owed it to them. Harley, Sue, and most of her restaurant staff would arrive later. When she entered the building a few minutes before the visitation, the funeral home director was already waiting by the door, somber and looming.

All funeral directors reminded her of Lurch from *The Addams Family.* It wasn't fair, and this gentleman looked nothing like him, but the association always stuck and caused giggles to surface at awkward moments. While the thought was absolutely inappropriate, it kept her mind occupied while approaching the open coffins.

She cherished their final moments together. They had given love, support, and hope—gifts she could never repay, nor would they want her to. Lou would miss them, but she was ready for her second chance. She gave each hand a little squeeze.

"Auf Wiedersehen."

Lou walked away to collect herself and read the cards on the many flowers. She knew Otto and Gertrude had a full life outside her restaurant, but she always felt she had them all to herself. The flowers were evidence of how wrong she was. She turned to see many people cautiously entering the room. Some distant great-nieces and nephews collected in one corner. Lou offered her condolences and introduced herself. She didn't think they really knew much about their great-aunt and uncle, not beyond the chitchat at family functions.

Lou wandered the room to find some photo albums and posted pictures. In every single image, they touched each other: holding hands, a hand on a shoulder or knee, or a full embrace with cheeks squished together. That was her favorite, something you expected teenagers to do, and it was one of their more recent pictures. They ate food in a lot of pictures, too, sitting side by side at picnic tables or lounging on a blanket in the grass.

The room filled up quickly, so she settled into a back chair, hoping there'd be enough seats for any of her former staff that came. Sue and Harley eventually arrived, as did many waitstaff and busboys. They surrounded her in their corner of the room, a phalanx protecting their lost commander. It felt good to be with her family, even in this sad setting; she'd missed them.

When the service began, Lou felt a tingle at the back of her neck. She turned to see Al enter the back of the room with a very hairy and rumpled man. He glanced her way, gave a nod of acknowledgment, and turned toward the minister. Lou turned back, too, not sure what to think about the newest mourner.

• • • • •

Don't look again. Don't look again. Whew—she turned around. If he looked at her again, he wouldn't be able to control himself; he'd be on his knees begging in an instant. He'd heard about Otto and Gertrude's death in the office. Hannah had called him in to ask whether he knew them. Their obituary was written based on a packet of information the deceased had wanted included. They wanted it known they frequently ate at the remarkable Luella's, owned by Lou Johnson. He'd only met them a few times, yet they'd left an indelible mark. The two together seemed unbeatable, impervious to the ups and downs of life. For them, it was only ups as long as they were together; they made sense. As a model of marital harmony, he could think of no better.

He intentionally entered just as the service began, bringing John as insurance. He meant to pay his respects, not harass Lou. But she looked so broken when their eyes met. Dark circles marked her face, and she looked too thin. All the chairs held bodies, heads facing the minister who talked about soul mates and shared happiness. Al didn't care much for funerals; they reminded him of his limited time to prove himself.

His parents had stayed for two weeks after the incident. He'd spent that time discussing his future with them, sharing many of the places Lou showed him: the art museum, The Good Land, Sprecher Brewery, and Miller Park. Alas, Northpoint Custard was closed for the winter, but they had one at the airport. When he drove his parents for their flight home, they had left early to eat at the custard stand. He had ordered everything and set it on the table in front of them, a communal feeding trough for the family.

"That's lovely. It smells just like the fish 'n' chips shop by the house," his dad had said.

"I know. But this is quite a bit better. Try the perch. So much tastier than cod."

They had sampled in silence, with a break to mutually agree the deep-fried cheese curds represented genius—evil genius, but genius.

"So, you're staying then?" his mum asked.

"Of course. Why wouldn't I?"

"You seemed reluctant to come, and then with the misunderstanding." Katherine waved her hand and continued, "We thought you might want to come back to England."

"Mum, it was a screwup, not a misunderstanding."

"Language, Alastair."

"Anyway, I thought about leaving. I could make a fresh start, create a new identity. But I like who I've become and I like this place. I fit here. I've made new friends, and it has an exciting, eclectic food scene I want to watch grow. I'm not proud of how I started, but I found myself here. I'm not going to leave and risk getting lost again. So, I'm afraid you'll just have to visit soon. Though try the summer next time." It went unspoken, but he knew they were thinking that Milwaukee also housed the woman he loved.

• • • • •

The noise of many people moving at once brought Al out of his memories. The service ended and people filtered out into a large dining room, forming a line at the *Spanferkel* buffet.

"You coming?" John pointed a finger toward the food.

"No, not hungry."

John joined the line as Al noticed Lou in her seat, waving her friends toward the food, her head down, and a wadded tissue swatting at tears. He'd taken a step in her direction when he saw Devlin sit down next to her. Al stepped into the foyer to watch. He should've left. But he didn't.

Lou stiffened but nodded when Devlin spoke. She stood to walk away. This time when his lips moved, she turned and strode toward the bathroom.

Devlin rose and stalked toward the exit but noticed Al hovering in the entry.

"You. You screwed it all up," he said, pointing his finger into Al's chest. Al didn't flinch.

"You don't get it, do you?" Al said, moving Devlin's finger off his body.

"Get what? That people don't leave me? That she belongs with me? I can take care of her."

"Lou can take care of herself." Al paused. "You dated her for a couple of years, right?"

"Yes."

"In all that time, you never once understood who she was. She has a gift, one you've never appreciated. She has too much talent to hide away in your kitchen preparing fancy meals. She's not a private chef you can shag after dinner."

For someone who grew up at an all-boys school as the son of a teacher, Al possessed a surprising lack of knowledge about how to take a punch. So when Devlin threw a hammer fist at his face, Al's reflexes didn't know to duck. He heard a sound like a lobster cracking open. Hot blood streamed from his nose, leaving an iron taste in his month.

"I guess I hit a nerve," Al said, trying to stanch the flow with his thumb and index finger.

Devlin pulled back his fist to deliver another punch, when Al held up his hand.

"One more question. Why did you send me that note card suggesting I review Luella's? You expected me to skewer it, right?"

Devlin dropped his arm, guilt on his face.

"That's what I thought," Al said. "You were so used to getting your way, you didn't care if it destroyed your own fiancée's dreams."

His eyes lifted to see Lou standing in the doorway, her brows knitted together. He nodded to her, then turned and walked out, pulling a white handkerchief from his pocket to mop up the damage.

• • • • •

Lou stepped forward to go after him, then stopped. It wasn't the right moment. She needed more information and time. Her wounds still stung from his lies. But Devlin. It should surprise her that he had urged the infamous A. W. Wodyski to review her restaurant, but it didn't. At the least, she should feel something, but she just didn't care about him anymore. She was more concerned about the bloodied writer who ran out into the snow.

At least Devlin's hand looked like it hurt, too. He rubbed it and stretched the fingers, working out the pain from punching with enough force to break Al's nose. Devlin turned around to see Lou watching him.

"Lou, you need—"

"No." Lou held her hand up to stop his prattling. "How dare you take my choices away from me. After all this time, you still know nothing about me. I've never wanted your vision. You've always pushed me toward a mold you thought I should fit into. But I'm not a little housewife, content to entertain your colleagues over dinner parties, staying home to raise children I'm not sure I want. And I'm not your mother, working at a job I hate to pay the bills. Quit trying to make me into someone else. I'm me. A chef, complete with burns, freakishly strong forearms, and an affinity for brightly colored plastic footwear." Lou paused. "I'd thank you for coming to the funeral, but you never even met Otto and Gertrude."

Lou stepped forward to give Devlin another piece of her mind when Harley appeared and loomed in front of him, arms crossed, face foreboding. Behind him appeared the scruffy guy who came in with Al, though his pose of disdain didn't induce the same level of intimidation as Harley's. Sue rounded out the trio. They glared at Devlin until he retreated to the door and out into the snow.

Lou joined the three enforcers in time to hear the new guy speak.

"He really is a tool, isn't he? Who punches a diplomatic guy like Al?"

Lou put a hand out and said, "Hi, I'm Lou."

A grin split the man's beard, reminding her of a Muppet.

"I'm John." Lou was about to ask how he knew Otto and Gertrude when he added, "I work with Al at the paper."

Sue laughed. "He told us in line he's the style editor."

Trying to process him as a style editor distracted Lou from all the questions she had about Al and the note card from Devlin that he'd mentioned.

"Really?" Lou scanned him up and down. "I always pictured someone more like Tim Gunn."

"That's why I don't usually tell people, but I felt honesty would be a better approach given recent events. I'm now regretting that decision."

He glared at Sue, who giggled even more. Even Harley suppressed a laugh.

After seeing Al in person, coupled with the voice mail he had left, Lou had questions about him and his motivations. John could probably answer those questions.

"It's nice to meet you, John. We need to talk. Tell me, how do you feel about *Spanferkel*?"

. . . . .

Lou tapped her foot on the coffee table as she and Tom waited for the lender to retrieve them. Her business plan sat in her lap, along with her loan documents. A woman with straight, brown hair and a friendly smile greeted them.

"Hi, Ms. Johnson, I'm Lisa. Why don't you follow me to my office?"

Lou and Tom trailed after her, settling into a small room. Pictures of children lined the bookshelf and manila envelopes were stacked on every surface. Lisa began flipping through the folder in front of her.

"Now, let's start with where we are. You've already missed a few payments on the loan with us for your current restaurant, Luella's. Correct?" Lou nodded. "Unfortunately, I'm under pressure from the loan committee to declare it a default and accelerate the final payment. I'm assuming you're here to discuss that?"

Lou's stomach curled. She hated this part, the negotiating, the possible rejection. Tom kicked her. She swallowed.

"Yes." Her voice squeaked. "I'd like to propose a second chance. One that would let me keep my loan, avoid an auction, and get payment back on track."

Lou felt sweat dripping down her back. If her nerves didn't let up, she'd leave a puddle on the chair.

"I like that as an idea, but what has changed?"

Lou laid out her new business plan and flipped to a page covered in figures.

"Recently, I inherited a house. I plan to sell it and use the proceeds to help cover some of my debts. I've also acquired an investor." Lou pointed at Tom, who grinned at the lender.

Lisa smiled back, then studied the numbers.

"This does seem to solve your cash problem, but I don't see how this will help with the restaurant you just closed."

"I'd like to restructure the loan for a new restaurant. The business plan outlines everything."

Lisa paged through the papers.

"The last thing the bank wants to do is seize and take back collateral, then try to sell it. I like that you're here, fighting for your business, and your plan seems viable. And having one of the most successful chefs in the city on your side doesn't hurt." Lisa grinned at Tom. "While I can't lend you additional money, we do want to see you succeed. If the numbers work and your new business plan is sound, we should be able to work out something. We'll review everything and call you in a few weeks, but from where I sit, it looks good."

Lou exhaled slowly. Lisa looked from her to Tom.

"Don't you want to add anything?"

Tom's smile expanded.

"I'm the silent partner."

After so much rejection and disappointment, Lou let the sweet relief spread. Her numbers were accurate. She would get the loan restructured. She would get her kitchen. She would get her second chance.

• CHAPTER TWENTY-SEVEN •

Lou spread the last of the frosting onto the cake. She could never get it as even as Harley did, but that's what the toasted coconut was for—to hide the flaws. She pressed the crunchy topping onto the sides and top of the cake, pausing to toss a pinch into her mouth.

She boxed up the cake and attached the note, her heart thumping with worry that her plan wouldn't work.

She poked her head down the hall and shouted.

"John, are you almost done? It's ready to go."

"Almost," he shouted back.

Lou poured herself a cup of coffee and flipped through a stack of papers on her counter. She pulled out Al's review of The Good Land. She'd reread it a few weeks ago. He described the food lovingly, taking the time to explain why it excelled, not just that it tasted good. No wonder he had found such success as a food critic. The beginning reminded her how much Al had changed since they first met:

> Milwaukee is all too often the butt of a joke, derided as a northern suburb of Chicago, the dreaded fly-over country. The streets are paved with cheese, rivers flow with beer, and cows run wild in the streets. Every native Wisconsinite can milk a cow, wears overalls, and drives a tractor. It's a blue-collar town of simple tastes and simpler hobbies.
>
> And in many ways, it is all of those things, but if you stop there, you'd be selling the city (and state) short, as well as denying yourself a true pleasure. As Alice Cooper explained so patiently to Wayne and Garth, mee-lee-wah-kay is Algonquin for "the good land." And it is.

He really wasn't the same man who had eviscerated Luella's almost a year ago, who'd written all the biting critiques before that. After the funeral, she spent time with John and learned Devlin's role in A. W. Wodyski's review. John had confirmed her realizations. Al—the man who had fallen in love with her and her hometown, who had confessed to his complete asshattery, and who took a punch to the nose for her—deserved a second chance.

John walked into the kitchen and Lou gave a soft whistle.

"You look lovely," Lou said, smoothing his hair a bit. "Make sure to call when you arrive so I know you got there safely. And remember, I'm a size ten."

John's smile distracted her a little. He looked so handsome—great hair, sparkly eyes, even his teeth impressed her.

"What do you think of the outfit?" John asked, crinkling the shirt in his hands.

"Stop wrinkling everything. You do that all the time."

"Sorry, old habit."

"Your clothes match your look perfectly. No need to mess them up."

"Really?"

John's brow furrowed.

"Trust me. I love the way you look."

"I'm not used to having a female opinion."

"Get used to it, because I can't give any other kind. We could call up Harley to ask his opinion if you'd like. I'm sure he'd be flattered and full of useful dressing tips."

"Funny." John checked his watch. "Oops. I should get going."

"Okay. You have the box and know what to do?"

"Fear not, dear lady." John picked up the kelly-green box, pecked Lou on the cheek, and headed out her apartment door.

She'd better hurry or she'd be late, too.

• • • • •

The spring sun lit up the newsroom, forcing the pallid writers to squint at their screens. But after the long winter, no one wanted to suggest closing the blinds. Al noticed people escaping on coffee runs just to get outside on the first warm day in months.

"So, will you visit?" Al said into his phone.

"You really want me to come? To Milwaukee? You seemed quite against it last time," Ian said.

Al smiled. "It's grown on me. A lot."

"Brilliant. I've been reading your reviews and I want the grand tour."

"You read my articles?" Al sat up straighter, like he did during school when he answered a question correctly.

"Of course I do. It's the only way I find out what you're up to. Speaking of, I like that you're using your real name now."

"Me, too."

"So, when should I visit?"

"How about mid-August, for Irish Fest? You'll love it."

"I can't wait. I'll let you know when I make the arrangements."

"And you're staying with me. No hotel."

Ian laughed. "Perfect."

"Later."

Al set the phone down and smiled, thinking of all the places he wanted to show Ian. He glanced at his Brewers schedule to see what home games fell during his brother's visit.

With a happy sigh, he looked toward the sun-filled windows and started his electric kettle; no outside runs for him today. He'd been working on a feature article for the last few months, the idea planted by Lou on one of their nondates. He'd researched how the different ethnicities within the city influenced the growing food culture, with an emphasis on the ethnic fests, his favorite part of Milwaukee's summers.

It had been over three months since he saw Lou at the funeral. His eyes slid to the cast-iron pan now hanging in his cubicle, covered in magnets, one for each special memory with Lou. He brought it to the office now that he spent more time here. It tracked not only his love for her but his love of the city.

He looked at the clock: four hours until deadline. He

should make it. He stood, bent over to touch his toes, now covered in clean black Converse sneakers. He wore blue jeans and a T-shirt with a sport coat covering the back of his chair. His Brewers cap sat on the edge of his desk; he usually wore it when he went out to restaurants or bars, unless it was a nicer place. His polos and khakis were buried in his full closet, all his suitcases unpacked. Al sat back down to finish his column.

He heard a noise behind him and assumed John finally showed for work. He rarely arrived so late in the day.

"Hey, John," Al said without turning. "Everything okay?"

"This is for you," John said. He saw John's arm set something green on his desk, elegant black-and-silver cuff links blinking at the end of an Italian wool sleeve. Al barely registered what the arm held because he struggled to merge the posh clothing with John's voice. He spun around to confirm it was actually John. Al's mouth fell open.

In front of him stood an impeccably dressed man: crisp Italian suit, subtle lavender dress shirt, matching pocket square, creased trousers, and polished black leather loafers. His honey-brown hair was cut neatly, emphasizing the solid, beard-free jawbone and strong facial features. Al's first instinct was to ask where John had gone.

"Are you going to see who it's from?" John said, pointing at the box.

Al's mind started clunking into motion, and a smile emerged in anticipation of the entertainment to come.

"What happened?" Al finally said.

"Come on, dude; don't make a big deal."

"Don't make a big deal? This is a very big deal. You have a

face." Al's voice got louder and other staff started popping up to see what had happened. The women didn't pop back down. John started looking uncomfortable with the staring.

"Please," John said.

"This is what you were hiding. I thought a dog bit half your face off, or you had a mole the size of Hong Kong. Mate, you're a looker."

John sighed, pulled out his chair, and plopped into it.

"This sucks. I feel naked." He rubbed his face with his hands. "I'm actually colder now. I need more clothes because the breeze makes my face cold. How dumb is that?"

"So why the change?"

"Paris."

"I thought fashion season was over."

"I'm doing a piece on how the houses translate their haute couture into prêt-à-porter. I'm going to Louis Vuitton, Catherine Malandrino, Givenchy, Chanel. I don't know how Hannah did it, but she got me ins at the best."

"It's because I'm the best editor in the world and you two will never forget it," Hannah said as she walked into their cubicle. "You look hot. If I didn't know what you looked like yesterday, I'd consider cuckolding my husband."

John looked horrified.

Hannah laughed.

"Buck up, pretty boy." She turned her attention to Al and said, "So Al, what's in the box? It smells incredible."

Al hadn't noticed; he'd been too fixated on John's transformation. He took a deep breath and sniffed.

It couldn't be.

But please, God, let it be.

He swiveled to face the box, a bold kelly green, the color grass yearned to attain, tied with a piece of white string. Taped to the top was a crisp white envelope with a small bulge. He carefully peeled it off, enjoying the smell, the rising optimism in his chest. He pulled out a heavy white stock card, the kind wedding invitations were printed on. It revealed a sample menu for a new restaurant named A Simple Twist, featuring an eclectic, ever-changing menu that caused his mouth to salivate. The only constant from day to day would be an amazing coconut cake. Al smiled.

Something fell out onto the desk. It looked like a black oval. When he flipped it over, he realized it was a magnet: a pristine white coconut cake on a matching stand, set against a background the same color as the box. He mentally cleared a spot in the middle of his cast-iron skillet and added the magnet to his collection, leaving ample black space around it.

With reverence usually reserved for a favorite toy or Grandma Eileen's Waterford Crystal goblets, Al untied the box and lifted the cover. Coconut teased him with tropical deliciousness; then the vanilla he so often smelled on Lou's neck wafted up. He ached to hold her, smell that spot right behind her ear. The cake, frosted and covered with toasted coconut, beckoned, wanting to be cut and eaten immediately.

What did this mean? Had she forgiven him? He checked the envelope for a note, a hint, anything to tell him how to proceed.

He turned the menu over. Written on the back in Lou's inconsistent scrawl was an address and three words: "Bring the Cake."

This time Al laughed.

"What?" Hannah and John said at the same time.

"I'm taking the afternoon off." With that, Al grabbed his coat, picked up the cake box, and headed toward the exit. Hannah stepped in front of him.

"You have a deadline."

"And where are you going with the cake?" John asked.

Al looked straight at Hannah and said, "I'm sorry. I've never missed a deadline. I know this one's important, but I couldn't finish it now if I tried. I've got to know what this means." Al lifted the cake. "I'll take any consequence you give me. I'll write obits for a month, report on traffic court—I don't care. I'm going."

Hannah stepped aside with a nod, and he jogged as fast as he could without jostling the box.

The address on the menu was only a few blocks from the paper. He arrived in minutes, breathing hard, though not from the fast pace. Outside, thick green curtains covered the window, hiding the construction within, with the exception of a small table covered in matching kelly green. On the table sat a white cake stand with the words "A Simple Twist, Coming Soon" painted in green.

Al yanked on the door, his palms slipping on the silver handle, his heart pounding.

• • • • •

Lou looked up from the open kitchen when she heard the door jingle. Earlier, she had hung up the bells she had rescued from Luella's. At A Simple Twist, watching the chefs work would be an integral part of the experience. Not to mention, she'd also get to watch the guests. She smiled when her eyes met Al's unsure gaze as he stood in the restaurant's entrance staring at her, not quite believing she had really summoned him here.

"I like the name," Al said. He took a few more steps into the restaurant.

"Thanks." Lou noticed he had the box. "Thank God—I worried the office vultures would discover it before you did. Or that John might drop it." She walked around the counter carrying a plate, a knife, and two forks.

"John? You saw John?"

"Of course. Didn't he deliver it? He was supposed to. Doesn't he look amazing? Who knew all that was hiding under the bushman? Poor guy doesn't know what to do with all the attention." She worked hard to keep her voice casual. She hadn't been sure he would come, that he still felt the same. She still didn't know about the latter.

Lou noticed Al struggling to keep up. Warmth for him bubbled to the surface, but not enough to enlighten him immediately.

"How is this possible?" Al asked, turning his head to look around the restaurant.

Lou's eyes misted and her voice cracked as she said, "Follow me."

She led him to a table standing in the center of the dining room. On it sat a silver framed picture of Otto and Gertrude, their cheeks squished together, making them look decades younger than they had been. Al's eyes watered a bit when he noticed, making Lou feel even better about the decision she'd made to take Gertrude's advice.

Lou reached for the frame and opened the back, pulling out a folded paper.

"Before Gertrude and Otto's funeral, their attorney contacted me about their will. They had left me their house. It wasn't enough to pay for a new restaurant, but enough to reignite the dream—which was their intention. The money came with two requests. One was that I reserve a table in the center of the restaurant for them."

Lou looked at the picture of the smiling faces. God, she missed Gertrude's optimism and Otto's steadfastness.

"What was the second?"

"That if I got a second chance, I needed to give one, too."

Lou cut a piece of cake and set it on the plate.

"Where did the rest of the money come from?"

Lou smiled.

"I did it the old-fashioned way—hard work, creativity, and help; in my case that means Chef Tom and the bank."

Al nodded, unsurprised by her accomplishment.

"There's one more thing," Lou said, looking serious again. She reached into her apron pocket and set the red leather ring box Al had given her on the table.

"You gave this to me. You should have it back. . . ."

"I don't want it back. I gave it to you because—"

"Let me finish. You should have it back until you know what you want to do with it."

Al's face melted from anger to relief to understanding. He reached for the box, and Lou worried for a moment he meant to take it back. That wasn't supposed to happen. Things were going so well. Instead of pocketing the ring, Al got down onto one knee, popped open the box, and pulled out the ring he bought months ago.

A little awed, he slowly looked up at Lou, giving himself time to gather his words.

With a deep breath he said, "Lou. My feelings have not changed at all. I've hoped for this chance and I'll be damned if I'm not taking it. I love you. I love you for the million kindnesses in your heart, your infectious enthusiasm, your search for the perfect deep-fried cheese curds. I love that you take apart a recipe, look at the parts, then put it back together better than before. I love that my first memory of you is the smell of vanilla, coconut, and bacon. I love that you wear Crocs in the kitchen and heels when we go on dates. I want to fill a wall with magnets for all our special memories. I want to carve the Thanksgiving turkey using your hand-painted carving set every year for the next fifty. I want to cook with you, laugh with you, make love to you, and most of all, I want to spend the rest of my life with you. Elizabeth Luella Johnson, will you marry me?"

Al's voice wavered with emotion toward the end, but as far as proposals went, he nailed it. Her answer was much simpler.

"Yes."

Al slid the ring on her finger. He stood and pulled her to him, taking her face in his hands. Neither could contain their silly grins. Al studied her face as if searching for any changes he needed to memorize right away. Would he kiss her already?

Lou grew impatient. Sick of waiting for him to give her what she wanted, Lou pulled him in for a proper kiss.

• • • • •

A bit later, they sat at Otto and Gertrude's table, neither wearing shoes, and Lou hadn't picked up her apron from where it lay crumpled.

She took a forkful of cake and offered it to Al. With their eyes on each other, he took the bite off the fork. With his mouth full, he said, "Perfect. I've waited a year to taste this cake. So worth it."

"Is that an official review?" Lou raised an eyebrow.

Al squirmed. "Um . . ."

Lou laughed, then leaned in to kiss him again. She rose, buttoned on her chef's coat, slipped her feet into the spongy green shoes, and picked up her apron. As she retied it, settling it into the ideal spot on her hips, she looked at Al, still sitting in front of the cake, shaving slices off, then tossing them into his mouth like tequila shots.

"Do you need to get back to work?" Lou asked, twirling the new ring around her finger and chewing her lip.

Al got to his feet, looking around the empty restaurant, boxes stacked in corners, books and notebooks filling the empty tables, and pots and pans scattered among fresh vegetables and meats in the open kitchen. He stood in front of Lou, looking into her melted chocolate eyes.

"I'll stay as long as you'll let me. I can't imagine a better place to spend my time. Can I do something to help? Or will I be in your way?"

Lou's infectious smile spread to Al's face, even though he didn't know the reason for it yet; he was just happy he helped put it there.

"How would you like to sample some truffle and foie gras sausages?" Lou grabbed his hand, led him to the kitchen, and wrapped a crisp white apron around his waist.

"Truffles? Fantastic."

Lou pulled the bow taut and stepped back to admire her new fiancé standing in the middle of her new kitchen, eager to taste her dishes. She noticed a bit of frosting on the edge of his lip, so she kissed it off.

Gertrude had been right. Second chances are good, and they taste like coconut cake.

• GRANDMA LUELLA'S • COCONUT CAKE

Though Harley says to weigh the ingredients, I'm giving the instructions the way Grandma Luella gave them to me. If you prefer to weigh, you can find nifty conversions on the Internet.

Make sure to bring all the ingredients to room temperature before mixing.

5 large egg whites (save the yolks to make homemade pudding—yum)

¾ cup cream of coconut

¼ cup coconut milk—make sure to stir the contents very well to recombine before measuring (save the leftovers for Thai food or your coffee)

1 large egg

1 tsp coconut extract

2 tsp vanilla extract (I've been known to use more—make sure it's REAL vanilla. I prefer Mexican vanilla, but use what you like)

2 ¼ cups cake flour

1 cup sugar

1 tbsp baking powder

¾ tsp table salt

12 tbsp unsalted butter, softened, cut into 12 pieces

1 recipe Coconut Frosting (see p. 313)

- Preheat oven to 325 degrees. Brush or rub melted butter onto two 9-inch cake pans (you can use cooking spray, but the butter will taste better), then line the pan bottoms with parchment paper (trust me, this makes cake removal so much easier). In a medium bowl, whisk the egg whites, cream of coconut, coconut milk, whole egg, and extracts together until combined and set aside.

- In a large bowl, whisk together the flour, sugar, baking powder, and salt. With a mixer on low speed, beat in the butter, one piece at a time, until the mixture resembles coarse crumbs, 2 to 5 minutes (about 2 minutes for a stand mixer, closer to 5 minutes with a handheld mixer).
- Increase the speed to medium-high and add 1 cup of the egg mixture. Beat until light and fluffy, about 45 seconds (a little longer with a hand mixer). Add the remaining egg mixture in a steady stream and continue to beat until the batter is combined, about 30 seconds. Scrape down the bowl and beaters as needed.
- Divide the batter evenly between the two cake pans and smooth the tops with a spatula. Bake until a wooden skewer inserted in the center of the cakes comes out with a few crumbs, about 30–35 minutes. All ovens vary, so be careful not to overbake. Rotate the pans halfway through baking.
- Let the cakes cool for 10 minutes on wire racks. Run a knife around the edge, then flip out onto the racks. Remove the parchment paper, flip the cakes upright, and let them cool completely before frosting.

• COCONUT FROSTING •

You can toast the coconut however you like: oven, microwave, or stovetop. I like to do it in a nonstick skillet on medium-low, stirring every few minutes. Careful once it starts to brown, as it can go from toasty goodness to burnt crud very quickly. I spread it out on paper towels to cool and save any leftovers to put on ice cream.

2 tbsp coconut milk

1 tsp coconut extract

1 tsp vanilla extract

pinch of table salt

16 tbsp unsalted butter, softened

¼ cup cream of coconut

3 cups powdered sugar

2 cups toasted coconut

- Stir the coconut milk, extracts, and salt together until the salt dissolves.

- Beat the butter and cream of coconut in a large bowl at medium-high speed until smooth, about 20 seconds. Reduce the speed to medium-low and slowly add the powdered sugar. Beat until smooth, about 2 to 5 minutes. Beat in the extract mixture. Increase the speed to medium-high and beat until the mixture is light and fluffy, about 4 to 8 minutes.

- Set one layer of cake on a cake stand or plate. You can use a daub of frosting to keep it in place. Take 1 cup of frosting and spread over the bottom layer (an offset spatula works well for this). Sprinkle with toasted coconut. This gives a nice crunch in the middle of the cake.

- Set the second layer on top of the first. Scoop out the remaining frosting onto the top of the cake. Spread the frosting to the edge of the cake, working it over the sides and down, spinning the stand or plate as needed to frost all sides of the cake. Don't worry about making it too pretty—the toasted coconut will help hide the flaws.

- Press the toasted coconut onto the sides of the cake, and sprinkle it over the top.

- Cut and hide a piece immediately because people will soon arrive to swipe your cake—I'm looking at you, Harley and Al.

· ACKNOWLEDGMENTS ·

The journey from first scribbles to finished book takes years of work by many, many people. Here's my attempt to thank them. I'm sure I'll forget someone important, so my apologies if I left your name off—it isn't because you aren't valuable, or you don't deserve credit, but because I'm flawed and have a sucky memory. I'll keep better notes for book two—I promise.

There's something special about that first person in the publishing community who pulls your story out of the slush and proclaims it worthy, something other people need to read. A huge and hearty thank-you to Rachel Ekstrom of the Irene Goodman Literary Agency for pulling *C3* out of the slush, washing it off, and seeing its potential. You worked your ass off to find *C3* a home.

Speaking of home, to my brilliant editor Kate Dresser at Gallery, thank you for falling in love with *C3*. Your enthusiasm shone through in all your comments, coaxing out the best in *C3*, and making it so much better than I ever thought possible. I couldn't have asked for an editor with more excitement and passion for my book. I'm still giddy that my words are in your very capable hands.

Thank you to Gallery for making my book Real (with a capital *R*). Louise Burke, Jennifer Bergstrom, Ciara Robinson, Jaime Putorti, Kristin Dwyer, Susan Rella, and anyone I may be forgetting—I am grateful you believed in me and my book. Your hard work makes me feel like my book was the only one you were working on. I'm a lucky author to be in the Gallery family.

Thank you to Regina Starace for designing my beautiful and perfect cover. I couldn't love it more.

Thank you to Baror International, Inc., for selling foreign rights.

Both Erin Niumata and Jessica Sinsheimer offered incredible feedback on my manuscript and query, without which I'm not sure the book would have made it to publication. You are both shining examples of the generosity and good-spiritedness in the publishing world.

Ann Christensen at *Milwaukee Magazine*—thank you for answering all my questions about restaurant reviews. You were more than generous with your time. You inspired all of Al's good behavior. Any errors are mine.

To all the chefs I have worked for, thank you for such good fodder for what happens in a kitchen. I edited out most of the cursing.

Andrew Heacock—you made me a beautiful website. I love it!

My local friends Val and Bob Wisniewski, Pam Gosenheimer, Courtney Marschalek, Lynnette Gunville, Jill Walworth, Joan Folvag (who also owns a magnificent coffee shop), and so many more I know I'm forgetting. You all kindly asked about and listened to my woes and successes during this long process.

My backside deserves a shout-out—it survived lengthy hours in uncomfortable chairs to finish this book. I promise I'll get you more exercise in the future.

Kelly Johnsen, thank you for reading an early draft, but more importantly, for taking my stunning author photo. I'm sure there are very technical explanations for how you capture the beauty in all your subjects, but to me it's magic!

To Erin Reichert, my awesome and bilingual sister-in-law, who not only read my book, but also provided me with German terms of endearment. You are my *Liebchen*!

And to Tom Reichert, thank you for being a supportive and enthusiastic brother-in-law.

To all my beta readers, Sue Molin, Brandi Manthas, Maria Cancino, Kate Clausen, Paula Kabara (who also keeps my hair looking fabulous), Sarah Cannon, Carla Cullen, and Sarah Henning, your helpful feedback made me a better writer. Especially those of you that read the early drafts when I had no idea what I was doing—your time was an invaluable gift.

Melissa Bielawski and Mark Benson, not sure what I would do without our ongoing conversations—you have saved my sanity more than once. Every writer should have friends as loyal and willing to call "bullshit" as you both are. *boob bump*

Ann Garvin—you are my writing guardian angel. You're the first writer who read my work, kindly patted me on the hand, and told me I had a lot of learning to do. We are kindred spirits and I'm so happy we found each other all the way in NYC.

My mother-in-law, Sandy Reichert—a writer couldn't ask for a more supportive and enthusiastic cheerleader!

To my siblings, Pam Lehman (also my bingo partner-in-crime), Steve Guertin, Paul Guertin, and Cathi Alonzo. One of my favorite childhood memories is each of us in a separate corner of the cabin reading our book of choice. I love that I'm part of a book-loving family and I love that a family gathering isn't complete without a lively book discussion.

To my mom, the matriarch of our book-loving family—your nightstand is never without a book or two. You've shown me over and over again that we Guertin women can do anything—so I did. I love you!

My beautiful and patient children, Ainsley and Sam—so much of what I do is to inspire you both, to show you that you can do anything with hard work and persistence. My proudest moments are when I hear you tell people that your mom is an author. And yes, using Twitter is working.

John Reichert, my husband, best friend, first reader, and most trusted consigliere—sharing this with you is one of my greatest joys. When I first told you I was writing a book, that's when it became real for me—a thing I was doing. That's when I knew I would see it through to the end. You've been supportive from that moment on, with helpful feedback, taking the kids out of the house when I needed work time, and understanding that I'm probably just going to get weirder—and loving me more because of it.

G

GALLERY READERS GROUP GUIDE

The Coincidence of Coconut Cake

· · · · · ·

AMY E. REICHERT

INTRODUCTION

The last thing Lou, a talented and tireless Milwaukee chef, expects to lose when she dumps her cheating fiancé is her beloved restaurant, Luella's. But when an off night in the kitchen—fueled by heartbreak and frustration—coincides with an anonymous visit from an exacting critic from the local newspaper, one scathing review is all it takes to see her promising business suddenly facing closure.

As the city's most infamous restaurant critic, Al prefers to keep his professional identity a secret. A recent transplant from England, he runs into Lou as she's drowning her sorrows in a pub and playfully challenges her to show him the best of Milwaukee. As Al and Lou explore the sights and sounds of her hometown, they begin to fall for each other—until Al realizes that it was his review that put the future of Luella's in jeopardy. When the truth comes out, the two star-crossed foodies must find a way to overlook the past in order to forge a new future together.

TOPICS & QUESTIONS FOR DISCUSSION

1. It's clear from the opening chapter of the book that Devlin and Lou have divergent plans for the future. What do you think drew them together in the first place? Did you find Devlin, with his good looks and promise of financial stability, alluring or stifling?

2. On page 86, Lou considers the following quote: "Delight is indeed born in the heart. It sometimes also depends on its surroundings." Do you think this holds true throughout the book? How do Al and Lou's surroundings impact their happiness? Do you think that your surroundings dictate your own happiness? Or are your perception and attitude more important?

3. Both Al and Lou have fond memories of their grandmothers' cooking, from Luella's famous coconut cake to the rusty cast-iron skillet that Al still holds dear. What are some of your favorite culinary memories or traditions? How have they evolved—or not—over the years?

4. As Lou plays tour guide to Al and opens him up to a wealth of new experiences, she gradually smooths over his gruff exterior. How does your perception of Al change throughout the book? Was there a specific moment where you started to find him more likeable?

5. *The Coincidence of Coconut Cake* is as much a love letter to Milwaukee as it is the love story of Lou and Al. What is your fa-

vorite stop on Lou's tour of the city? Which of their meals are you most eager to try?

6. On page 254, Devlin says to Lou, "I may shape and bend the facts in my favor or make tactful omissions, but I don't lie." Were you surprised to hear Devlin's explanation for the scantily clad intern in his apartment? Do you think he was telling the whole truth?

7. What do you think about Al's decision to keep his identity a secret from Lou, particularly after he learns that Luella's is her restaurant? Are his lies more forgivable than Devlin's behavior? How would you have handled the situation if you were in Al's shoes?

8. On page 136, Lou reflects on the fate of Luella's: "The fault was hers and hers alone. Taking responsibility gave her control. Taking responsibility gave her hope she would find happiness again." What do you make of this sentiment? Do you think that Lou is being too hard on herself—that she's just the victim of circumstance—or is she to blame for the restaurant's closure?

9. *The Coincidence of Coconut Cake* features a vibrant cast of secondary characters, from John, the fashionista in disguise, to Harley, the loveable, tattooed pastry chef. Who is your favorite secondary character? How does he or she influence events or help to move the story along?

10. Gertrude emphasizes the importance of second chances to Lou. "Don't let your heart get too hard," she says. "[Al] made you happy. That was not an act. Try to forgive him—promise me" (page 281). Do you agree with Gertrude's belief that a

person deserves forgiveness as long as his or her intentions are good? What personal experiences have shaped your own attitude toward second chances?

11. What do you think the future holds for Lou's new restaurant? What important lessons has she learned from Luella's?

12. While the story of Luella's is fictional, it's not uncommon for a new restaurant to fail because of negative press—particularly in the age of crowd-sourced online reviews. Did the book make you more sympathetic to the plight of struggling business owners and the impact of online reviews?

ENHANCE YOUR BOOK CLUB

1. Host a book club potluck! Have each member bring his or her favorite family dish and describe the origin of the recipe.

2. Plan a day of sightseeing or activities in your hometown. What would you want an out-of-towner to experience?

3. Have each book club member write a review praising his or her favorite restaurant—or emulate A. W. Wodyski and pan a terrible meal.

4. Learn more about author Amy E. Reichert by visiting her website (http://amyereichert.com) or following her on Facebook (https://www.facebook.com/amyereichert) and/or Twitter (@aereichert).